continued . . .

THE
wHoLe CaT AnD
CaBoodLe

A SECOND CHANCE CAT MYSTERY

Sofie Ryan

AN OBSIDIAN MYSTERY

OBSIDIAN
Published by the Penguin Group
Penguin Group (USA) LLC, 375 Hudson Street,
New York, New York 10014

USA | Canada | UK | Ireland | Australia | New Zealand | India | South Africa | China
penguin.com
A Penguin Random House Company

First published by Obsidian, an imprint of New American Library,
a division of Penguin Group (USA) LLC

First Printing, April 2014

For Patrick

Acknowledgments

This book began as a "what if" while I was prowling around one of my favorite thrift stores. I owe a huge hug and an equally huge thank-you to my friend, author Lynn Viehl, for her support and encouragement while I was writing it, and for her friendship, always. No matter what wild idea I come up with, fellow writer Laurie Cass will always say, "You should write that," and then help me work out the details. Thanks, Laurie. Thank you to my agent, Kim Lionetti, who is one of my biggest cheerleaders. Thank you as well to everyone at my publisher, Penguin, who, as always, put their best efforts into this book. A special thank-you to my editor, Jessica Wade, who makes everything I write a little—and sometimes a lot—better.

I am indebted to Lauri McGivern and Phyllis Middleton, who generously answered my questions about medical examiners' investigators. Any errors or deviation from real-world procedures are because reality didn't fit the fictional world.

And most important, thank you to Patrick and Lauren for never complaining about all the times I walk around the house talking to imaginary people. Love you.

Chapter 1

Elvis was sitting in the middle of my desk when I opened the door to my office. The cat, not the King of Rock and Roll, although the cat had an air of entitlement about him sometimes, as though he thought he was royalty. He had one jet-black paw on top of a small cardboard box—my new business cards, I was hoping.

"How did you get in here?" I asked.

His ears twitched but he didn't look at me. His green eyes were fixed on the vintage Wonder Woman lunch box in my hand. I was having an early lunch, and Elvis seemed to want one as well.

"No," I said firmly. I dropped onto the retro red womb chair I'd brought up from the shop downstairs, kicked off my sneakers, and propped my feet on the matching footstool. The chair was so comfortable. To me, the round shape was like being cupped in a soft, warm, giant hand. I knew the chair had to go back down to the shop, but I was still trying to figure out a way to keep it for myself.

Before I could get my sandwich out of the yellow vinyl lunch box, the big, black cat landed on my lap. He wiggled his back end, curled his tail around his feet and looked from the bag to me.

"No," I said again. Like that was going to stop him.

He tipped his head to one side and gave me a pitiful look made all the sadder because he had a fairly awesome scar cutting across the bridge of his nose.

I took my sandwich out of the lunch can. It was roast beef on a hard roll with mustard, tomatoes and dill pickles. The cat's whiskers quivered. "One bite," I said sternly. "Cats eat cat food. People eat people food. Do you want to end up looking like the real Elvis in his chunky days?"

He shook his head, as if to say, "Don't be ridiculous."

I pulled a tiny bit of meat out of the roll and held it out. Elvis ate it from my hand, licked two of my fingers and then made a rumbly noise in his throat that sounded a lot like a sigh of satisfaction. He jumped over to the footstool, settled himself next to my feet and began to wash his face. After a couple of passes over his fur with one paw he paused and looked at me, eyes narrowed— his way of saying, "Are you going to eat that or what?"

I ate.

By the time I'd finished my sandwich Elvis had finished his meticulous grooming of his face, paws and chest. I patted my legs. "C'mon over," I said.

He swiped a paw at my jeans. There was no way he was going to hop onto my lap if he thought he might get a crumb on his inky black fur. I made an elaborate show of brushing off both legs. "Better?" I asked.

Elvis meowed his approval and walked his way up my legs, poking my thighs with his front paws—no claws, thankfully—and wiggling his back end until he was comfortable.

I reached for the box on my desk, keeping one hand on the cat. I'd guessed correctly. My new business cards were inside. I pulled one out and Elvis leaned sideways for a look. The cards were thick, brown, recycled card stock, with SECOND CHANCE, THE REPURPOSE SHOP, angled across the top in heavy red letters, and SARAH GRAYSON and my contact information, all in black, in the bottom right corner.

Second Chance was a cross between an antique store and a thrift shop. We sold furniture and housewares—many things repurposed from their original use, like the tub chair that in its previous life had actually been a tub. As for the name, the business was sort of a second chance—for the cat and for me. We'd been open only a few months and I was amazed at how busy we already were.

The shop was in a redbrick building from the late 1800s on Mill Street, in downtown North Harbor, Maine, just where the street curved and began to climb uphill. We were about a twenty-minute walk from the harbor front and easily accessed from the highway—the best of both worlds. My grandmother held the mortgage on the property and I wanted to pay her back as quickly as I could.

"What do you think?" I said, scratching behind Elvis's right ear. He made a murping sound, cat-speak for "good," and lifted his chin. I switched to stroking the fur on his chest.

He started to purr, eyes closed. It sounded a lot like there was a gas-powered generator running in the room.

"Mac and I went to look at the Harrington house," I said to him. "I have to put together an offer, but there are some pieces I want to buy, and you're definitely going with me next time." Eighty-year-old Mabel Harrington was on a cruise with her new beau, a ninety-one-year-old retired doctor with a bad toupee and lots of money. They were moving to Florida when the cruise was over.

One green eye winked open and fixed on my face. Elvis's unofficial job at Second Chance was rodent wrangler.

"Given all the squeaks and scrambling sounds I heard when I poked my head through the trapdoor to the attic, I'm pretty sure the place is the hotel for some kind of mouse convention."

Elvis straightened up, opened his other eye, and licked his lips. Chasing mice, birds, bats and the occasional bug was his idea of a very good time.

I'd had Elvis for about four months. As far as I could find out, the cat had spent several weeks on his own, scrounging around downtown North Harbor.

The town sits on the midcoast of Maine. "Where the hills touch the sea" is the way it's been described for the past 250 years. North Harbor stretches from the Swift Hills in the north to the Atlantic Ocean in the south. It was settled by Alexander Swift in the late 1760s. It's full of beautiful, historic buildings, award-winning restaurants and quirky little shops. Where else could you buy a blueberry muffin, a rare book and fishing gear all on the same street?

The town's population is about thirteen thousand, but that more than triples in the summer with tourists and summer residents. It grew by one black cat one evening in late May. Elvis just appeared at The Black Bear. Sam, who owns the pub, and his pickup band, The Hairy Bananas—long story on the name—were doing their Elvis Presley medley when Sam noticed a black cat sitting just inside the front door. He swore the cat stayed put through the entire set and left only when they launched into their version of the Stones' "Satisfaction."

The cat was back the next morning, in the narrow alley beside the shop, watching Sam as he took a pile of cardboard boxes to the recycling bin. "Hey, Elvis. Want some breakfast?" Sam had asked after tossing the last flattened box in the bin. To his surprise, the cat walked up to him and meowed a loud yes.

He showed up at the pub about every third day for the next couple of weeks. The cat clearly wasn't wild—he didn't run from people—but no one seemed to know who Elvis (the name had stuck) belonged to. The scar on his nose wasn't new; neither were a couple of others on his back, hidden by his fur. Then someone remembered a guy in a van who had stayed two nights at the campgrounds up on Mount Batten. He'd had a cat with him. It was black. Or black and white. Or possibly gray. But it definitely had a scar on its nose. Or it was missing an ear. Or maybe part of a tail.

Elvis was still perched on my lap, staring off into

space, thinking about stalking rodents out at the old Harrington house, I was guessing.

I glanced over at the carton sitting on the walnut sideboard that I used for storage in the office. The fact that it was still there meant that Arthur Fenety hadn't come in while Mac and I had been gone. I was glad. I was hoping I'd be at the shop when Fenety came back for the silver tea service that was packed in the box.

A couple of days prior he had brought the tea set into my shop. Fenety had a charming story about the ornate pieces that he said had belonged to his mother. A bit too charming for my taste, like the man himself. Arthur Fenety was somewhere in his seventies, tall with a full head of white hair, a matching mustache and an engaging smile to go with his polished demeanor. He could have gotten a lot more for the tea set at an antique store or an auction. Something about the whole transaction felt off.

Elvis had been sitting on the counter by the cash register and Fenety had reached over to stroke his fur. The cat didn't so much as twitch a whisker, but his ears had flattened and he'd looked at the older man with his green eyes half-lidded, pupils narrowed. He was the picture of skepticism.

The day after he'd brought the pieces in, Fenety had called to ask if he could buy them back. The more I thought about it, the more suspicious the whole thing felt. The tea set hadn't been on the list of stolen items from the most recent police update, but I still had a niggling feeling about it and Arthur Fenety.

"Time to do some work," I said to Elvis. "Let's go downstairs and see what's happening in the store."

The cat jumped down to the floor and shook himself, and then he had to pause and pass a paw over his face. Elvis knew *store* meant "people," especially tourists, and *tourists* meant "new people who would generally take one look at the scar on his face and be overcome with the urge to stroke his fur and tell him what a sweet kitty he was."

I put on some lipstick and gave my head a shake. I'd gotten my thick, dark brown hair from my father and my dark eyes from my mom. I'd just cut my hair in long layers to my shoulders a couple of weeks previous. If we were moving furniture or I was going for a run I could still pull it back in a ponytail. Otherwise I could pretty much shake my head and my hair looked okay.

One of my part-time staff members, Avery, was by the cash register downstairs, nestling three mismatched soup bowls that had gotten a second life as herb planters into a box half-filled with shredded paper. Her hair was the color of cranberry sauce, and she'd shown up that morning with elaborate henna tattoos covering the backs of both hands. They were beautiful. (She claimed the look was all part of her "rebellious teenager" phase.) Avery worked afternoons in the store—her progressive private school had only morning classes—and full days when there was no school, like today.

I'd had a few rebellious moments myself as a teenager, so Avery's style didn't bother me. She was smart and hardworking, and even though one of the main reasons I'd hired her was because she was the granddaughter of one of my gram's closest friends, I kept her because she did a good job. And my customers seemed to like her.

Mac, the store's resident jack-of-all-trades, was showing a customer a tall metal postman's desk that we'd reclaimed from the basement of a house near the harbor. We'd had to cut the desk apart to get it up the narrow, cramped steps and through the door to the kitchen. Mac had banged out all the dents, put everything back together and then painted the piece a deep sky blue, even though I'd voted for basic black. I watched him hand the customer a tape measure, then give me a knowing smile across the room.

I could see the muscles in his arms move under his long-sleeved gray T-shirt. He was tall and fit with close-cropped black hair and light brown skin. Avery had given Mac the nickname Wall Street. He'd been a financial planner but had ditched his high-powered life to come to Maine and sail. In his free time he crewed for pretty much anyone who asked. There were eight windjammer schooners based in North Harbor, along with dozens of other sailing vessels. Mac was looking for space where he could build his own boat. He worked for me because he said he liked fixing things.

Second Chance had been open for a little less than four months. The main floor was one big open area, with some storage behind the staircase to the second floor. My office was under the eaves on the second floor. There was also a minuscule staff room and one other large space that was being used for storage.

Some things we offered in the shop were vintage kitsch, like my yellow vinyl Wonder Woman lunch box—with matching thermos. Some things were like Elvis—working on a new incarnation, like the electric blue shelving unit that used to be a floor-model TV console. Everything in the store was on its second or sometimes third life.

Our stock came from lots of different places: flea markets, yard sales, people looking to downsize. Mac had even trash-picked a metal bed frame that we'd sold for a very nice profit. A couple of Dumpster divers had been stopping by fairly regularly and in the last month I'd bought items from the estates of three different people. So far, rummaging around in boxes and closets I'd found half a dozen wills, a diamond ring, a set of false teeth, a stuffed armadillo and a box of ashes that thankfully were the remains of someone's long-ago love letters and not, well, the remains of someone.

We sold some items in the store on consignment. Others, like the post office desk, we'd buy outright and refurbish. Mac could repair just about anything, and I was pretty good at coming up with new ways to use old things. And if I ran out of ideas, I could just call my mom, who was a master at giving new life to other people's discards.

Elvis had headed for a couple that was browsing near the guitars on the back wall. The young woman crouched down, stroking his fur and making sympathetic noises about his nose. The young man moved a couple of steps sideways to take a closer look at a Washburn mandolin from the '70s, with a spruce top and ebony fingerboard.

Avery had finished with the customer at the counter. She walked over and lifted the mandolin down from its place on the wall and handed it to the young man. "Why don't you give it a try?" she said. I knew as soon as he had it in his hands he'd be sold.

Avery glanced down at Elvis. He tipped his furry head to one side, leaning into the hand of the young woman who was scratching the top of his head, commanding all her attention, and it almost looked as though he winked at Avery.

A musical instrument was the reason I'd ended up with Elvis—that and his slightly devious nature. I'd taken a guitar down to Sam for a second opinion on what it was worth. Sam Newman and my dad had grown up together. I could play, and I knew a little about some of the older models, but Sam knew more about guitars than anyone I'd ever met. I'd found him sitting in one of the back booths with a cup of coffee and a pile of sheet music. The cat was on the opposite banquette, eating what looked suspiciously to me like scrambled eggs and salami.

Sam had moved his mug and the music out of the way, and I'd set the guitar case on the table. Elvis studied me for a moment and then went back to his breakfast.

"Who's your friend?" I asked, tipping my head toward the cat.

"That's Elvis," Sam said, flipping open the latches on the battered Tolex case with his long fingers. He was tall and lean, his shaggy hair a mix of blond and white.

"Really?" I said. "The King of Rock and Roll was reincarnated as a cat?"

Sam looked at me over the top of his dollar-store reading glasses. "Ha, ha. You're so funny."

I made a face at him. Elvis was watching me again. "Move over." I gestured with one hand. To my surprise the cat obligingly scooted around to the other side of the plate. "Thank you," I said, sliding onto the burgundy vinyl. He dipped his head, almost as though he were saying, "You're welcome," and went back to his scrambled eggs. They were definitely Sam's specialty. I could smell the salami.

"Is this the cat I've been hearing about?" I asked.

Sam was engrossed in examining the vintage Fender. "What? Oh yeah, it is."

Elvis's ears twitched, as though he knew we were talking about him.

"Why Elvis?"

Sam shrugged. "He doesn't seem to like the Stones, so naming him Mick was kinda out of the question." He waved a hand in the direction of the bar. "There's coffee."

That was Sam's way of telling me to stop talking so he could focus his full attention on the candy apple red Stratocaster. I got up and went behind the bar for the coffee, careful to keep the mug well out of the way of the old guitar when I brought it back to the table. Elvis had finished eating and was washing his face.

"What do you think?" I asked after a couple of minutes of silence. Sam's head was bent over the neck of the guitar, examining the fret board.

"Gimme a second," he said.

I waited, and after another minute or so he straightened up, pulling a hand over the back of his neck. "So, tell me what you think," he said, setting his glasses on the table.

I put my coffee cup on the floor beside my feet before I answered. "Based on what the homeowner told me it's a 1966. It belonged to her husband. It's not mint, but it's in good shape. There's some buckle wear on the back, but overall it's been taken care of. I think it's the real thing and I think it could bring twelve to fifteen thousand."

Beside me Elvis gave a loud meow.

"The cat agrees," I said.

"That makes three of us, then," Sam said.

I grinned at him across the table. "Thanks."

When I got up to leave, Elvis jumped down and followed me. "I think you made a friend," Sam said. He walked me out to my truck, set the guitar carefully on the passenger's side, and then wrapped me in a bear hug. He smelled like coffee and Old Spice. "Come by Saturday night, if you're free," he said. "I think you'll like the band."

"Old stuff?" I asked, pulling my keys out of the pocket of my jeans.

"Hey, it's gotta be rock-and-roll music if you wanna dance with me," he said, raising his eyebrows and giving me a sly smile. He looked down at Elvis, who had been sitting by the truck, watching us. "C'mon, you. You're gonna get turned into roadkill if you stay here." He reached for the cat, who jumped up onto the front seat.

"Hey, get down from there," I said.

Elvis ignored me, made his way along the black vinyl

seat and settled himself on the passenger's side, next to the guitar case.

"No, no, no, you can't come with me." I leaned into the truck to grab him, but he slipped off the seat, onto the floor mat. With the guitar there I couldn't reach him.

Behind me, I could hear Sam laughing.

I blew my hair out of my face, backed out of the truck and glared at Sam. "Your cat's in my truck. Do something!"

He folded his arms over his chest. "He's not my cat. I'm pretty sure he's your cat now."

"I don't want a cat."

"Tell him that," Sam said with a shrug.

I stuck my head back through the open driver's door. "I don't want a cat," I said.

Ensconced out of my reach in the little lean-to made by the guitar case, Elvis looked up from washing his face—again—and meowed once and went back to it.

"I have a dog," I warned. "A big, mean one with big, mean teeth." The cat's whiskers didn't so much as quiver.

Sam leaned over my shoulder. "No, she doesn't," he said.

I elbowed him. "You're not helping."

He laughed. "Look, the cat likes you." He rolled his eyes. "Lord knows why. Take him. Do you want him to just keep living on the street?"

"No," I mumbled. I glanced in the truck again. Elvis, with some kind of uncanny timing, chose that moment to tip his head to one side and look up at me with his big green eyes. With his scarred nose he looked . . . lonely.

"What am I going to do with a cat?" I said, bouncing the keys in my right hand.

Sam shrugged. "Feed him. Talk to him. Scratch under his chin. He likes that."

I glanced at the cat again. He still had that lonely, slightly pathetic look going.

"You two will make a great team," Sam said. "Like Lennon and McCartney or Jagger and Richards."

"SpongeBob and Patrick," I muttered.

"Exactly," Sam said.

I was pretty sure I was being conned, but, like it or not, I had a cat.

I looked over now toward the end wall of the store. My cat had apparently helped sell a mandolin. The young man was headed to the cash register with it. Elvis made his way over to me.

I leaned over to stroke the top of his head. "Nice work," I whispered. I wasn't imagining the cat smile he gave me.

The woman who had been looking at the post office desk was headed for the door, but there was a certain smugness to Mac's expression that told me he'd made the sale. I walked over to him. "Go ahead, say 'I told you so,'" I said.

He folded his arms over his chest. "I can't. I'm fairly certain she's going to buy it. She just wishes it were black."

I laughed. "I guess black really is the new black," I said. "I'm about ready to leave. I have to pick up Charlotte, and Avery is going to get her grandmother. Do you need anything before I go?"

I was doing a workshop on color-washing furniture for a group of seniors over at Legacy Place. North Har-

bor was full of beautiful old buildings. It was part of the
town's charm. The top floors of the old chocolate factory
had been converted into seniors' apartments. There were
a couple of community rooms on the main level, where
the residents had various classes like French and yoga
and got together to socialize. We were using one of them
for the workshop since many of the class participants
lived in the building. Eventually I wanted to renovate
part of the old garage next to the Second Chance building for workshops; for now, when I did classes for the
general public, I had to settle for renting space at the
high school. Luckily the hourly rate was pretty good.
This workshop was a freebie my gram had nudged me
into doing.

Mac shook his head. "I've got everything covered."
He narrowed his brown eyes at me. "Are you sure it's a
good idea to make Avery go with you?"

"Actually she volunteered."

"Avery volunteered to help you teach a workshop for
a bunch of senior citizens?" One eyebrow shot up. "Seriously?"

"Seriously. She's good with older people. They'll be
feeding her cookies and exclaiming over her hair color,
and before you know it she'll have wangled an invitation
to go prowl around someone's attic." Avery had a thing
for vintage jewelry, and thanks to her grandmother Liz's
friends, was building a nice collection.

I pressed my hands into the small of my back and
stretched. I was still kinked from crawling around that
old house all morning. "You know, I used to hang around
with some of those same women when I was Avery's

age." I'd spent my summers in North Harbor with my grandmother as far back as I could remember. The rest of the time I'd lived first in upstate New York and then in New Hampshire. "Liz taught me how to wax my legs and put on false eyelashes."

"I could have gone the rest of my life not knowing that," Mac said dryly.

"And I know the secret to Charlotte's potpie," I teased.

"You're not going to say it's love, are you?"

I shook my head and grinned. "Nope. Actually it's bacon fat."

My father had been an only child and so was my mother, so I didn't have a gaggle of cousins to hang out with in the summer. My grandmother's friends, Charlotte, Liz and Rose had become a kind of surrogate extended family, a trio of indulgent aunts. When I'd decided to open Second Chance, they'd been almost as pleased as my grandmother, and Charlotte and Rose had come to work for me part-time. Now with Gram out of town on her honeymoon, the three women fed me, gently nagged me about working too much and pointed out every single man between twenty-five and, well, death. When Gram had asked me to offer one of my workshops to her friends, how could I say no?

I glanced at my watch. "I don't expect to be more than a couple of hours," I said. "And I have my cell."

"Elvis and I can hold down the fort," Mac said. "Are you going to take another look at that SUV?"

I'd been thinking about replacing the aging truck we

used to move furniture with an SUV, if I could get it for the right price. "I might," I said.

"Well, take your time," Mac said. "It's Monday afternoon. Nothing ever happens in this town on a Monday."

Of course he was wrong.

Chapter 2

The second thing I noticed when I stepped into the room we were using at Legacy Place was that nothing had been set up for the workshop. The first thing I noticed was Alfred Peterson. He was naked. Let's just say it wasn't a good look for him; he was somewhere between seventy-five and eighty. That's not to say there aren't people close to eighty who look good with their clothes off, but Alfred Peterson definitely wasn't one of them.

I exhaled slowly, sent up a silent prayer—*Please don't let me see anything*—and headed across the floor, keeping my gaze locked on the old man's blue eyes.

"Good afternoon, Sarah," he said with a slight dip of his head as I got close to the center of the room where he had . . . arranged himself. "What are you doing here?"

"Good afternoon, Mr. Peterson," I said. "I'm doing a workshop. What, ah . . . are you doing?"

"I'm posing, my dear."

I could see that. I was fairly certain he was trying to imitate the Farnese Atlas, a marble sculpture in which

Atlas is partly down on one knee, holding the world on his shoulders, except Mr. Peterson was holding a red-and-white-striped beach ball with the logo of a beer company instead of the world, and he had two pillows under his bent knee. I was pretty sure he was sitting on a cardboard box, but I wasn't going to look behind him to find out for sure.

I gave him what I hoped looked like a sincere smile. "But why exactly are you . . . here . . . like this?"

"Sammy called. There's a busload of tourists down at the pub and they're running behind schedule, so he's not going to get here, and I thought, *Why don't I just take his place instead*?" He frowned. "I though Sammy said Eric was teaching the class, though."

Eric was one of Sam's bandmates. The rest of the time he was an artist.

"Alfred Peterson, where on earth are your pants?" a voice said behind me. It was Charlotte coming from the small kitchen at the end of the main hallway, where she'd gone to put the kettle on for tea. The room rental came with access to the communal kitchen.

"In the gentleman's lavatory," Mr. P. said with a slight superior edge to his voice.

"Apparently you left your common sense in there, as well," Charlotte retorted. She frowned at him, hands on her hips. Even in flats she was an inch taller than I was, and she had the posture and steely glare of a high school principal, which is what she'd been. "What on earth are you doing in the middle of Sarah's class as naked as the day you were born?"

"This is Eric's art class, 'Sketching the Human Form.' "

The old man held his head high, chin stuck out. "Sammy couldn't make it so I'm the model. I may not be a spring chicken but I've still got it."

Charlotte's mouth twitched and I realized she was trying not to laugh. "Be that as it may," she said. "There's no reason to be putting it all on display for the rest of us. And didn't Sam tell you? Eric's class is in the small room next door today, and they're drawing hands."

"Hands?"

"Hands."

"But the class is called 'Sketching the Human Form,'" Mr. P. said stubbornly.

It seemed pretty clear to me that getting him back into his clothes wasn't going to be easy.

"And hands are part of the human form." Charlotte made a move-along gesture with hers. "So that's all we need to see. Go put your pants on before the class gets here and the mystery's gone."

Mr. Peterson seemed deflated. He handed me the beach ball, while Charlotte headed back to the kitchen down the hall. "Hands? Really?" he asked me.

I had no idea but I nodded, anyway.

The old man slowly straightened up, and I realized that the washrooms were off the outside hallway, too. I thrust the beach ball back into his grasp. "Why don't you take this with you?" I said. It at least made the front view G-rated as he headed for the door. I couldn't exactly say the same for what was bringing up the rear.

Avery and her grandmother, Liz French, came in just as Mr. P. got to the door. He nodded as they passed. The two women crossed the floor to join me, Liz's high heels echoing on the wooden floor. As usual Liz was elegantly dressed, in a lavender tunic over navy pants. Her soft blond hair curled around her face.

"Hello, Sarah," she said. She handed me a cardboard box and leaned in to kiss my cheek. "I baked."

That really meant she'd been to Lily's Bakery.

Liz had a gleam in her blue eyes and I knew she'd have some comment about Mr. Peterson's attire—or lack of. "Was Alfred naked, or did his suit just really need ironing?"

Beside her Avery made a face. "Geez, Nonna," she said. "That joke's older than I am." She turned to me. "Why was Mr. P. . . ." She paused and gestured with one hand.

"Naked as a jaybird?" Liz interjected. "Hanging the moon?"

"Sam got held up with a busload of tourists at the pub," I said. "Apparently he was supposed to be the model for an art class. Mr. Peterson decided he'd help out by taking Sam's place. He just got the room and the dress code wrong."

Avery rolled her eyes and folded her arms over her chest. "You guys do get that right now Mr. P. is walking all the way down the hall to the men's bathroom, past that whole big wall of windows?" She paused, probably for effect. "You know, windows that overlook the parking lot?"

Liz gave me a sweet—and fake—smile. "Given all the cars in the lot, half the town's probably seen Alfred's as—"

"Assets," I said, raising my voice to drown her out. I held out my keys to Avery. "Would you start unloading the truck, please?"

"No problem," she said. "It's probably not a good idea for me to stay here. I'm young and impressionable." She headed for the door.

Liz shook her head. "She's impressionable, and this is my original hair color."

"It's not even close."

Liz and I turned.

Rose was standing in the doorway. "Do you want to know what your original hair color was?" she asked.

Liz made a dismissive gesture with one hand. "No, I do not. Like my real age, some things should not be discussed in public."

Rose came across the floor to us. She was barely five feet tall, with cropped white hair and warm gray eyes. She was dwarfed by the neon orange tote bag over her shoulder. Rose's bags reminded me of Mary Poppins's carpetbag. I never knew what she was going to pull out of one of them.

"Hello, sweetie bug," she said with a smile, reaching up to pat my cheek. "Welcome to Shady Pines."

"Shady Pines?" I asked.

"Don't encourage her," Charlotte said. She'd come from the kitchen again, carrying a tray loaded with teacups, napkins and a small glass bowl filled with sugar cubes.

I hurried over to take it from her, setting Liz's cookies on a stack of napkins, and immediately realized I had nowhere to put the whole thing down.

"She's not encouraging me," Rose said. "She just asked a question." She looked at me. "I call this place Shady Pines because it's just like living in an old folks' home. All anyone wants to talk about is how many pills they're taking and when they last had a bowel movement."

Liz smirked at me. "You were warned," she said. She turned to Rose. "Will you please come and live with Avery and me so we don't have to listen to you talk about other people's ailments and bodily functions?"

Rose crossed her hands primly in front of her. "Have you actually forgotten Vermont?" She looked over at me. "Liz and I shared a room when we went on a bus tour to Vermont. I seriously considered smothering her with a pillow while she slept."

"I'm not suggesting we share a room," Liz said, making a sweeping gesture with her hands. "I have that big house. We could probably go for a day or two and not even see each other."

"No." Rose shook her head vigorously. "The key to us having been friends for the past fifty years is never spending that much time together. I'm not about to ruin a beautiful friendship now." She gestured at the long, multipaned windows on the side wall of the room. "We should open a couple of these. It's going to get stuffy in here."

"Is Alfred putting his clothes on?" Charlotte asked me in a low voice.

"I sincerely hope so," I whispered. I set the tray on the floor and headed for the supply closet at the far end of the room.

By the time I had the cups set out on a table under the tall windows, the other women in the class were coming in. Avery had spread the drop cloths on the floor and was carrying in the various little wooden tables I'd collected for the class to work on. She'd set a cardboard box over by the wall. I was trying to remember what was inside when one of the top flaps, which hadn't been folded flat, seemed to . . . move.

"Avery," I said, making a get-over-here gesture with one finger, my eyes fixed on the carton.

She came to stand in front of me. "What?"

I pointed at the box. "Tell me you didn't," I said.

She shrugged. "Okay, I didn't."

The chance that I would have believed her was pretty much zero, anyway, but Elvis chose that moment to poke his head up out of the box and look around.

"Okay, so maybe I did," she said. "But, c'mon, he gets lonely hanging out in the store all day."

The cat jumped out of the box, shook himself and came to sit in front of me, all green-eyed innocence. "Don't think I don't know your part in all this," I said, glaring at him and folding my arms across my chest. In the few months I'd had the cat I'd learned he wasn't above doing his Sad Kitty routine to get what he wanted. It had even worked on me a couple of times—okay, maybe six or seven times—before I got wise. "Avery, Elvis is a cat. His life is eat, sleep in the sunshine and get scratched behind his ears."

Elvis gave a short, sharp meow and narrowed his gaze at me.

"And be the enforcer when it comes to mice, birds, bats and the occasional Junebug. You shouldn't have brought him."

Avery jammed her hands in the pockets of her black jeans. "You take him with you lots of times."

"That's different. That's work."

"So is this," she immediately countered, bending down to pick up the cat.

"How is this work?" I said.

"Public relations. People meet Elvis. They like him. They come to the store. It's good for business."

The cat actually leaned his furry face against Avery's cheek and half closed his eyes. She gave me her sweetest smile.

"Oh, for heaven's sake," I muttered. I knew when I was beaten. "He's your responsibility," I said sternly. I narrowed my eyes at the cat. "Stay out of the paint."

Elvis closed his eyes and shook his head, almost as though he'd understood what I'd said and was offended at the suggestion that he'd get paint on his sleek black fur.

I headed out to the truck to get the paint and the trash cans we'd be using to mix the color wash, since Avery had her hands full. The sun was streaming through the wall of windows that made up the east side of the old factory, making checkerboard squares of light on the plank floor of the hallway. Legacy Place had been the Gardner Chocolate factory—"A little bite of bliss in a little gold box"—until the company's new manufacturing plant had been built just on the outskirts of North Harbor.

The building had had a number of incarnations in the next twenty years, and then about three years ago the

Gardner family had renovated the space into a much-needed apartment complex for seniors. The fact that it all happened at the same time that a tabloid had published photos of Hank Gardner, the CEO of the company, boogying at a club with an exotic dancer while wearing a certain item of her clothing as earmuffs was just coincidence. (Gardner had explained it all by saying, "It was January and my ears were cold.")

The chocolate factory and tourism were the main industries in town and that made for an eclectic mix of people that was part of North Harbor's appeal. There were musicians, artists, sailors and fishermen, small business owners, factory workers, young people and senior citizens.

I glanced in at the art class as I passed by the room. Mr. Peterson was dressed—thankfully—in a long-sleeved, navy blue golf shirt, gray pants hiked up almost to his armpits and running shoes. He was posed on a stool in the middle of the room, circled on three sides by easels.

Avery had found a chair somewhere and Elvis was perched on it, holding court when I returned with the paint. I set her to work opening the cans and did a quick head count. Eight women had signed up for the class. We were missing someone. I scanned the room. "Does anyone know where Maddie is?" I asked when I realized one of my gram's longtime friends hadn't shown up yet.

"Probably with her new boyfriend," someone said. The speaker was a tiny woman, more petite than Rose, wearing a flowing shirt covered with blue and green parrots.

"Maddie has a boyfriend?" I said.

"Uh-huh. She's smitten," Liz said, pulling a men's faded chambray shirt over her tunic. Liz dressed for every occasion. I'd never seen her in a sweatshirt or yoga pants, unlike most of the other women her age.

Charlotte took a sip of her tea. "Elizabeth is right. Maddie's like a young girl when he's around." She handed me a cookie.

I couldn't picture sensible, practical Maddie getting giggly over a man. On the other hand, I hadn't seen her in a long time.

"I was looking forward to seeing her today," I said. "When I was little, Gram and I would walk to Maddie's house for lemonade in the summertime. She had an incredible garden behind her house. Gram said there were fairies living there and I was always trying to find them." I took a bite of the cookie.

Charlotte smiled. "That's Maddie. She was born with a green thumb."

Liz nodded her agreement. "I got a poinsettia plant at Christmastime. The thing turned brown—I don't know what the heck happened to it—but Maddie pulled it out of my kitchen garbage can and brought the darned thing back from the dead."

"You probably forgot to water it," Rose said.

"No, I didn't," Liz retorted as she fastened the snaps on her paint-streaked shirt. "I definitely remember I gave it the last of the coffee a couple of times."

Rose sighed. "Well, I don't think that was a good idea."

Liz made a dismissive gesture with one hand. Her nails were painted a deep royal purple. "Clearly, since the danged thing turned brown."

Charlotte shook her head. With her height and perfect posture she might not have fit every grandmother stereotype, but she had a huge, loving heart. She and my own grandmother had been friends since they were girls. "Maddie met her beau, Arthur, at a fund-raiser for the Botanic Garden. She's still in the rose-colored-glasses stage when it comes to him. She probably just got caught up in whatever his latest plans are and forgot to call you."

"Arthur?" I said slowly.

"Yes," Charlotte said. "Arthur Fenety."

Arthur Fenety.

Maddie was seeing the man who had brought in the silver tea set and then wanted to buy it back a day later. The man I'd thought was a little too smooth, a little too charming.

And it was really none of my business.

Avery had the paint cans open and had brought in a couple of big buckets of water. I looked at my watch. It was almost twelve o'clock. Time to get started. Maybe Maddie would arrive in a few minutes.

The ladies were eager to learn. I explained how to make the color wash by diluting the paint. Then we tested the depth of the color on some scrap wood. We got started by dipping the legs—which I'd detached from the underside of each little table—using a brush to pull the color upward and create a faded effect.

I was glad I'd brought Avery along. She had a great

eye for color, she didn't mind getting her hands dirty and she might have had an opinion on well, pretty much everything, but a lot of her insights were dead-on. Elvis stayed on his seat, watching intently but happy to be away from the paint.

The hour-long class was over before I knew it. A couple of times I couldn't help glancing over at the door from the hall, hoping Maddie might show up late, but she didn't.

When the class ended, Avery helped me pack everything and prop up the color-washed table pieces so that they weren't lying on the drop cloths as the paint finished drying. There was nothing happening in the room for the rest of the day, so we'd be able to pick up the completely dry tables in the morning and the ladies could retrieve them from the shop later in the week. We carried the rest of our supplies back out to the truck. Mr. P., whose posing duties had ended at the same time as the workshop, held open the door to the parking lot. The only spot I'd been able to find was at the far end of the space—the parking area of the office building next door was being paved and their clients were using the Legacy Place lot—so I tried to carry as much as I could in each trip.

Once everything was loaded, Avery left with her grandmother. I could hear the two of them arguing about what they were going to have for supper. Liz wanted to order a pizza and Avery seemed to be making the case for fermented vegetables.

I walked back to the building. I'd found a heavy canvas tote in the truck that I used at the market and it was over my shoulder, Elvis's head poking out of the top. Mr. P. held the door for me. "Thank you," I said. "That was the last load."

He smiled. "You're welcome, my dear." He reached over and stroked the top of the cat's head. Then he pulled a tiny spiral notebook and an equally tiny pencil out of his pocket. He tore a page out of the book and offered it and the pencil to me.

"What's this for?" I asked.

"You've been repeating the same three names under your breath. Why don't you write them down?"

I felt my cheeks get warm. "Thank you," I said. "They all wanted me to say hello to Gram next time I speak to her and I was afraid that I'd forget somebody's name. I hadn't realized that I was talking out loud."

My grandmother was somewhere on the Atlantic Canadian coast with her new husband, John, in an RV that wasn't much bigger than a minivan. John looked like he could be actor Gary Oldman's older brother. He had the same brown hair, streaked with gray, waving back from his face, and the same intriguing gleam in his eyes. There were thirteen years between them, which had raised some eyebrows, but Gram didn't seem anywhere near her seventy-three years and, even more importantly, she didn't care what other people thought.

I took the pencil and paper from Mr. P. and scribbled down the three women's names before I forgot them.

"At your age when you talk to yourself it's charming," Mr. P. said. "When you do it at my age they start asking if you eat enough roughage, and watch to make

sure you're not wearing your underwear on the outside."
He hiked up his pants and gave me a wink and a smile.
"Sometimes I do, just to mess with people."

I watched him head down the hallway, nodding at
Charlotte as she came from the kitchen. I wasn't sure if
the old man might have been messing with me.

Charlotte smiled as she walked up to me. Like Mr. P.,
she reached over to pet the top of Elvis's head. "The
class was lovely, Sarah. Thank you. I know Isabel roped
you into it."

"It was fun," I said, taking the fabric tote she was carrying. "Is this everything?"

She glanced in the top of her bag and then nodded.

"Where could I drop you?"

"Oh, I don't mind walking," she said as we started
across the parking lot. "I don't have that far to go," she
pointed at the carryall, "and my bag's not that heavy."

I pulled my keys out of my pocket. "I have time."

Charlotte's glasses had slid down her nose, and she
frowned at me over the top of them. "Thank you, dear,
but I'm perfectly capable of getting an empty cookie can
and a canister of tea bags home."

"I know that," I said. "I also know that no matter
what you said, you're worried because Maddie didn't
show up and you plan on going to check on her. I thought
maybe I could go with you."

She fingered one of the buttons on her rose-colored
sweater. "I know I'm being an old worrywart. It's just
not like Maddie to not call if she wasn't coming."

My mother had always told me to trust my instincts.

Now I was wishing I'd paid more attention to the funny feeling I'd had about Arthur Fenety and at least asked Sam if he'd heard anything about the man. Because he owned The Black Bear, Sam knew pretty much everything that was happening in North Harbor. Maddie had been a nurse and she was one of the most responsible people I'd ever met. I wasn't going to ignore my gut feeling again.

"You're not being an old worrywart," I said. "I want to check on Maddie, too. We might as well go together."

Charlotte patted my arm. "All right, let's go see what's going on."

"Does she still live at the end of your street?" I asked as I slid onto the front seat of the truck. I set Elvis down and he settled himself in the middle, between us.

She nodded. "Oh yes. That house has been in her family for close to a hundred years. I can't see her selling it."

In North Harbor a hundred years didn't really make a house that old. There were lots of buildings that dated back to the late 1700s and early 1800s.

Charlotte fastened her seat belt and reached over to give Elvis a scratch under his chin. "We're probably worrying about nothing."

"Probably," I agreed. "But it doesn't hurt to check." Once we got there I'd decide how to sound Maddie out about Arthur Fenety.

I backed out of my parking spot, made a tight turn in the tiny lot and pulled out onto the street.

"You drive like your grandmother," Charlotte said,

folding her hands in her lap. Elvis was looking straight ahead out the windshield.

"That's probably because she's the one who taught me how to drive," I said. "Do you remember that old one-ton truck she had? She called it Rex."

"Heavens, yes," Charlotte said, with a shake of her head. "Don't tell me she taught you how to drive on that old rust bucket."

"She did," I said, grinning at the memory of being behind the wheel of the old green truck for the first time, front seat squeaking as we bounced down a pothole-pocked dirt road just on the outskirts of town. "Liam took driver's ed, but the class was the same time as honors math, so I was going to have to wait an entire term to learn to drive. I didn't want him to get his license months before I did."

There's only a month between my brother—well, strictly speaking, my stepbrother—Liam and me. My mom and his dad had gotten married when we were in second grade. One moment he'd be a pain-in-the-butt, overprotective big brother, making it pretty much impossible for me to date anyone, and in the next he was covering for me when I set the vacuum cleaner on fire. (Another long story.)

Out of the corner of my eye I saw Charlotte shoot me a skeptical look. "Your mother agreed to let Isabel teach you how to drive?"

"Well, I didn't exactly tell her."

"And I'm thinking you didn't exactly tell Isabel that you didn't have your mother's permission for driving lessons."

"Pretty much." I stopped at the corner and looked

over at Charlotte. Elvis seemed to be as interested in the story as she was.

She closed her eyes for a moment and shook her head. "I can't believe I've never heard this story. So, what happened?"

I grinned. "I got my license two hours before Liam did."

"And?" Charlotte prompted.

"And I was grounded for two weeks and couldn't drive for a month."

She laughed. "So was it worth it?"

"Absolutely," I said. "Not only did I get my driver's license before Liam got his, I could drive a stick and he couldn't."

Charlotte pushed her glasses up her nose. "Let me guess," she said. "Isabel taught him how to drive that old truck, too."

I nodded. "You know Gram. She's big on being fair."

Gram was my dad's mother. She had no biological connection to Liam, but she'd always considered him to be her grandchild, too.

I put on my blinker and turned onto Charlotte's street.

"That's Maddie's car," she said, pointing through the windshield.

"Maybe she's here, then," I said. I pulled up to the curb in front of the little stone house. It looked just the way I remembered it, like it belonged on a winding lane in the English countryside, not on an East Coast, small-town street.

Maddie's wasn't the only house in town with a beautiful garden. Even though the growing season was short in Maine, there seemed to be flowers everywhere in the late spring and summer; in window boxes and planters in front of the shops and in backyards like Maddie's.

I'd seen Maddie only twice, briefly both times, since I'd been back in North Harbor. She'd been visiting her son, Christopher, in Seattle when I arrived and since she'd gotten back we hadn't had much of a chance to spend time together. Probably because of her new romance, I realized now.

"Stay here," I told Elvis. He meowed what I hoped was agreement.

Charlotte and I got out and walked up to the front door. She turned the antique crank doorbell and we waited.

"I don't think she's here," she said after a minute or so.

I knocked on the yellow-paneled door with the heel of my hand. There was no response to that, either. "Maybe she went somewhere with her friend," I said. I tried to keep the little twist of anxiety spinning in my chest out of my voice.

"That's probably it." Charlotte pressed her lips together, and I knew she wasn't completely convinced.

I looked around. A stone walkway led around the side of the house to the backyard. "Or maybe Maddie was working in the garden and just lost track of time. Why don't we go take a look?"

Charlotte exhaled slowly. "I'm acting like an old busybody, I know, but this is just not like her."

I gave her arm a squeeze. "You're not a busybody; you're just worried about a friend. Let's take a look.

Maybe we'll find her in the backyard, attacking the weeds." I was trying to convince myself as much as Charlotte, because the Maddie I remembered wouldn't have not shown up without calling—unless something was wrong.

Maddie *was* in the backyard. We found her sitting in a chair pulled up to a round teak table that looked as though it had been set for lunch. For a moment, until she wrapped one arm across her body, I wasn't sure she was all right. I couldn't say the same about the man in the chair beside her. It was pretty clear Arthur Fenety was dead.

Chapter 3

Charlotte made a strangled sound in the back of her throat. "Maddie—oh, my word! What happened?" she asked, bending down and laying one hand on the other woman's arm.

Maddie turned her head at the sound of her friend's voice. "Charlotte," she said. She closed her eyes for a moment. When she opened them again I could see they were bright with unshed tears. "Arthur's gone."

Charlotte looked at me. I pressed two fingers to Arthur Fenety's wrist, even though I was already certain he was dead. There was an abrasion on the back of his left hand. It was red and raw but it wasn't bleeding. His skin had an ashen pall that told me it was too late to do anything for him.

There was no pulse.

I shook my head. Had Maddie been sitting out here with a dead body? Clearly she was in shock.

Maddie focused on me then. "Sarah." She managed a tiny smile. "I missed your workshop. I'm sorry."

"It doesn't matter," I said. "Are you all right?"

She nodded. But she obviously wasn't.

"I want you to go wait with Charlotte. I'll take care of things here."

"I can't leave Arthur alone," she said. I noticed she avoided looking directly at the body, although she reached toward it.

I caught her hand, sandwiching it between both of mine. It was icy-cold. "He won't be alone. I'm going to stay with him. It's okay."

I had a flash of memory—the night my father died—when Maddie had taken a bewildered five-year-old's hand and told me to go with my grandmother. She'd promised to stay with my dad. Her hazel eyes locked on to mine and I wondered if she was having the same memory. "All right," she said softly.

"I'll take her inside," Charlotte said.

I shook my head again. "Take her out to the truck. There's a blanket behind the seat."

She frowned. "The truck?"

"We shouldn't touch anything. Out here or inside."

She took a deep breath and let it out. "You're right." I let go of Maddie's hand and Charlotte helped her to her feet, putting one arm around her friend. I stepped into Maddie's sight line so she couldn't see the body any-more, just in case she decided to turn in that direction.

Charlotte looked back over her shoulder as they started around the side of the house. "Sarah, call nine-one-one and then call Nicolas, please," she said. She re-cited a phone number.

I waited until the two of them were out of sight and then I pulled out my cell phone and called 911. After I'd hung up, I took a couple of steps closer to the body. It was slumped to the side in the teak chair, head sagging toward the right shoulder, eyes closed. There was a little foam at the right corner of the mouth, and the lips looked blue and waxy. I noticed that there was a ceramic bowl filled with fruit salad in the center of the table and a coffee cup, half-full, at Arthur Fenety's place. I'd had a bad feeling about the man from the moment he'd brought the tea set into Second Chance, but I'd never expected things to end like this.

I pulled a hand back over my hair and punched the number Charlotte had given me into the phone. Nick Elliot was Charlotte's son and a former EMT. He'd know what to do for someone in shock. I got his voice mail. After a moment of awkward hesitation, I explained who I was and where I was, and hung up.

Nick had been back in town only a few weeks after working for a couple of years in New Hampshire, and since North Harbor wasn't a very big place, I was surprised I still hadn't run into him.

I heard the wail of sirens getting closer and followed the walkway to the side of the house. I could see Charlotte and Maddie in the front seat of the truck. Elvis had climbed onto Maddie's lap and she was stroking his fur. All of a sudden I was glad Avery had brought the cat along.

In a couple of minutes a black-and-white pulled in behind my truck and an officer got out. I raised my hand to catch his attention and he walked across the grass to me.

"Ms. Grayson?" he asked. He wore the standard

patrol-officer uniform and his hair was buzzed close to his scalp, so all I could see was dark stubble.

I nodded.

"You reported a body."

I pointed into the backyard. "At the table, just around the corner."

"Please wait here," he said.

I stuffed my hands in my pockets and stood there while he went to have a look. In less than a minute he was back, just as an ambulance pulled in behind the police car. He held up a hand to me and walked across the lawn to meet the paramedics. I waited while he showed them the body and then came back to me again.

"Ms. Grayson, what were you doing here?" he asked.

I explained about Maddie not showing up and how Charlotte and I had come to check on her. "I think Mrs. Hamilton's in shock," I said, gesturing at the truck. "I thought it was better if she waited there instead of staying where the . . . body was."

"I'll get one of the paramedics to check on her."

The officer, whose last name was Whalen, according to his name tag, asked more questions and I answered them as best I could. He nodded after everything I said and made notes in a small spiral-bound pad. I couldn't read anything in his face.

"I'm going to need you to hang around for a little while, until I talk to the other two ladies," he said finally, closing the notebook and tucking it into his shirt pocket.

"That's all right," I said, thinking I should call Mac and tell him I was going to be a while, but maybe not why.

I turned back to the street as a dark blue sedan squeezed in curbside in front of my truck. At the same time a black SUV parked at the end of the line of vehicles, and a man got out and started up the sidewalk. It wasn't until he came level with the house that I realized I was looking at Nick Elliot.

"Please wait here," Officer Whalen said to me. He headed across the lawn toward the blue car, stopping for a moment to speak to Nick. It was obvious the two men knew each other.

Nick had always been tall, but he was well over six feet now. He was wearing a navy Windbreaker over a sky blue polo shirt and black pants with multiple pockets on the sides. Charlotte got out of the truck on the driver's side and walked around to him. He said something to the police officer and then turned his attention to his mother, putting one hand on her shoulder.

I felt a little silly just standing there next to what looked like a bed of daylilies, but I didn't want to intrude on Nick and Charlotte's conversation. Finally I saw Charlotte point in my direction and Nick turned my way for the first time. He said something to his mother, gave her shoulder a squeeze and started toward me.

It had been years since I'd seen him and it looked as though those years had been good to him. The sandy hair was the same, only shorter. And he was still built like a big teddy bear—but now the bear seemed to have the shoulders of a defensive lineman. He wasn't quite the shaggy-haired, wannabe musician I remembered from all the summers I'd spent in North Harbor when I was growing up. He definitely wasn't the same guy I'd French-kissed at fifteen.

Then he smiled at me and I caught a glimpse of the boy I remembered. "Sarah, hi," he said.

I smiled back. "Hi, Nick," I said, taking a couple of steps forward to meet him. "You got my message."

"You left me a message?" He frowned and felt in his pocket for his cell phone, setting down the boxy silver case he was carrying. I wondered what had happened to the black nylon backpack full of first-aid supplies that he'd used to carry everywhere.

I looked at him uncertainly. "If you didn't get my message, then what are you doing here?"

He gestured over his shoulder at the car angled at the curb in front of my truck. "I'm here because Michelle called me."

From the time I was twelve years old until I was fifteen, Michelle Andrews had been my best friend in North Harbor. Each summer we'd just pick up again where we'd left off. Then right after my fifteenth birthday, all of a sudden, she stopped talking to me. I still didn't know why. I'd known Michelle had become a police officer, but somehow it felt different to *see* her as a police officer.

"Michelle?" I said stupidly, even though I could see her getting out of the driver's side of the car. She was wearing gray pants, an emerald green shirt and a black leather jacket. Her red hair was pulled back into a smooth ponytail.

Nick nodded. "She caught the case."

I'd known things were going to get complicated—just

not this complicated. I'd realized that as soon as the first police officer saw the body, with its blue lips and blood-specked froth at the corner of the mouth, he'd call for a detective.

I had no idea how Arthur Fenety had died, but I was certain it wasn't from natural causes.

Chapter 4

I stared at Nick for a long moment—which wasn't hard to do. "I don't understand," I said. "Michelle called you? Why?" I gave him a small smile to soften the words. "No offense."

He smoothed a hand over the back of his head and gave me a wry smile. "You haven't heard."

I had no idea what he meant. "I guess not," I said.

"I'm working for the medical examiner." He half turned and I saw the words *State Medical Examiner's Office* on the back of his jacket.

I narrowed my eyes at him. "Doing what?"

Nick shrugged. "Death investigator."

"I thought you were taking a job teaching EMT classes in Standish." For the past four-plus months I'd spent all my time either working at Second Chance or working on my house, so I was a little out of the loop as far as what was going on around North Harbor, but I hadn't thought I was *that* out of it.

He glanced over at my truck and then his gaze came back to me. "I turned it down," he said quietly.

Nick had a degree in biology and I knew that for a while he'd thought about going to med school. He'd worked as an EMT to put himself through college. I was about to ask him why the change in plans when Michelle joined us.

"Hello, Sarah," she said. Her smile was cool and professional.

"Hi," I said. It was the first time I'd seen Michelle face-to-face since I'd come home to North Harbor and I suddenly realized that she had to have been avoiding me for the past six months. Outside of tourist season the town was just too small not to bump into pretty much everyone.

An awkward silence hung between us for a moment. At least it felt awkward to me.

Michelle looked at Nick. "I know it's not part of your job description, but before you look at the body would you mind checking on Mrs. Hamilton?" she asked. "See if she needs to go to the hospital?"

"Of course." He looked at me then. He didn't smile exactly, but the warmth in his eyes was hard to miss. "Good to see you, Sarah," he said, reaching down to pick up his case.

I nodded. "You too, Nick."

He headed across the grass, and Michelle waited until he reached the curb before she turned her attention back to me. "How have you been?" she asked. Her tone was polite, almost formal.

For a moment I thought about waving a hand in front of her face and reminding her that it was me, reminding her about the time Gram had taken us to Portland over-

night and we'd snuck out to buy padded bras to enhance
our boyish fourteen-year-old, pretty much nonexistent
figures. Gram hadn't been fooled by the old pillows-
under-the-blankets trick. And I don't think she'd really
bought our story that Michelle had "forgotten" to pack
any clean underwear, either. But then Michelle had
pulled a pair of white cotton underpants—granny panties, really—out of her hot pink faux-fur-trimmed bag.
Our alibi, she'd called the underwear when she'd dragged
me into a dollar store to buy it on the way back to the
hotel.

But I didn't. We'd already had a very melodramatic
version of that conversation years ago and it hadn't
changed anything. So all I said was, "Things are going
well."

She gave a slight nod and took a small notebook and
a pen out of the pocket of her jacket. "What were you
and Mrs. Elliot doing here?" she said.

I told her about the workshop, how Maddie hadn't
shown up and Charlotte and I had decided to check on
her. I explained how we'd found Maddie and how I'd
sent her with Charlotte to wait in the truck while I called
911.

Michelle nodded silently and made notes. "Did you
see anyone else?" she asked, when I stopped talking.

I shook my head.

"Did Mrs. Hamilton say anything?"

"No. Just that Arthur Fenety was dead. I could see
that she was right, but I checked for a pulse just to be
sure."

She frowned. "Did you know him?"

"He came into the shop a couple of days ago. I bought a silver tea set from him. The next day he changed his mind and wanted to buy it back."

"I'll send somebody over to get that." She looked over my shoulder toward the backyard and then her gaze settled on my face again. "Is there anything else?"

"I don't think so," I said, absently rubbing my hands together.

Her expression softened a little. "I, uh, heard about your radio show," she said. "I'm sorry. I used to listen to it."

For a moment I could see a glimpse of the fifteen-year-old who used to be my best friend. I gave her a wry smile. "Thank you. According the new station owner most of my listeners were over-the-hill hippies who wore Birkenstocks and ate tofu."

Michelle glanced down at her stylish black boots, then back at me. "Well, I do like the orange-ginger tofu stir-fry at McNamara's," she said, and a hint of a smile flashed across her face.

I didn't talk much about my former late-night syndicated radio show. When the radio station had changed hands I'd been replaced by a music feed from California and a nineteen-year-old with a tan and ombré hair who gave the temperature every hour. Or, as my brother Liam derisively called it, Malibu Ken and a computer.

There was an awkward silence, and then Michelle fished in her pocket and held out a business card. "If you think of anything else, please call me."

"I will," I said, taking the little card stock rectangle without even looking at it. I glanced toward the truck. "What about Charlotte and Maddie?"

"They can go, as well," she said. She turned toward the back of the house.

"It was good to see you, Michelle," I said.

She stopped and looked back at me over her shoulder. "Yeah, it was good to see you, too."

I stuffed my hands in my pockets and walked across the front lawn to my truck. Nick was standing by the curb, talking to his mother. Maddie was in the cab of the truck, talking to Elvis and stroking his ebony fur. Her color was better. Elvis was giving her his full attention and, knowing the cat, probably making little murps of acknowledgment from time to time. I figured that whomever the cat used to belong to had talked to him a lot. Somewhere Elvis had learned the art of listening, cocking his head to one side, focusing his green eyes on the speaker's face and making encouraging sounds to keep the conversation going.

Nick and Charlotte both turned as I approached them. "We can go," I said. I gave Nick an inquiring look. "Is Maddie okay?"

He nodded. "I think so, but keep an eye on her."

"We will," I said. I looked at Charlotte. "Would you like to go to your house?"

"Please," she said.

"I'll take them," I said to Nick. "I'm guessing you have work to do."

He nodded. "Thanks." He put one arm around his mother's shoulders and leaned over to kiss her cheek. "Call me if you need anything. Otherwise I'll be in later."

Charlotte laid a hand against his cheek and gave him a small smile. "I'm just fine," she said.

Nick smiled back at her. "I never doubted it," he said. He straightened up and turned the smile on me. "You have my number now. If they need anything—or if you do—call me. Please."

"I will," I said. I sensed another awkward moment coming on.

"I'm so glad I finally got to see you," he said. "Even if it had to be like this."

"Me too," I said.

He was gone, cutting across the lawn with long steps, before we got to the awkward part. I watched him pull a pair of latex gloves from his pocket, thinking that he was a very good-looking man. I gave a little shake of my head. And that was a very inappropriate thing to be thinking with Nick's mother standing beside me, not to mention Arthur Fenety's dead body still in the backyard.

I put one arm around Charlotte's shoulders. "Why didn't you tell me Nick was working for the medical examiner?" I asked, keeping my voice light.

She pursed her lips and sighed. Then she looked at me. "Because I was hoping he wouldn't take the job."

I could tell from the expression on her face that she was serious. "Why?" I said.

Her gaze slid off my face. She looked across the yard. Nick was just disappearing around the side of Maddie's house. I waited in silence until Charlotte looked at me again. She answered my question with a question. "What did Nick say to you?" she asked.

"Just that he was working for the medical examiner's office and he turned down the job teaching the EMT course."

Charlotte nodded. "We had . . . words." Her mouth moved but she didn't say anything else.

"You wanted him to take it."

"Do you know how many close calls he's had in all the years he's been an EMT?" she asked.

I shook my head.

"I'm proud of him for wanting to help people. I just thought maybe he could do it in a classroom for a change." The color rose in her cheeks. "And I thought maybe being in a classroom might inspire him to think about medical school again. It doesn't make me a very nice person, does it?" she said.

I gave her shoulder another squeeze. "Don't talk like that," I said. "You're one of the nicest people I know."

"I know Nicolas is a grown man, more than capable of taking care of himself."

"But he's still your baby," I finished.

She nodded again. "And I don't think this is going to be easy. Nick has some strong opinions. Not everyone is happy he got this job. And while I think everyone has a right to express their opinion, if your opinion is critical in any way of my child, well, let's just say we're going to have a little problem."

"Nick is a lovely, lovely man," I said, deadpan, to lighten the mood.

Charlotte smiled at me then. "He is," she said, "and, you know, he's not seeing anybody."

"Don't start," I said, with a mock glare. "You sound like Gram."

"That's because she wants great-grandchildren before she's too old to enjoy them."

I shook my head. "She told me she wanted them before she was too *dead* to enjoy them."

"Yes, well, that too," Charlotte said. Her expression grew serious. "We should get Maddie away from all of this." She gestured with one hand.

"Michelle said we could all leave," I said. "I'll run you over to the house."

"If it's not too much trouble. Maddie and I could walk."

"It isn't," I said. "Let's go."

I walked around the front of the truck. Through the windshield I could see Elvis sitting on Maddie's lap while she stroked his black fur. It looked like she was talking to him as well. She seemed more like herself.

I climbed into the driver's side of the cab and Maddie turned to me. "We can't stay, can we?" she asked.

I shook my head. "No, I'm sorry. We can't," I said.

Charlotte had gotten in on the other side. "You can stay with me," she said.

Maddie took a deep breath as though she were going to say something, argue maybe. Then she let it out and all she said was, "Thank you."

I drove around the loop and out to Charlotte's little yellow house at the bottom end of the court. Elvis stayed on Maddie's lap and when she climbed out of the truck she carried him with her. I'd been planning on leaving Elvis in the truck, but Maddie seemed to be finding some comfort in the cat and I didn't think Charlotte would mind.

As soon as we stepped through the door Charlotte headed for the kitchen and Maddie and I—and Elvis—

trailed behind her. "Sit," Charlotte said. She washed her hands at the sink and filled the kettle, setting it on the stove with one hand and lifting down a canister that I knew held tea bags with the other.

"Charlotte, you sit," I said.

"I'm just going to make the tea," she said over her shoulder. Like my grandmother, Charlotte thought tea fixed everything from a broken bracelet clasp to a broken heart.

"I'm capable of making a cup of tea," I said, pulling off my jacket and draping it over the back of a chair. Charlotte gave me a skeptical look. "I am," I insisted. "Gram may not have been able to teach me to cook but I can make a decent cup of tea, so sit."

"Don't fuss over me, Charlotte," Maddie said. She'd taken a seat at the table. Elvis was on her lap, head cocked to one side as he took in all the scents of Charlotte's kitchen.

Charlotte opened her mouth to say something, and there was a knock at the front door.

"It's only me," a voice called. Liz appeared in the doorway. "I heard what happened," she said. She leaned sideways to look in Maddie's direction and held out a small white bakery box to me. "I cooked," she said, her blue eyes flicking momentarily in my direction. "Are you all right?" she asked Maddie.

Maddie nodded. "I was just telling Charlotte not to fuss."

Liz made a dismissive wave with one perfectly manicured hand. "Nobody's fussing," she said. She glanced at me again.

I held up both hands. "I'm just making tea. Have a seat."

"Heaven help us," Liz muttered almost under her breath. She sat down at the end of the table, reached across and gave Elvis a scratch on the top of his head, and then took one of Maddie's hands. "What can I do?" she asked.

I took the container of tea bags out of Charlotte's hands and all but pushed her toward the table. "I've got this," I said. I warmed the teapot with a little hot water from the kettle, dropped the tea bags inside and turned around to find Charlotte poking her head in the refrigerator.

I leaned over her shoulder. "What are you doing?" I hissed.

"I'm looking for the chicken." She straightened up, holding a small blue-and-white casserole dish.

"Of course," I said. "Tea with milk and sugar, tea with lemon or tea with chicken."

"Isabel obviously fell down on the job when it came to teaching you some respect for your elders," she said tartly. I knew from the gleam in her eye that she wasn't really annoyed with me. And I knew why she'd gone foraging for that chicken.

"I failed that day," I countered, taking the container from her. "Number one, that cat does not need a piece of chicken. Number two, sit down, please."

"It's not fair for all of us to have something and not give Elvis a little treat."

"Oh, for heaven's sake," I muttered. She glared at me. I glared at her. I won. She sat.

I could see Elvis out of the corner of my eye. He had a nose like a truffle hog and it was twitching in my direction. I put the chicken on the counter, put the cookies Liz had brought on a plate, made the tea, poured the tea and served everything to the ladies, the whole time being followed by a pair of deep green eyes. I knew if I didn't give the cat a piece of that chicken Charlotte would be on my case. She may have been as tough as a boiled owl, to use one of my grandmother's expressions, but I knew her well enough to know that she'd been shaken at finding Maddie with Arthur Fenety's body.

I cut four tiny bites of chicken for Elvis, set them on a piece of paper towel on the floor and crooked my index finger at the cat. He rubbed the side of his face against Maddie's wrist, jumped down and came across the floor to me. Being a well-mannered cat, he gave a soft meow of thanks before he started eating.

I poured a cup of tea for myself, added lots of milk and sugar and took the last seat at Charlotte's table. Liz lifted her cup and nodded with what I took to be approval of my tea-making abilities. I hadn't been exaggerating when I'd told Charlotte it was the only thing Gram had been able to teach me to do in the kitchen.

"Sarah, what's going to happen now?" Maddie asked. Both of her hands were wrapped around the china teacup. She had long fingers, the nails cut short and square, the opposite of Liz's immaculate manicure.

I ran my finger around the rim of the cup. I didn't want to tell Maddie or the others about my suspicions. "There'll be an autopsy," I said, finally. "The police will have more questions for you. They'll need to contact his family."

Maddie put a hand to her throat. "Oh, my word," she said, the color that had come back to her face draining away. "I forgot about Daisy."

I looked at Liz, raising an eyebrow.

"Arthur Fenety's sister," she whispered.

Charlotte put a hand on Maddie's arm. "The police will take care of that," she said.

"I should call her."

Charlotte shook her head. "You can call her later."

"Why don't you tell us what happened?" Liz said, tracing the loop of the teacup handle with one finger.

Maddie exhaled slowly. "I don't really know what to tell you," she said. "I invited Arthur for brunch. He says it's the best parts of breakfast and lunch put together and the time is more civilized." Her voice trailed away. She cleared her throat and when she spoke again her voice was stronger. "He arrived between quarter after twelve and twelve thirty. We talked for a few minutes; then I went in to start cooking. I was going to make an omelet for the two of us to share when the phone rang. Everything took longer than I meant it to. When the omelet was ready and I went back outside, Arthur was . . . gone." She looked across the table at me. "I couldn't find a pulse. I . . . I should have called an ambulance. I don't know what came over me. It was only a couple of minutes and you and Charlotte showed up, thank heavens."

"How long were you in the house?" I asked. Elvis had finished his snack and had started washing his face. He paused, one paw raised, as though he wanted to hear Maddie's answer, too.

She turned to look at me, fingering the collar of her tailored yellow blouse. "I don't know, really. I didn't look at the clock. No more than about fifteen or twenty minutes, I'm guessing. I . . . I shouldn't have left him alone for so long."

Liz immediately spoke up. "Don't think like that. Arthur wasn't a young man. This kind of thing can happen at our age." She'd put a cookie on her napkin and broken it into several pieces, but I noticed she hadn't eaten any of them.

I nodded agreement that I didn't completely feel. I didn't see the point in saying that I didn't think Arthur Fenety had died of natural causes. "Liz is right," I said. "There's no point in speculating. Let the police do their job." I glanced at my watch. "Is there anything else I can do for you before I head back to the store?"

She shook her head. "No. I'm in good hands here." She looked at Liz and Charlotte before her gaze met mine again.

I pushed back my chair and got to my feet. Charlotte stood up as well and came around the table, wrapping me in a hug. "Thank you, sweetie," she whispered against my ear.

"If you need anything, call me," I said softly.

She nodded.

I leaned down and put my arm around Maddie's shoulders. "I'm so sorry this happened," I said. "But I'm very glad that I got to see you."

She reached up and covered my hand with hers. "I'm glad I got to see you, too, Sarah," she said.

I straightened up and Liz was on her feet. "I'll walk out with you," she said. "I think I blocked you in."

I scooped Elvis up off the floor, gave Maddie and Charlotte one last smile and headed for the front door with Liz right behind me.

Liz's car was parked at the curb. It wasn't blocking my truck in any way.

"I can back out just fine," I said to her.

She crossed one arm over her midsection. "Well, look at that," she said. She gave a small shrug.

"Yes, look at that," I repeated. Elvis leaned sideways in my arms and gave Liz a look that could only be described as skeptical.

"I'm glad you were with Charlotte," she said.

I opened the driver's door of the truck and set Elvis on the seat. He immediately sat down and looked expectantly up at Liz.

I turned to face her. "Okay, what's going on?" I said.

She brushed a stray thread off her lavender shirt. "Nothing's going on. I just wanted to ask you what happened without Maddie sitting right there."

I explained how Charlotte and I had ended up at the little stone house, how we'd gone looking for Maddie and found her in the backyard with Arthur Fenety's body.

"Why didn't she call for help?"

I'd wondered the same thing myself. "I don't know," I said. "Shock, I guess."

Liz narrowed her blue eyes. "Do you think he had a heart attack?"

I didn't want to lie to her. Plus I wasn't very good at it. "I don't know," I said, fishing my keys out of my pocket.

"He was slumped to one side. I felt for his pulse and I couldn't find one."

She nodded, seeming satisfied with my answer. "I should get back inside," she said.

"Call me if Maddie or any of you need anything."

"I will." Liz reached over and patted my cheek. "I'm glad you're here, Sarah." She turned then and headed back up the driveway.

I climbed in the truck and waited until she was inside before I backed into the street. I looked down at Elvis next to me on the seat. "There's something Liz wasn't telling me," I said.

He gave a short, sharp meow. I decided to see it as him agreeing with me.

I reached over and gave the top of his head a scratch. "So what's her secret?" I said. "And what does it have to do with Arthur Fenety?"

Elvis made a sound close to a sigh.

Clearly he didn't know, either.

Chapter 5

Rose was going through boxes when I got back to the store. The double doors to the storage area were open so she could keep an eye on the store, but there were no customers. The first couple of days of the week were always quiet. I set Elvis down and he made a beeline for Rose. Poking his nose and a paw into boxes was kind of his hobby.

She was unpacking a collection of vintage Fiestaware. I knew of at least two collectors who would be interested in the brightly colored cream soup and onion soup bowls. She smiled at me, pushing her glasses up her nose. "Hello, dear," she said. "Did you go see Maddie?"

I nodded.

She immediately noticed my serious expression. "Is Maddie all right?"

"She's fine. It's her . . . friend. Arthur Fenety. He's . . . dead."

"Oh, good gracious," Rose said, closing her eyes for a brief moment. "Where's Maddie?"

"She's at Charlotte's. Liz is there, too."

Rose nodded. "Good."

"If you want to leave now, it's all right with me," I said.

She set the forest green bowl she'd been holding down on the table. "Thank you, but Maddie's in good hands. I'll stop in on my way home." She brushed bits of newsprint from the front of her red apron. "Do you know what happened to Arthur?"

I shook my head. "Not really. There'll be an autopsy to find out for sure."

"That's so sad for Daisy," Rose said. "She's Arthur's sister. I don't know if there's any other family."

"Why didn't you tell me that Nick had taken a job with the medical examiner?" I asked.

"It wasn't my place."

"Charlotte told me they disagreed."

Rose pushed her glasses up her nose. "That's one way to put it," she said.

I looked around. There were two very large boxes on the floor, holding open one of the doors. Elvis was poking one of the flaps with a paw, trying to get it open. "Get out of that," I said.

He turned to look at me over his shoulder and then went back to scraping at the cardboard. "Hey!" I snapped. "Stop it!"

He didn't even bother glancing back at me.

"Jessie's coming to pick up those two boxes," Rose said. "Elvis can't get them open. He can't hurt anything."

"That's not the point," I said, dropping my bag to the floor so I could go grab the cat. "I told him to stop. He acts like he can't hear me."

Rose took another paper-wrapped bowl from the box at her elbow. "Oh, he can hear you. He just doesn't have any intention of listening." She smiled without looking up. "He's a cat."

"He's a very bad cat," I said, picking him off the floor. "You're bad," I said, sternly, shaking my finger at him.

His response was to sniff it. Behind me Rose laughed.

I set Elvis down just inside the store. I pointed to the steps. "Go upstairs." I made a shooing motion with my hand for emphasis. He looked at me unblinkingly. Then he made a wide circle around me and went back into the storage room, in search of Mac—or more boxes he could paw his way into.

"Where's Mac?" I said to Rose.

She dipped her head toward the back of the space. "He's in the shed."

I headed for the door along the back wall. Elvis had jumped onto a metal plant stand. He looked a little like some Egyptian cat-god statue.

I found Mac out back in what we called the shed. The outbuilding had most likely been a two-car garage originally. It had been built much later than the house and had had at least two other lives that I knew about—as an appliance repair business and a pottery studio. My long-term plans were to fix the roof, add some insulation and use the space for more formal workshops, along with badly needed extra storage.

Mac was crouched down in front of a long dresser. It had two long drawers, two short ones, and it sat on four squat, curved feet. The wood, which we thought was elm, was in pretty decent shape. Really the only problem was the fact that it had been painted an unfortunate shade of orange that I thought was reserved just for traffic cones.

"What do you think?" I asked.

He squinted up at me. "The joints are all solid. There's no sign of mold or worms, although it does smell pretty strongly of mothballs and, if my nose is correct, Evening in Paris perfume."

"Some time in the sun will get rid of a lot of the smell," I said. I took a couple of steps to the front of the chest so I could get the full effect of the orange.

"What are you going to do for a finish?" Mac asked, getting to his feet and brushing the dust off his hands. He'd rolled back his sleeves and I could see the muscles in his arms. Mac was all lean, strong muscle. A couple of times I'd thought about inviting him for a run but I was a bit afraid he'd leave me behind.

"I'm not sure yet," I said. "I'm going for a distressed look but I'm not sure about the color."

"That orange is pretty distressing," Mac said with a smile as he came to stand beside me.

I rolled my eyes. "You've been spending too much time with Avery."

He smoothed a hand over his head. "Actually, I wanted to talk to you about Avery."

I raised an eyebrow. "What did she do?"

"Nothing. I was thinking maybe we should see if she'd be interested in helping me do some work in here."

"You mean repurposing some of the pieces?" I said. I looked around. Between Mac and me there were probably a dozen refurbishing projects in various stages of completion and maybe eight or nine more waiting to be worked on.

"She has a good eye for color."

I had been thinking the same thing. "Okay," I said, rubbing my left shoulder with the other hand. "I trust your judgment." I squinted at the chest of drawers, trying to picture it in some other — any other — color. Green, maybe.

Mac frowned at me. "Everything okay?"

I blew out a breath. "I'm not sure. One of the women didn't show up for the workshop. Madeline — Maddie — she's a friend of Gram's. I've known her since I was a little girl." I stretched my left arm up over my head trying to work out the stiffness. "Charlotte and I went to check on her."

"Was she okay?"

"She was. But her gentleman friend wasn't. He was . . . uh . . . dead."

"Dead?" Mac said. His brown eyes narrowed with concern. "What happened?"

"I'm not sure." I headed for the door and he followed. "The police came, and after that I took Maddie and Charlotte over to Charlotte's house. That's what took me so long."

We swung the wide doors shut and I made sure they were both closed tightly and locked securely. "Do you remember that older man who came in the other day with the silver tea set?" I asked Mac.

"White hair, mustache, nice suit. I remember," he said, bending down to snag a plastic grocery bag that was blowing across the pavement. "Wait a minute. It was him?"

I nodded. "Arthur Fenety. Which reminds me, the police will be by to get that tea set. It's in my office."

Mac shook out the bag and dropped it in the recycling bin by the back door of the shop. "So, how did the workshop go?"

"Good," I said. "Except Avery brought Elvis with her."

"Why?"

"She says he's good advertising for the shop."

He smiled. "What was her plan? Put a little signboard on him and have him walk up and down the sidewalk?"

"Don't say that out loud," I said. "It's just the thing Avery would be apt to try."

Elvis was back at the boxes propping open the door, trying diligently to work one paw under a flap of cardboard on the top of the box.

"Don't do that," Mac said.

Elvis immediately pulled his paw back and sat down on his haunches.

"I'll start bringing things in from the truck," Mac said, heading for the front door.

"I'll be right there," I said. I looked down at Elvis, who had come to sit by my feet. "So, him you listen to?"

He looked up at me and blinked, all green-eyed innocence.

Rose was showing a customer the little teacup gardens—tiny, hardy Haworthia or chives, planted in odd china cups with saucers. I inclined my head in her direction. "Go help Rose," I said. To my surprise Elvis headed purposefully across the floor in her direction. Sometimes I got the feeling that cat was messing with me.

Mac and I unloaded the truck and put everything back in the storage room. Rose sold four teacup gardens and I helped her wrap them while Elvis entertained the customer. By the time we had finished it was five minutes past store closing time. Rose walked around tidying up the displays while I ran the vacuum over the floor and Mac swept the storage room.

"If you talk to Jess tonight tell her those boxes of clothes are ready, please," Mac said, pulling on his denim jacket.

"I will," I said.

Jess was my closest friend in North Harbor—closest friend of my age, anyway. I'd known her casually when we were teenagers, but we'd gotten close after we became roommates in college. She had a great sense of funky style, and with a sewing machine and a pair of scissors she could make over just about any piece of clothing. Everything she restyled ended up in a little used and vintage clothing shop on the waterfront. She'd also started making one-of-a-kind quilts from recycled fabric. I'd had two of them in the shop and they'd sold within a week.

Mac picked up Rose's canvas tote bag. "I'll see you in the morning," he said. Now that sailing season was over I wondered what Mac would do with his free time. In the four months we'd worked together I'd learned very little about him. Any questions about his private life usually got only a one- or two-word answer.

Rose stopped to give me a hug. "Thank you for taking

care of Maddie today," she said. "Give Isabel my love when you talk to her."

"I will," I promised. I felt in my pocket for the little piece of paper Mr. P. had given me to write down the names of the women who had passed on messages to Gram. It was still there.

I locked the door behind Mac and Rose. Then I did a circuit around the store, trailed by Elvis, looking to see what was selling and what might need a little more tweaking. There were only three of the teacup gardens left. I knew there were cups in the storage room and more tiny plants upstairs in my office.

"Wanna help me do some planting?" I said to Elvis. He tipped his head to one side as though he was considering the question and then meowed. I took it as a yes.

I set up outside on an old, paint-spattered table we kept by the back door. Elvis jumped up and immediately began poking his whiskers in everything. He had to sniff the cups and the plants, and when I took the lid off the pail of potting soil he stood on his hind legs, put his front paws on the edge and pushed his face down inside before I could stop him.

And immediately sneezed. And sneezed. And sneezed. He shook his head vigorously, meowed indignantly and swiped at his nose with one paw.

I struggled to keep a straight face. Even though Elvis was a cat and not a person, it seemed mean to laugh at him.

"Let me see," I said. I reached for him and used the hem of my shirt to wipe some of the dirt from his black fur. He sneezed one more time and glared at me as if somehow this whole thing was my fault. I fished in my pocket for a Kleenex to try to clean his face a little better.

"I don't think he's going to blow his nose," a voice said behind me. I turned around to see Michelle standing a few feet away, hands in her pockets, a small smile on her face.

"He's pretty smart," I said.

"Oh, it's not that I think he couldn't. It's just from his expression I don't think he's going to."

Elvis was leaning sideways, watching Michelle intently as she crossed the space between us. He still had a slightly sour look on his face. I took advantage of the fact that his attention had shifted to clean his fur. He shook his head and took a swipe at my hand with his paw, but his claws weren't out so I knew he wasn't really that mad.

"What's his name?" Michelle held out her hand so the cat could sniff it.

"Elvis."

He sniffed a couple of times and seemed to like what his nose told him.

"What happened to his nose?" she asked, gesturing to the long, ropy scar that almost bisected the cat's nose.

"Nobody knows," I said with a shrug. "The best guess the vet could give is that he got into a fight with something that was probably a lot bigger than he is. The cat, I mean, not the vet."

Elvis butted her hand with his head, kitty shorthand for "Give me a scratch." Michelle obliged, stroking the top of his head, brushing away the last bit of soil and peat moss clinging to his fur. His eyes narrowed into slits and he began to purr.

"You have a friend," I said.

She smiled. "I like cats. Is Elvis the cat that was wandering around downtown for a while?"

I nodded. "Uh-huh."

"How did you end up with him?" Elvis was leaning against her arm, rumbling like a well-tuned motorboat engine.

"Sam," I said, brushing potting soil off my shirt.

"That explains a lot," she said, her smile widening. "The animal-control officer tried for weeks to capture this cat. He set up a cage in the alley by Sam's place. All he ended up catching was one very pissed-off seagull."

I laughed. "I'm sure Sam had nothing to do with that."

Michelle rolled her eyes. "I'm sure." She smiled down at Elvis, who was nudging her hand because she'd stopped scratching behind his ear. "Well, I'm glad he ended up with you."

I didn't know what else to say to her. Silence settled between us like a large rock. Then I remembered the silver service. That was probably why Michelle was here. "You came for the tea set that Arthur Fenety wanted to sell," I said.

"I did," she said

"It's in my office," I said, gesturing at the back door. "Come in and I'll get it for you."

Elvis jumped down and followed us. To be more exact, he followed Michelle. When we stepped inside the store she stopped in the middle of the room and looked around.

"This is really nice," she said. "I should have come in before now." She looked at me and it was hard to read her expression. Was that guilt I could see in her eyes? I felt as if that rock had just landed in the middle of the room between us.

I cleared my throat. "You're welcome anytime," I said. "If I'm not here, Elvis usually is."

The cat gave an enthusiastic meow at the sound of his own name. We both laughed and it seemed to chase away some of the awkwardness.

I took Michelle upstairs to my office and gave her the box with the silver tea set. She looked quickly at each piece and then wrote me a receipt.

"You know this place was briefly a private smokers' club," she said as we headed back downstairs.

"That would explain the smell and the window boxes full of cigarette butts," I said.

"I'm glad you're giving the place a new life." She gestured at the sign by the door. "A second chance." Her expression grew serious. "I'm sorry if I made you uncomfortable before, when I brought up your show."

"It's okay," I said. "It was just a job." I held out a hand. "And now I have this."

"Not everyone bounces back as well as you did, Sarah," Michelle said. "Believe me. I've seen people at their worst."

I brushed my hair back from my face. "I'm lucky. I had a lot of people helping me. "

She nodded. "You are."

I walked her out to the small parking lot. She shifted the box with the silver from one arm to the other and bent down to stroke Elvis's fur. "Bye, puss," she said. She straightened up. "I'm glad you're back, Sarah." She turned then and headed toward the street.

I watched her go, and then I walked back over to the table. Elvis jumped up again, made a wide berth around the bucket of potting soil and ended up sitting down in the middle of the collection of little plants—the second-most inconvenient place for him to be. Even with him pretty much in the way the entire time I still managed to get all the plants transferred into the cups.

I was just coming back from putting the last teacup in the front window when Nick Elliot walked up the drive-way. "Hi," he said. "I was hoping I'd find you here."

"Well, you did." I realized how lame the words sounded as soon as I'd said them.

Elvis was eyeing Nick the same way he'd checked out Michelle.

"Elvis, right?" Nick said. "Mom told me you'd taken the cat that had been hanging around downtown."

"More like Sam and Elvis"—I gestured to the cat with the tray of plastic pots I was holding—"conspired to trick me into taking him."

Nick reached for the bucket of soil. "Sam tricked you?" he said, eyebrows raised.

"Yes," I said.

He smiled. "Yeah, I can see him doing that."

Nick followed me in the storage room, and I took the bucket from him and set it up on the shelf next to my pile of pots. He looked around. "You've done a lot of work here. How about a tour?"

"All right," I said. I held up both hands. "This is part storage room, part workroom. Anything that's really messy we do out in the old garage. It still needs some work."

I led him over to the doors that led into the shop.

"This is great," he said as he stepped into the space. "Are you using both floors?"

I shook my head. "No. I have an office upstairs and some more storage."

He nodded but one of the guitars on the wall had caught his eye. "That's a Rickenbacker," he said. "A 'sixty-five."

"Uh-huh. Sparkle inlays. All original." I walked over and lifted the guitar off the wall. It was the deep russet color of an autumn leaf. "Try it," I said.

His eyes narrowed. "Seriously?"

"Yes." I held out the guitar. "You still play, don't you?" I asked.

He gave me a wry smile. "Not as much as I used to, but yeah, I still play."

"So play something for me," I said.

Nick took the guitar from me and sat down on the steps to the second floor. I leaned against the wall while he tuned the strings and played some chords. Then he looked over at me. "I don't know," he said a little self-consciously, "but maybe you remember this." He bent his head and started to play.

I did remember. It was the first song Nick had taught me to play on guitar. "Comin' Back to You." He played the bridge and then he started into the first verse, sing-ing along softly with the music:

I'm comin' back to you,
Somehow I always knew
No matter what I do,
All roads lead back to you.

For a moment I was fifteen again, it was summertime and the night sky was filled with stars. The memory wrapped around me with the music. Nick played through to the end of the chorus, then looked up at me and smiled a bit sheepishly. "I'm a little rusty."

"You sounded great to me," I said.

"Do you play much?" he asked.

I pushed away from the wall and shook my head. "I've been a little busy."

"That's too bad." He got to his feet again and his gaze darted to my face for a moment. "Mom told me about your radio show being canceled," he said. "I'm sorry."

"Thanks," I said.

Nick didn't say anything for a moment, as though maybe he was waiting for me to say something more. Then he held out the guitar. "It's a nice instrument, Sarah. Thanks for letting me play it."

I raised an eyebrow at him as I took it, trying to lighten the mood a little. "You know, you qualify for the family discount."

He shrugged. "It should go to someone who would actually play it once in a while. I don't have a lot of time these days."

"That's too bad," I said, copying his words and the tone of his voice from before.

He smiled. "Touché."

I smiled back.

"Speaking of family," he said. "How's yours?"

"Good," I said. "Dad's teaching journalism now and still doing some writing, mostly longer pieces for magazines. Mom has a new book out next month." My mother wrote a series for elementary school kids about a talking gerbil named Einstein. "And Liam's pretty much focused on passive solar design now."

Nick nodded. "Yeah, he told me he's gotten involved with the small-house movement."

"I didn't know you guys stayed in touch," I said. I wondered why Liam hadn't told me.

Nick shrugged. "Off and on."

I hung the guitar back on the wall and turned to face him. "I'm thinking the reason you're here isn't because you wanted a tour of the shop or to catch up on my family."

"Yeah, I do have a few questions."

Elvis had wandered in from wherever he'd been. He twisted around my legs and I bent down and picked him up. "No offense," I said, "but isn't that Michelle's job?"

Nick leaned over to give the cat a scratch under his chin, which pretty much earned him a friend for life. "It's mine, too," he said. "The police are trying to figure out whether or not a crime's been committed. I'm trying to figure out how and why Mr. Fenety died. We overlap a little."

I explained about the workshop and Maddie not

showing up. Elvis was leaning sideways, his head nestled in the crook of my elbow. I shifted him slightly in my arms and he turned his head just enough to shoot me a look. "I knew Charlotte would go over there to check on Maddie. I went with her, just in case."

I recounted how we'd tried the front door and then decided to see if Maddie had been working in the backyard and just lost track of time.

"What did the body look like?"

I narrowed my eyes and pictured Arthur Fenety's body in my mind. "It . . . he was slumped to one side and his eyes were closed. There was something at the corner of his mouth." I raised a hand to my face.

"Where was Maddie?"

"She was just sitting there," I said. "I think she was in shock."

Elvis started to purr. Nick smiled at the cat. "Do you have any idea how long she'd been sitting there?"

"I don't know. A couple of minutes, I guess. She said she'd been making an omelet for the two of them. Then the phone rang." I paused for a moment, picturing the table and running Maddie's words through my head again. "When, uh, she went back outside Arthur Fenety was dead."

He caught my hesitation and his brown eyes narrowed. "What is it?" he asked. "Did you remember something else?"

"I just realized that I'm going to have to tell all of this to Gram over the phone."

Nick gave me a sympathetic smile. "Your grandmother and Maddie are close."

"They've been friends as far back as I can remember."

My left arm was starting to fall asleep. I set Elvis down on the floor again. He shook himself and started washing his face but I saw him dart little glances at Nick and at me, almost as though he wanted to listen to the rest of our conversation but didn't want us to know. I reminded myself that he was a cat and what he was probably thinking about was how he could get another scratch.

"Is there anything else you can tell me?" Nick asked.

"I don't think so," I said, brushing cat hair off my sleeve.

"If you think of anything, will you call me?" he said, pulling his keys from his pocket. "Please. You have my cell, don't you?"

"I do," I said. Elvis stretched and headed for the stairs.

"So, tell me about your new job," I said as we headed toward the back door. "You're not like the kind of crime-scene investigator I've seen on TV."

He laughed. "No one's like the crime-scene investigators on TV." He pulled a hand back through his hair. "I told you I'm working for the medical examiner's office."

I nodded.

"My official job title is medicolegal death investigator. It's my job to figure out the cause and manner of death when someone dies in this part of the state. Sometimes I have to investigate, like today. That means taking pictures, talking to witnesses, collecting evidence, working with the police. Other times it's as simple as taking a basic report and having the deceased's doctor sign the death certificate."

We stepped out into the parking lot. "So you're doing this because you're trained as an EMT?" I asked.

"It doesn't hurt," he said with a shrug. "But I actually took a course in St. Louis." He narrowed his gaze. "Mom didn't tell you."

"She left out a few details."

Nick shook his head. "She wanted me to take the teaching job. And she still has this fantasy that I'll go to med school eventually." He pulled a hand back through his hair. "She likes the sound of *my son the doctor*."

"She just wants you to be happy," I said, as we stepped outside.

He smiled. "I am." He still had that great mischievous little-boy smile, but I could see lines etched into the skin around his eyes. "How about dinner sometime down at Sam's? We can catch up." The smile widened into a grin. "And maybe it'll get my mother to stop asking not so subtle questions about my love life."

I smiled back at him. "Somehow I don't think it'll work, but dinner sometime would be nice."

"I'll call you, then." He pulled his car keys out of his pocket. "Have a good night, Sarah," he said, and then he headed for the street.

I went back inside. I found Elvis in my office, sitting next to my bag. "Ready to go home?" I asked.

"Meow," he said, and then he licked his whiskers in case it hadn't occurred to me that he was hungry.

Elvis rode shotgun all the way home. In the few months I'd had the cat I'd discovered that he liked riding around in the truck. It made me wonder what his past life had been like. When I'd driven him back to the shop from Sam's after he'd become my cat, I couldn't help laughing at the way he'd watched the traffic at every stop sign and how he'd twisted to look over his shoulder as I backed into my parking spot.

When I pulled into the driveway he jumped out of the truck without waiting for me to lift him off the seat and headed for the backyard. "Supper's in about fifteen minutes," I called after him.

He meowed in acknowledgment and kept going.

I gathered the mail and I let myself into the house. Standing in the entryway I found myself wishing Gram was upstairs in her apartment instead of in a van somewhere in the wilds of eastern Canada.

My house was an 1860s Victorian that had been divided into three apartments probably thirty-plus years ago. It had been let go when I bought it, but I could see that it had good bones. Liam, my dad, and I had done almost all of the work on my main-floor apartment and Gram's second-floor one. My mom had helped me decorate with yard-sale chic. The third small apartment at the back of the house still needed a little more work. It was where my parents or Liam stayed when they came to visit.

The house had been an incredibly good deal and for a while I'd told myself that's why I'd bought it: as an investment. But really North Harbor was the place that most felt like home to me and deep down I'd always known it was where I'd end up.

I unlocked the apartment door and dropped my

things on one of the high-backed stools at the kitchen counter. Then I opened the refrigerator door, hoping that somehow it had become magically filled with food. It hadn't.

I didn't feel like another egg and tomato sandwich for supper. I wanted to sit at the round wooden table in Gram's green-and-white kitchen and eat meat loaf with mashed potatoes or baked beans and brown bread. And I really, really wanted to talk to her about Maddie.

I looked at my watch. That I could do. But first I needed to let Elvis in. I found him sitting on the small verandah by the side door. There was a dried leaf stuck to his tail and a prickly brown burdock clinging to the fur on the middle of his back.

"Hang on," I said, as he tried to make his way around me. He made annoyed sounds low in his throat but he stood still, tail flicking through the air, as I worked the little spiky ball from his fur. "If you'd stay out of that back corner of the yard you wouldn't get these things in your fur," I said, for maybe the tenth time. "Why are you back there, anyway?"

He licked his lips.

"Well, in that case you don't need any supper."

He didn't even dignify my comment with a snippy meow; he just headed for the kitchen and I managed to grab the dead leaf from his tail as he went by. My kitchen, living room and dining room were one big, open space with tons of light from the double bay windows at the front of the house. The bedroom overlooked the back-yard, which would have been nothing but grass if it hadn't been for Gram and her friends. Instead I had a raised flower bed full of perennials and two hanging baskets by the back door.

I followed Elvis to the kitchen and gave him his dinner and a fresh bowl of water. Then I wandered in the living room, dropped onto the sofa and reached for the phone.

Gram answered on the third ring. "Hello, sweet girl," she said.

I couldn't help smiling at the sound of her voice. "Hi, Gram," I said, "How was your day?"

"Wonderful. I had the best blueberry pancakes I've ever eaten. I wish you'd been here."

"I wish I were there, too," I said, tucking my feet up underneath me.

"What's wrong?" she asked.

I took the elastic out of my hair and shook out the braid. "How do you do that?" I said.

"Grandmother's intuition," she said. "What is it?"

I sighed, softly. "It's not me. It's . . . do you know Maddie's gentleman friend?"

"Arthur," she said. "I've met him twice, I think." I could hear the caution mixed with curiosity in her voice.

"I'm sorry, Gram," I said. "He's dead."

"Oh, my word," she said. "Poor Maddie." I heard her turn to John and repeat what I'd just said. "What happened?" she asked when she came back to the phone. "Was it an accident? Did he have a heart attack?"

I took a deep breath, let it out slowly and gave her the short version of what had happened. About halfway through my explanation Elvis wandered in, jumped up on my lap and laid his head on my chest as though he was listening to me breathing.

"Are you all right?" Gram asked.

"I am," I said. Just talking to her made me feel better. "And Maddie is with Charlotte."

"What can I do?" I could hear her moving around and guessed that she was looking for a piece of paper and something to write with. That was Gram. Whenever something was wrong the first thing she did was look for a pencil and make a list.

I put one arm around Elvis and stretched out my legs. He tipped his head and his green eyes looked up at me. I started to stroke his fur and he closed them and began to purr. "There really isn't anything you can do," I said. "Maybe you could call Maddie. She'd probably love to talk to you."

"Okay, I'll do that," Gram said. "Now what can I do for you?"

"You've already done it," I said.

"Anytime, sweet girl," she said. I could feel the warmth of her smile coming through the phone somehow. "So, tell me how the workshop went?"

"It went very well." Elvis was purring so loudly I was surprised Gram couldn't hear him through the receiver. "I could have done without seeing Mr. Peterson naked, though."

For a moment there was nothing but silence. "Naked?" Gram finally managed to choke out. "Alf was . . . naked?"

"As the day he was born."

"Did he have some kind of breakdown or a stroke?"

I laughed. "No. It's a long story, but there was an art class in the room next door. Mr. Peterson was the model but he got the dress code and the room wrong."

"Oh, sweet girl, that would be enough to put a person off their food," she said. "No offense to Alf."

"Mr. P. doesn't strike me as the type of person who takes offense that easily," I said. "And it would take a lot more than the sight of his wrinkly backside to get rid of my appetite."

She laughed. "I miss you," she said.

"I miss you, too," I said. "Tell me more about your day."

Elvis suddenly lifted his head and licked the edge of the telephone receiver.

"And Elvis just sent you a kiss."

"Give him one from me."

I spent the next five minutes hearing about Gram and John's adventures along the coast of Nova Scotia. When I hung up I was still hungry, but not nearly as lonely.

I'd come to North Harbor to figure out what I was going to do next after my job had disappeared. I'd spent a week with my mom and dad, mostly feeling restless and out of sorts. My mother had suggested coming to Gram's. Mom had walked up behind me while I was standing, looking out the kitchen window, and put her arms around my shoulders.

"I love you, pretty girl," she'd said. "But I'm kicking you out."

I'd turned to look at her. "What do you mean? I don't understand."

She'd kissed the top of my head. "Your grandmother is expecting you for supper. North Harbor is where you need to be. You have a house there and, more importantly, that's where your heart is. Go figure out what you want to do next. Your dad and I are only a phone call away."

The next morning Gram had brought me breakfast in bed. She'd told me I had exactly one week to wallow. That had been a Wednesday. I made it until lunch on Thursday. I hated having unwashed hair, I'd gotten crumbs in the bed and my pajama bottoms had a hole in one knee.

How could I lie around feeling sorry for myself with Gram around? A lot worse had happened to her. She'd lost my grandfather. She'd lost my dad, her only child. And she could still find joy in the world. She'd told me once that it would be an insult to my dad's memory to give up on life because he'd been the type of person to grab onto it with both hands. And since I could still grab onto life pretty well with both hands that's what I was trying to do. Which was why, in the end, I hadn't told Gram what I also hadn't told Nick: I didn't know what had happened at Maddie's house this afternoon. I just knew she wasn't telling the truth about it.

Chapter 6

I couldn't cook. Whatever the cooking equivalent of a green thumb was, I didn't have it. In middle school I was voted Most Likely to Set a Kitchen on Fire after a term of culinary arts classes in eighth grade. But I did like to eat and I paid a lot of attention to food. I'd seen the glass bowl of fruit in the middle of the teak table in Maddie's backyard. And Arthur Fenety had had a cup of coffee, about half-full, at his place. What I hadn't seen was the omelet that Maddie had said she was making for the two of them to share.

Maybe I couldn't make an omelet—okay, definitely I couldn't make an omelet—but I knew they weren't something you whipped up, stuck in the refrigerator and then popped in the microwave later to warm up.

"So, where was it?" I asked Elvis. "Presumably she would have brought it outside to serve it to Arthur."

The cat stopped purring long enough to lift his head and give me a blank look. He didn't know, either.

I closed my eyes and pictured the round table again, set with sunny red, orange and white place mats and matching napkins. There hadn't even been any plates at either of their places, which made sense. When the omelet was finished, she would have just slid it onto the plates and served it. But she didn't. Why?

I didn't think for a moment that Maddie had killed Arthur Fenety. She wasn't that kind of person.

"She's hiding something," I said. "What? And why?"

He didn't have an answer to that question, either.

I looked at the phone. Should I call Michelle? And tell her what? That I knew Maddie wasn't telling the whole truth because she let some eggs get cold? What difference did that make, anyway? It was a police investigation. It was none of my business.

I was still hungry. I reached for the phone and punched in my friend Jess's number.

"Hey Sarah, what's up?" she said.

"Have you had supper?" I asked.

"No," she said. "Not unless you count three Tic Tacs fused together that I found in my pocket about an hour ago."

Unlike me, Jess could cook. It was just that she'd get busy sewing and forget. "How about supper at The Black Bear?"

"Umm, yes," she said. I pictured her at her sewing table, tucking her long brown hair behind one ear.

"Twenty minutes too soon?" I asked.

"Not for me. I'm doing over a wedding dress and I'm out of ideas. Maybe supper will inspire me."

"Nothing screams 'Marry me,' like a pub with a house band named The Hairy Bananas," I said, dryly.

Jess laughed. "You joke, but a couple of years ago a

guy actually proposed to his girlfriend at Sam's place. It was one of those elaborate public proposals and he did it during halftime of the Superbowl."

"Please tell me you're making this up."

"I am not," she said, a bit of indignation in her voice. "All I can remember is that it involved tortilla chips, bean dip and a pretty expensive diamond ring." She paused for effect. "The ring turned up a couple of days later."

I groaned. "Now I know you're making it up."

She laughed again. "I'll see you in a bit," she said, and ended the call.

I hung up the phone and gave Elvis a little nudge. He opened one green eye and looked up at me without lifting his head. "I'm going to meet Jess for supper," I said. "You have to get up."

He sat up, yawned and stretched and finally jumped down to the floor and headed to the bedroom. I went into the bathroom to wash my face, and when I walked into the bedroom Elvis was sitting on the white faux-leather lounger, looking expectantly at the TV.

I changed into a black sweater and my favorite pair of gray suede pull-on boots. A loud meow came from the chair by the window.

I looked over at the cat. "This is insane," I muttered.

He narrowed his eyes at me, and his tail slapped against the seat of the chair. Then he looked pointedly at the television again.

I checked my watch, even though I didn't really need to. I knew exactly what time it was. What I didn't know was how Elvis knew what time it was. And he definitely did know.

I grabbed the remote off the nightstand, turned on the TV and changed the channel just in time to hear Johnny Gilbert announce, "This is *Jeopardy!*"

Elvis made a noise that sounded a lot like sigh of contentment and stretched out on the lounge chair, chin on his paws.

The cat was a *Jeopardy!* junkie, something I'd discovered about a week after I'd brought him home. Elvis had been eating when suddenly his head came up as though maybe he'd heard something. He'd tipped it to one side like he was listening and then he headed purposefully for the bedroom. Curious, I'd followed him.

He had parked himself on the floor in front of the television and looked at me. When I didn't do anything he'd made a sharp meow. So I'd turned the TV on. The cat had studied the screen for a moment and then meowed again.

"What? You don't like *Star Trek* reruns?" I'd said.

That had gotten me a look that I would have called withering if Elvis had been a person. So I started working my way through the channels. It was strange enough thinking that the cat wanted to watch TV, so it wasn't that much weirder to think that he had a specific program in mind. The moment he'd seen Alex Trebek, Elvis had jumped up onto the chair and stretched out.

The same thing happened the next night, although I didn't channel surf. I went right to the show. The third night was a Saturday. When Elvis started for the bedroom, I'd said, "It's Saturday. No *Jeopardy!*"

He'd stopped in his tracks. I'd waited to see what he'd do. After a moment he'd turned and come back to his bowl. Not only did I have a cat that liked to watch quiz shows, but somehow he also knew it was a weeknight thing.

Luckily, the TV had a sleep timer so I could set it to turn off in thirty minutes, when the show was over. I pulled my hooded red sweater over my head and grabbed the beaded bag Jess had given me for my birthday.

"I'm leaving," I said to Elvis.

His eyes didn't move from the screen. His tail twitched once and he made a low murp that was probably the cat equivalent of "Okay. Fine."

The streets in North Harbor were spread out in no pattern that I'd ever been able to figure out. It seemed that as the town grew, streets were laid down wherever they seemed to be needed, so it wasn't always easy to get from one place to another in more or less a straight line. But that was part of the town's charm, too. I was only three blocks from the harbor front. An easy walk.

Jess had already snagged a booth along the back wall when I got to The Black Bear. One elbow was on the table, head propped on her hand, and she was staring at a basket of Sam's spicy corn chips.

"Why are you torturing yourself?" I asked as I slid onto the seat opposite her.

"It's not torture," she said, without looking up. "I'm expanding my sphere of willpower."

"Just because you're trying to eat healthier doesn't mean you can't have the occasional corn chip, Jess," I said.

Jess was trying to live a healthier lifestyle but it kept

getting derailed by her love of all things deep-fried and her loathing for any activity that made her sweat.

"I don't want a corn chip," she said in a flat voice, like she was repeating some kind of mantra. She was concentrating so hard there were frown lines between her blue eyes.

"Okay," I said. I reached over and pulled the basket across the table. I knew the crisp little tortilla triangles would be spiced with cracked black pepper and lemon. I grabbed two. They were delicious, still warm from the oven. I ate a third one.

"How can you sit there and eat those right in front of me?" Jess asked, an exaggerated aggrieved edge to her voice.

"I'm removing temptation from your sphere of willpower," I said, reaching for another chip.

She made a face at me and leaned against the back of the booth. She was wearing her long brown hair loose with a pumpkin-colored sweater, jeans and brown knee-high boots. She had a funky, eclectic style and she could find humor in just about anything.

Jess had grown up in North Harbor but we really hadn't been friends, probably because I was a summer kid. We'd gotten close when I put an ad on the music-department bulletin board at the University of Maine, looking for a roommate. Jess had been the only person to call. She'd been studying art history and I'd been doing a business degree and taking every music course I could fit into my schedule, but we'd hit it off. After we'd been living together for a couple of weeks she'd confessed that she'd taken the ad down about five minutes after I'd pinned it up.

"I would have put it back if I hadn't liked you," she'd said.

"What if I hadn't liked you?" I'd countered. We'd been out on the lawn, painting a trash-picked table we'd carried half a mile home, walking on the edge of the road like a couple of nomads.

Jess had grinned. "Now, what were the chances of that ever happening?"

"How was your day?" she asked me now.

I blew out a breath. "That's a long story," I said, looking around for a waitress.

"I already ordered for us," Jess said, waving one hand dismissively at me.

"Why?" I asked as I pulled my sweater off over my head. It was warm inside The Black Bear. Even though it was a Monday night the place was about half-full. Three tables had been pushed together in the center of the room for what I was guessing was a group of tourists, at least a dozen. There was another tourist, a woman wearing a Red Sox cap and sunglasses, in the booth behind Jess. The folded map on the seat beside her was a dead giveaway,

"Because I know you like Sam's fish chowder and Sam said they seemed to be having a run on it tonight. Did you want something else?"

I shook my head. "No, that's good. Did you order me some of those little cheese biscuits?"

She nodded. "I told Sam you'd figure out your own dessert."

I smiled at her. "Thanks."

She laced her fingers behind her head. "So, tell me the long story about your day."

"Let me see if I can sum it up for you," I said. "I got a great price on two boxes of Fiestaware. I saw a seventy-five-year-old man naked. And Charlotte and I discovered a dead body."

Jess blinked. "Wow," she said. "That beats the heck out of a seagull stealing my French fries at lunch." She leaned forward again, forearms on the table. "Start with the dead body."

"His name is—was Arthur Fenety."

"Wait a minute. Does he have a sister named Daisy?"

"Yes," I said, stretching my legs under the table. "Why? Do you know her?"

"I altered a dress for her. Silk. Beautiful, beautiful fabric. What happened to her brother?"

"I'm not sure," I said carefully. I explained how Charlotte and I had ended up at Maddie's house.

Jess shook her head. "Poor Maddie. She's such a nice person. You know those buckets of tulips that are out in front of the shop?"

I nodded.

"She helped me plant all of them. She gave me fertilizer to put in the water. She even told me when to water them. You know me—I can't even keep plastic flowers alive."

Our waitress arrived then with two oversize steaming bowls of Sam's fish chowder, a plate of cheese biscuits and a little pot of butter.

We ate for a couple of minutes in silence, cut only by our little murmurs of satisfaction. If there was fish chowder that was better than Sam's, I hadn't tasted it yet.

Jess set down her spoon and reached for a biscuit.

"So, how does the naked seventy-five-year-old man fit into this?" she asked.

I laughed. "He doesn't, really. Remember I told you I was doing a workshop for a bunch of Gram's friends down at the seniors' apartment building?"

Her mouth was full so all she did was nod.

"Well, it turns out there's an art class there at the same time."

Jess nodded and brushed crumbs off the corner of her mouth. "Isn't Eric teaching some kind of drawing class?"

"That's it," I said, scooping up a fat scallop with my spoon. "Do you know Alfred Peterson?"

"Little bald man? Pants are always up under his armpits?"

I nodded.

Jess paused, spoon halfway to her mouth. "Wait a minute. You saw Mr. Peterson naked?"

I nodded again.

"Did he know?"

"That he was naked or that I saw him?"

Jess thought for a moment. "Both."

I fished a chunk of red-skinned potato out of the bowl and ate it. "Yes and yes."

"So Eric's class is drawing nudes and Mr. Peterson is their model?"

"Not exactly," I said. I leaned sideways and looked around the room. Sam had just come from the kitchen. He gave me a sheepish grin when I caught his eye, and started over.

"I'm sorry," he said as he got close to the table, holding up both hands as though he was surrendering. "I really did think Alf knew Eric was just going to have the class draw hands." He was trying to keep the grin in check but it wasn't working. "Was he really completely . . . ?" The end of the sentence trailed off.

"In all his glory," I said solemnly.

Sam laughed. "I'm sorry, Sarah. If I'd had any idea that Alf didn't know, I would have told him. I swear."

"I believe you," I said. "I think."

"Are you playing Thursday night?" Jess asked. In the off-season the house band—Sam's band—played most Thursday nights with whoever was around and wanted to sit in.

He nodded. "Are you two coming?"

Jess looked at me.

"I think so," I said.

"We'll be here," Jess said.

"What if I have a date Thursday night?"

"You on a date." Jess tipped her head to one side, a thoughtful expression on her face as she studied me. After a moment she turned back to Sam. "Not likely. We'll be here," she repeated, reaching for a biscuit.

"Good," Sam said. He turned to me again. "Mac said you might have an old fiddle you're going to need an estimate on in a few days."

"Looks like it," I said.

"Okay, well Vincent knows a guy up in Limestone. So let me know and I'll set something up." He glanced over his shoulder. "I need to get back to the kitchen. There's rhubarb-strawberry pie, if you're interested."

Jess's eyes lit up. "I may possibly love you, Sam."

Sam laughed and headed back to the kitchen.

I was just spooning up the last bit of creamy broth from the bottom of my bowl when Katie, our waitress, appeared with pie and coffee for both Jess and me.

"Mmmm," Jess moaned after her first bite. "Why doesn't my pie ever turn out this good?"

I took a sip from my cup. "I can tell you, but you aren't going to like the answer."

She licked flakes of pastry from the back of her fork. "It's not going to be something corny, like Sam makes it with a song on his lips and love in his heart, is it?"

"Uh, no," I said, taking another bite and wondering if I could taste a hint of vanilla in the filling. "It's lard."

"Lard?" Jess frowned, her mouth twisted to one side.

"Uh-huh."

I could almost see the gears and cogs turning in her head. "Lard is animal fat," she said.

I nodded.

Her expression cleared. "Okay. *Animal fat* means 'meat.' Meat is a source of protein. Protein is part of a healthy diet. I'm good." She used her fork to spear another bite.

I reached for my coffee cup again. "You can rationalize pie but you couldn't rationalize a corn chip?"

"Yeah, the human mind is a funny thing, isn't it?" she said, around a mouthful of berries and rhubarb.

"Did you know Nick Elliot is working for the medical examiner's office?" I asked, deliberately changing the subject.

Jess looked up from her plate. "Seriously?"

I nodded.

"I thought he was taking a job teaching an EMT course."

I shrugged. "I guess he changed his mind."

"So how does Nick look these days?" Jess asked teasingly.

"Fine," I replied, maybe a little too quickly.

She smirked at me over her mug. "Only fine?"

"Well, maybe . . . very fine," I admitted, feeling my cheeks redden.

"I knew it," Jess crowed, waving her fork in the air almost as though she were conducting an imaginary symphony orchestra.

"Okay, so Nick is a very good-looking man. The fact that I noticed it doesn't mean anything. I can appreciate that just the way I'd appreciate a beautiful sunset over the harbor or a well-made guitar.

Jess leaned back against the padded vinyl. "Good thing I wore my boots," she said.

I narrowed my eyes at her across the table. "What are you talking about?" I said.

"Good thing I wore my boots," she repeated, "because all that bull crap you're spreading would have ruined my new shoes."

I made a face and she laughed.

"Getting involved with Nick Elliot. Now, there would be a bad idea," I said, wrapping my hands around my coffee cup.

Jess shrugged. "What's so bad about it?"

"Well, he just started a new job; that's going to be pretty stressful. I'm trying to get a business off the ground, and, as you like to point out, all I do these days is work." I held up a hand because I could tell from Jess's face that she was about to mount an argument to try to refute my objections. "And don't forget, Nick's mother works for me." I raised my eyebrows at her.

Jess pressed her lips together and after a moment she sighed. "Okay, you win. I don't have anything."

"How about you and Nick?" I said.

She shook her head. "He is not my type."

"Oh, really?" I set my cup back on the table and folded my arms across my chest. "And your type would be?"

She tilted her head back and looked up at the hammered-tin ceiling, putting one hand to her throat. "I like the sensitive, artistic type, the kind of man with the soul of a poet."

"Good thing I wore *my* boots," I said dryly.

Jess laughed.

I was so glad Jess was still in North Harbor. She was always bugging me about spending too much time working, but the truth was that without her dragging me out with the three-dimensional people, as she put it, I would have spent all of my time at the shop, working on the house or looking for new business.

We spent the next ten minutes or so with Jess catching me up on town gossip. Her sewing space and the little shop where she sold her repurposed clothing were right down on the waterfront and, like Sam, she knew everything that was happening in North Harbor.

As we got up to leave, Jess glanced at the woman in the booth behind us. She was still wearing the Red Sox baseball cap with bits of flaming red hair poking out from underneath, but she'd taken off the sunglasses for a moment and was rubbing the bridge of her nose with her thumb and index finger.

Jess tipped her head in the woman's direction. "If I can get tickets, do you want to drive down to Portland for a Sea Dogs playoff game?"

"Yes," I said.

"You mean you'd actually take an entire day off?"

"I would," I said as we walked over to the bar to pay our bills.

She gave me a self-satisfied smile. "You taking the day off. My work on this planet is pretty much done."

Jess and I walked up to Maple Street together. She rented a little cottage at the back of a much larger Federal-style house partway up the hill.

"If Charlotte or Rose needs some time off to be with Maddie, call me," she said. "I can come and help out."

"Thanks, Jess," I said. "And I'll let you know about Thursday."

She nodded. "Tell Mac I'll be up to get those boxes. Maybe after lunch tomorrow."

I hugged her and turned right while she went left.

Arthur Fenety's death was front-page news in the morning paper. They'd managed to dig up a lot of information about the man in less than twenty-four hours. A lot.

My eyes got wider and wider as I read the article. As Liz would have put it, Fenety had been a very, very bad boy during his time in New England. It turns out that Maddie hadn't been the only woman he'd been involved with. He also had a girlfriend in Portland, and four different wives—at least that they'd found so far. And it appeared he'd done more than break hearts: apparently he'd taken money and jewelry from several of the women.

Arthur Fenety was an old-fashioned con artist who used his charm, his manners and his distinguished demeanor to take advantage of women.

"Poor Maddie," I said to Elvis. He'd jumped onto my lap after he'd finished his breakfast. My breakfast had been coffee because I still didn't have any more food in the fridge than I'd had the night before.

The cat craned his neck forward as though he were studying the wedding photos of Fenety with his four wives.

I looked at the pictures myself. I could see why all the women had been scammed. It didn't mean they were stupid or gullible, just lonely. Arthur Fenety had been well-spoken, I remembered. Even though I'd thought he was a little too smooth, I hadn't suspected what he was really up to. In each of the photos he was well dressed, his white hair freshly barbered, mustache clipped. He looked exactly like what he'd said he was: an educated, affluent, former financial advisor.

I thought about the time we'd discovered that a customer's valuable heirloom oil painting was nothing more than a paint-by-number forest scene in a very expensive frame.

"You can put a pink tutu on a bear," Rose had said, "but that doesn't make him a ballerina."

Arthur Fenety had dressed in expensive suits but that didn't mean he was a gentleman.

Something about the image of Fenety with his second

wife caught my eye. I leaned over for a closer look and so did Elvis.

"Wait a minute. I've seen her," I said to the cat, tapping the paper with one finger.

He looked at the photograph and then looked at me, tipping his head to one side.

"Yes, I'm sure," I said, feeling a little silly that I was having a conversation with a cat. At least I wasn't talking to myself.

I grabbed my phone and called Jess.

"Do you have the paper?" I asked.

"Ummmm, let me see. Yes," she said. I was guessing she was in her sewing space and had to look around to find where she'd set it down.

"Second page. Picture in the middle. Does that woman look familiar?"

"Hang on," she said. I heard the newspaper rattle and Jess take a long drink from something, probably a cup of black coffee so strong you could strip paint with it.

"Oh yeah," she said after a moment. "That was the woman in the booth behind us last night."

"Are you positive?" I asked. Elvis kept craning his neck in the direction of the phone, as though he were trying to hear Jess's half of the conversation.

"Of course I'm positive," she said. I heard her take another sip of her coffee. "Same chin, same nose, same eyes, and she even had on the same earrings that she's wearing in the photograph." There was silence for a moment. "Wait a second," she said. "How many wives did this guy have?"

"I have a feeling the final count isn't in yet," I said. "Thanks, Jess. I'll talk to you later."

I set the phone on the counter and looked at Elvis, who seemed to be looking at the pictures again.

"I'm betting Arthur Fenety had more than four wives," I said. Elvis bobbed his head up and down, almost as though he were nodding. I picked him up and set him on the floor.

"The bigger question is, did one of them kill him?"

Chapter 7

I wasn't sure if it was important or not, but I called and left a message for Michelle at the police station, telling her that Jess and I had seen one of Arthur Fenety's former wives at The Black Bear last night.

I realized I'd forgotten to ask Sam about the Rickenbacker guitar I'd let Nick play, so Elvis and I headed down to The Black Bear instead of up to the shop. I knew Sam would probably be in the kitchen. His apartment was over the pub and he did almost all his cooking in the pub kitchen.

I pounded on the heavy metal back door, and after a minute I heard the dead bolt turn and Sam opened the door.

"Hi, kiddo," he said, a smile spreading across his face. "I thought you were the laundry. What are you doing here?"

"We got a new guitar in on consignment and I thought it might be something you'd be interested in. I completely forgot to tell you about it last night."

Sam smiled. "Yeah, I heard about what happened." He studied my face. "Are you okay?"

I nodded. "I'm good."

"Do you have time for breakfast?" he asked.

"Meow!" Elvis said loudly. I was carrying him in an old gym bag slung over my shoulder and his head was poking out of the top. As long as he could see what was going on he was happy to stay in the bag and get carried around.

"Yes, we know you have time for breakfast," I said.

Sam gave me an inquiring look. "Blueberry pancakes," he said.

My stomach gurgled. "Well, I wouldn't want Elvis to have to eat alone," I said with a smile.

"C'mon," he said.

I followed Sam through the kitchen into the pub itself and slid into the same booth where I'd first encountered Elvis. He wiggled his way out of the bag as soon as I set it on the floor and hopped up onto the seat beside me. He sat down and looked expectantly at Sam.

"Do you have pictures of the guitar?" Sam asked.

I patted my pocket. "They're on my phone."

"Okay," he said, wiping his hands on his long white apron. "Give me a minute and I'll make your pancakes; then I can take a look." He gestured toward the bar. "Help yourself to some coffee."

I slipped past Elvis and got myself a mug of coffee; then I walked around the pub, looking at the photos that were everywhere in the room. After a moment Elvis jumped down and trailed behind me.

Sam had been making music pretty much his whole life and he'd known my dad—my biological dad—just about as long. In their early twenties—back before marriage, Mom and me—Sam and my father had been in a band called Back Roads. They'd even had a minor hit, "End of Days." Even though I had Peter, and he was as much my dad as he was Liam's, Sam still took on a kind of fatherly role in my life. When it came to music and musical instruments I trusted him more than I did anyone else.

One of my favorite photos of Sam and my dad hung behind the bar. I bent and picked up Elvis and walked over to look at it. They were squinting into the sunshine, grinning, with their arms around each other's shoulders.

Sam came out of the kitchen, carrying a large, round tray. I walked back to the booth, set Elvis on the seat and slid in beside him. Sam had brought me two blueberry pancakes and a bowl of chopped apples, oranges and grapefruit. For Elvis there was a little dish of shredded chicken. I set the dish next to me on the vinyl seat. Elvis leaned around me to look at Sam, almost as though he were saying thank you, and then he eyed my plate.

"Keep your paws off my pancakes," I warned. He made a huffy sound and dropped his head over his own food.

"Isn't this breaking about a dozen health department rules, having him in here?" I asked Sam, cutting part of a pancake with my fork.

He was getting himself a cup of coffee. "Oh, probably," he said, adding sugar to his cup. "But I wash those booths down every day, and I can promise you a cat eating breakfast isn't the most unsanitary thing that's happened in here."

I held up a hand. "I'm eating. I don't want to know."

Sam laughed as he sat down opposite me. "Okay, girl. Let me see those pictures." He held out his hand and I slid my phone across the table to him.

Sam scrolled through the photos of the Rickenbacker while I ate.

"I'm tempted," he said, rubbing his bearded chin with one hand. "What are you asking?"

I named a price.

He reached for his coffee. "I didn't ask you what the seller wanted. I asked for your price."

I set my fork down and picked up my own mug. "You're family, Sam."

He shook his head. "Doesn't matter, Sarah. This is business. Your business."

I picked up a section of grapefruit with two fingers and ate it. "So, does that mean you're going to charge me for these pancakes?"

"That's not the same thing and you know it," he said.

Elvis had stopped eating and was watching us, almost as if he could follow the conversation.

I reached for my fork again. "How many instruments have you checked out for me in the past four months?"

Sam shrugged. "I don't know. Half a dozen, maybe."

"Eight," I said. "You haven't charged me a cent. And it's not like I've even make you a thank-you cake or a plate of cookies."

"And I'm very grateful for that," he said with a smile.

I made a face at him. "So don't give me a hard time about the price."

"Okay."

"Okay, you're not going to argue with me, or okay, you want the guitar?" I said.

Sam held up both hands. "Okay, you win, and okay, yes, I want the guitar."

I grinned at him across the table. "Good. It's beautiful and I wanted somebody to have it who would play it more than a few times a year. The man who owned it didn't think he played well enough to get it out very often so it spent most of the time in a closet."

Sam shook his head. "That's criminal." He took one last look at the guitar and then pushed the phone back across the table to me. "A great instrument like that is meant to be played and enjoyed."

"You're just going to have to play it a lot to make up for that," I said. I wondered if Sam was thinking about my father's guitar that hadn't been out of my closet in more than a year. If he was, he didn't give any sign of that on his face.

Sam leaned against the back of the booth. "So, how did you come to find that Fenety man's body?" he said.

"I drove Charlotte over to Maddie's house."

Elvis had finished eating. He climbed over my lap, jumped down and went around to the other side of the booth, settling himself next to Sam.

"Had you seen him around town?" I asked, starting in on my second pancake.

"A few times." He tented his fingers over the top of his cup. "And Fenety and Maddie Hamilton were in here for lunch a couple of days ago." He took a deep breath and let it out slowly.

"What is it?" I asked.

Sam shook his head. "There was just something about the guy that I didn't like. He was just a little too perfect, if you know what I mean." He leaned forward, both elbows on the table. "I saw the paper this morning. Do you think she knew?"

"That Fenety was a polygamist?" I said. "She didn't say anything. And it's kind of hard to imagine they'd be having a cozy little brunch for two at Maddie's house if she'd found out he was just scamming her."

"That's true," Sam said.

I swallowed the last bite of pancake and checked my watch, snagging a chunk of apple from the bowl at the same time. "I have to get to the shop," I said. Elvis's head came up when I said *shop*. He shook himself and jumped down to the floor. I stood up, as well.

Sam got to his feet and hugged me. He smelled like coffee and Old Spice aftershave. There was something very comforting about that combination.

"Thanks for breakfast," I said.

"Anytime," he said. "Thank you for the guitar. It'll probably be tomorrow before I can come get it. There's another fall-foliage tour scheduled for a late lunch here this afternoon."

Elvis was already headed for the door. He settled on the passenger's side of the front seat as I pulled out of my parking spot, and looked out the side window as though checking for oncoming cars. I wondered how he'd liked the new—well, new to me—SUV that I was planning on trading the truck for. He seemed to like driving around in the truck, which fit with the theory that he'd used to belong to the guy in the camper van.

I stopped at Legacy Place to pick up the tables the ladies had dipped the day before. I wrapped them carefully in the tarps I'd brought with me and set them in the back of the truck. Mac was already at the shop when we got there. He helped me carry the tables inside and I helped him carry a long farm-style table out and set it on a drop cloth.

"Are you sure you want to strip off the old paint?" I said, standing back to look at the table. It was painted olive green.

"I am," Mac said. "I'm almost positive it's oak. There's some beautiful wood underneath all those layers of paint."

"I hope you're right," I said.

Elvis had been circling the table and now he stopped and meowed loudly at me.

I laughed. "Okay, so you've convinced him."

"Good to know you have my back, Elvis," Mac said to the cat.

Rose was heading toward us. "I'm going to open things up," I said. "Rose can handle the shop and—"

Elvis meowed again.

"Excuse me," I said. "Rose and Elvis can handle the store, and I'm going to work on an offer for the pieces I want from the Harrington place."

Mac was already rolling up his sleeves. "I think we could do something with that sleigh bed."

"Me too," I said. "And I think I'll make an offer on those quilts we saw."

"Good idea," Mac said. "They always sell."

I nodded in agreement. "Oh, and Sam's buying the new guitar, the Rickenbacker. I'll take it up to my office. And Jess is going to try to come get those boxes this afternoon."

He nodded. "All right." He was eyeing the table and I knew his attention was already there.

I walked over to meet Rose and took the quilted bag she was carrying.

"Good morning," I said. "How's Maddie?"

"She's still upset, although she's trying to hide it. She stayed the night with Charlotte." She looked up at me. "How long do you think it will take to settle all of this?"

"A few days, at least. They'll be an autopsy to figure out just how Arthur Fenety died." I didn't say that once the police knew what the man had died from, things might just get a lot more complicated.

The quilted tote bag was a lot heavier than it looked. "Rose, what do you have in here?" I asked as we walked over to the back entrance, Elvis leading the way.

"Tea bags," she said. "And a cherry coffee cake." She smiled. "And coffee, of course, because I know Mac isn't that crazy about tea. Oh yes, and some cloth napkins. I really don't like using so many paper ones. And my fertility-goddess statue."

I had been just about to unlock the door. I paused, keys in one hand. "Excuse me?" I said. "A what?"

"A fertility-goddess statue," Rose repeated.

"Why are you carrying around a fertility-goddess statue?"

She looked at me like I was just a little bit dense. "Well, for Avery, of course."

I sighed, figuring I was probably going to regret asking my next question. "Why does Avery need a fertility statue?" I knew I couldn't think of any good reason. I unlocked the door, flipped on the light switch and let Rose and Elvis go ahead of me into the storage room.

"It's for her history class," Rose said over her shoulder as I hurried to catch up with her and Elvis. She moved surprisingly fast for a woman who was almost seventy-five.

I was already in deep so I decided to ask the next obvious question. "And why does Avery need a fertility statue for her history class?"

Rose bustled ahead of me into the store, stopping to turn on the overhead lights. I went across the room to switch on the tall floor lamp with the elegant cranberry glass shade that sat by the cash register. It cast a warm, rosy glow on that part of the store.

I set the bag down and Elvis started sniffing at it.

"Well, dear, it's a little complicated," Rose said as she unbuttoned her jacket. "Avery is studying religious artifacts and symbols in her history class, and you know how she likes to put her own stamp on things."

I smiled. "Yes, I do."

"She decided she wanted to write about fertility statues. The problem was, she'd never actually seen one." Rose gestured at the bag by my feet. "So I brought mine for her to see."

She came over to me, rummaged in the bag and pulled out what I was guessing was the statue, wrapped in a big blue bath towel. She unwrapped it and handed it to me. It was clearly the figure of a woman, robust, with heavy breasts, an ample belly and wide thighs. It stood about four inches high, and was carved from a single piece of rust-colored stone.

"It looks old," I said, turning over the little figure in my hands. Its curves and edges had been worn smooth by time and weather.

"I think it is," Rose agreed. "I found it in a little open-air market in Vienna twenty years ago. The man who sold it to me didn't seem to know anything about its history."

"You should get someone to look at this," I said, handing the statue back to Rose. "It could be worth a lot of money."

"Oh, heavens, I wouldn't want to know that," Rose said as she wrapped the towel around the stone figure. "I wouldn't feel right putting her up on the window ledge by the sink if I knew she was worth money, but I'd miss seeing her when I'm doing the dishes."

"All right," I said as she settled the statue next to the box of tea bags, but I made a mental note to warn Avery to be careful.

I carried Rose's bag upstairs to the lunchroom, put my things in my cubbyhole office and went back downstairs to open the shop while Rose made coffee and tea, supervised by Elvis.

When I finally got back upstairs there was a cup of tea and a piece of coffee cake waiting on my desk. I had a hard-shell case for Sam's guitar, and I laid it inside.

I spent a good part of the morning working out what

I could afford to pay for the items I wanted to buy from Mabel Harrington's house. Mac looked over the numbers and made a couple of suggestions for changes.

At lunchtime I cleaned out the truck and went to pick up the new-to-me SUV. Just as I returned the woman came back for the old postmaster's desk and Mac and I—with some help from Avery—padded and wrapped it and helped load it into the back of the pickup the woman was driving.

"Nice work," I said to Mac as we passed the formerly olive green table on our way back into the shop.

He brushed off his hands and smiled. "Thanks. Do you think we can find some chairs to put with the table? I think it would sell better."

"Do you want six of the same?" I asked, as we walked into the storage area. "There are those two with the back spindles—they haven't been finished yet—and there are four more out back with just a plain back panel. What were you thinking of for a finish?"

"What do you think about a black semigloss?" he said, swiping a hand over his neck.

We walked into the shop, talking about the merits of black paint versus a dark stain. Charlotte was standing by the cash desk with Rose. I knew at once from their body language that something was wrong.

"Sarah," she said when she caught sight of me.

"Excuse me a second," I said quietly to Mac.

He nodded and I left him and walked over to Charlotte and Rose.

"Is everything all right?" I asked.

Charlotte shook her head and I could see the concern

in the tight lines around her mouth. "No, everything most decidedly is not all right," she said sharply, and I realized it wasn't concern I saw on her face, it was anger. "The police have arrested Maddie. They say she killed Arthur Fenety."

Chapter 8

I heard the words but for a moment they were only words, and then the meaning sank in. Arthur Fenety had been murdered, just as I'd suspected.

"I thought Arthur had a heart attack," Rose said. "I can't believe someone killed him. Could it be a mistake?"

I shook my head. I knew Nick wouldn't make that kind of a mistake.

"Maddie didn't kill Arthur, Sarah," Charlotte said. "How could they arrest her? It's ridiculous."

I put a hand on her arm. "What happened, exactly?"

She was twisting her watch around and around her left wrist. "The bell rang. When I went to the door it was Michelle Andrews and another police officer. They asked to speak to Maddie. I took them into the living room. Michelle asked Maddie some questions and then she arrested her. They put handcuffs on her!" Anger flashed in her eyes. "She's seventy-three years old. They didn't need to do that."

"Maddie will be fine," Rose said. "She's strong." She

flashed a look at Avery, who had been leaning on the counter, listening to everything, and the teen headed for the stairs.

"Does she have a lawyer?" Mac asked.

Charlotte shook her head. "I don't think so."

"She needs a lawyer, Sarah," Mac said quietly.

"The Evans boy," Rose said at once.

"Josh Evans?" I said. I held my hand out at my waist, palm down. "Little Josh is a lawyer?"

"He's not little anymore, dear," Rose said.

Mac had already moved behind the counter and pulled out the phone book. Avery was coming down the stairs, carrying a china cup and saucer.

"Charlotte, did you call Nick?" I asked, raking one hand back through my hair.

She nodded, one hand still twisting her watch. "All I got was his voice mail. Not that he can do anything, anyway. I just wanted to know what on earth was going on and why he hadn't called me."

It struck me that while we were standing there talking, Maddie was at the police station, probably without a lawyer. I felt certain she was hiding something, but I just couldn't believe she had killed Arthur Fenety. Not deliberately.

"Give me a couple of minutes and I'll see what I can do," I said.

Charlotte opened her mouth to say something else, but Rose didn't give her a chance. "Let Sarah see what she can do to help," she said, steering Charlotte in the direction of the tub chair.

Avery handed Charlotte the cup of tea she'd brought

downstairs, and then she leaned against the bottom stair post.

Mac gestured at her. "Avery, go get a cup of tea for Rose, too, please." She nodded and ran up the steps again.

I rubbed the space between my eyebrows with the heel of one hand. Then I checked the number Mac had looked up and reached for the phone, crossing my fingers—literally—that little Josh Evans would remember me.

He did. I explained about Maddie being arrested and filled in what few details I knew.

"I'll go," he said. "Give me a number and I'll call you when I know what's going on. It'll probably be a while, though."

"I understand," I said, feeling some of the tension seep out of my body. I gave him my cell number. "Thank you," I added.

"I'm happy to help," he said. "You can buy me dinner when this gets straightened out, and catch me up on your life."

"Absolutely," I said.

I thanked him again. He repeated his promise to call me when he had news, and I hung up.

"Maddie has a lawyer," I announced.

Rose smiled at Charlotte and gave her arm a squeeze. "See?" she said. "Everything's going to be fine."

Charlotte got to her feet, still holding her cup of tea. "Thank you, Sarah. I don't understand what the police are thinking. And Nicolas." She shook her head. "He's known Maddie since he was a little boy." She smoothed the sleeve of her jacket. "I should go down to the police station."

Rose leaned just a little to the left, caught my eye and shook her head almost imperceptibly.

I walked over to Charlotte and put my arm around her shoulders, leaning my head against her. "I care about Maddie, too," I said. "I've known her since I was a little girl. But right now we need to let Josh handle things."

She looked at me, lips pressed together. "Maddie didn't kill Arthur Fenety," she said. I could see the fear etched into the tight lines on her face but there was no trace of it in her voice.

"I know that," I said. I glanced at my watch. Everyone was looking at me. I wished Gram wasn't on her honeymoon. She'd handle this a whole lot better than I could. I took a deep breath and pasted on a positive face, even though I didn't exactly feel it.

"It's time to close up," I said, grateful there hadn't been any customers in the past fifteen minutes or so. "It'll be a while before I hear from Josh. There isn't anything that we can do right now that will help Maddie." I gave Charlotte's shoulders another squeeze. "I'm going to Sam's for supper. Who wants to come with me?"

"Meow," Elvis said. He was sitting on the stairs about halfway down. His enthusiastic response broke the tension.

"Elvis is in," I said, looking around. "Anyone else?"

"I'll come," Mac said.

I shot him a look of gratitude.

"Me too," Avery chimed in.

Rose got to her feet. "What a good idea," she said, tugging the bottom of her apron to straighten it out. "Everything will look better once we've had something to eat."

"You always say that," Charlotte said, and I thought I saw a tiny hint of a smile.

Rose shrugged. "I'm old. I repeat myself sometimes."

Charlotte shook her head and this time I did see a smile.

"Since you're here you could help me refold the quilts," Rose said.

"The front window needs a little rearranging, too," Charlotte said.

Rose turned, hands on her hips, to consider the wide, high window behind her.

Mac caught my eye. "I have some things to put away." He pointed toward the back.

I nodded. "I'll get the deposit ready." Avery was already pulling out the vacuum without even being asked.

"Thank you," Charlotte said softly to me.

I smiled. "Anytime," I said. "Once when we were kids, Josh got five of us free chocolate-dip cones at Hawthorne's because he argued that their sign was deceptive. It read FREE KIDS' CONE WITH ADULT PURCHASE. They forgot to put the apostrophe before the s in *kid's*."

I couldn't help smiling at the memory of a ten-year-old Josh, with his spiky haircut, standing his ground with an annoyed Nathan Hawthorne. "Josh was smarter than most adults when he was ten," I said. "Maddie will be okay." I headed over to the cash register.

Avery was plugging in the vacuum cleaner. "Nonna's

going to pick me up," she said, shaking her hair back off her face. "Is it okay if she comes, too?"

"Of course," I said. I knew Liz would help lighten the mood.

I had the deposit ready when Mac came back in. "Shed's locked," he said. "And I can drop off the deposit on the way to Sam's."

"Thanks," I said, leaning against the counter, "and thanks for coming with us for supper. I know you probably have better things to do." When Mac wasn't working he was generally crewing for someone or hanging around the boatyard, learning everything he could about wooden boats so he could eventually build his own. He was a very private person. I'd never been to his apartment in the four months we'd worked together, and if he was seeing anyone, I had no idea who it was.

"I like Charlotte," he said, looking over to where she and Rose were rearranging several stone flower urns in the window to the left of the door. "There isn't anywhere else I want to be." He smiled at me. "And Sam makes a great cheeseburger."

"Oh yeah, he does," I agreed, thinking about Sam's cheeseburger with two kinds of cheese, onions, mushrooms and a spicy tomato sauce that could spoil you forever for generic ketchup.

"So, you and this lawyer, Josh Evans, knew each other when you were kids?" Mac asked, pulling a hand over his neck.

"Yeah." I traced the curved edge of the counter with one finger. "He was a summer kid like I was at first, and then his parents moved here full-time. Josh was a pretty persuasive little guy." I sighed and pushed myself upright. "I hope he can convince the police that Maddie didn't do this."

Mac looked down at the floor for a moment and I heard him exhale softly.

"What is it?" I asked.

His dark eyes met mine. "Sarah, please don't take this the wrong way, but are you one hundred percent positive she didn't?"

Chapter 9

Liz arrived to pick up Avery and agreed to join us all at Sam's. I pulled her aside for a moment. "You suspected, didn't you?" I said.

"Suspected what?' she asked.

"That Arthur Fenety wasn't what he seemed."

She brushed lint off the front of her sweater. "I thought maybe he was married," she said. "If I'd had any idea of the truth . . ." She shrugged. "I wouldn't have killed him but he would have been singing soprano."

I slipped away to my office and called to give Sam a heads-up that we were coming and why. I hesitated and then I punched in Nick's number, hoping I wasn't inter-fering in something that I should be keeping my nose out of. I got his voice mail.

"Hi, Nick," I said. "It's Sarah. Call me, please." I hesi-tated. "Or just call your mom." I recited my cell number in case he hadn't kept it.

I looked at Elvis, who was sitting on the edge of my desk. "I suppose you really do want to come with us," I said.

He murped his acknowledgment.

"You have to go in my gym bag."

He blinked at me, jumped down from the desk and walked over to the nylon bag sitting on the floor of the tiny closet tucked under the eaves.

"You'll have to stay in the truck—I mean the SUV," I warned. He really seemed to think about it, wrinkling up his face and scrunching his whiskers.

"Meow," he said finally. He put a paw on the top of the bag and scratched at the fabric.

"I can't believe I'm doing this," I muttered as I unzipped the top of the black gym bag and pulled out my running gear. I'd been planning to run after work today. *Tomorrow,* I promised myself. Elvis stuck his head through the opening and sniffed, whiskers twitching. Then he looked up at me.

"All those things were clean," I said. "It smells fine." He put a paw inside and gave me his best pathetic cat look, head tipped to one side so it was impossible to miss the scar on his nose.

I leaned down so my face was just inches away from his furry one. "Do I need to remind you that the only way you're going to get to come with us is in this bag?"

He blinked, climbed into the bag and sat down, looking expectantly up at me. Some days I had the feeling the cat understood every single word I said to him. Other days I figured that while he pretty much got what I was saying, he just wasn't listening.

When I got back downstairs Rose and Charlotte were at the cash counter with Avery. The fertility statue was unwrapped, sitting on the blue towel. Charlotte was saying something and Avery was listening intently.

Liz had been standing by the window but she walked over when I came down the stairs. "I hear you got Maddie a lawyer," she said. "Thank you."

"Calling Josh was Rose's idea," I said, watching her turn over the carved stone figure to show Avery something on the back of the statue.

"And you're the one who made the call," Liz said. She gave me a long, appraising look. "If Maddie needs bail you tell Josh to call me."

"Oh, Liz," I said, and then I had to stop because all of a sudden there was a lump in my throat.

"Don't 'Oh, Liz' me," she said, making a sweeping gesture in the air with one hand. "We take care of each other and we stick together."

I put my arms around her and gave her a hug, resting my head on her shoulder.

She shook a finger at me. "And it goes without saying, my dear, that it stays between the two of us."

I nodded. I had no idea exactly how much money Liz actually had. I was pretty sure it was more than her friends realized. Liz had come to the rescue with her checkbook before, without most people knowing, and I felt certain there were probably times I wasn't aware of.

"You're taking the cat?" Liz asked, pointing at my gym bag.

Elvis narrowed his green eyes at her as though he was offended by her question.

I opened my mouth to explain that if I tried to leave

him behind the cat wasn't above retaliating, when she raised a hand and waved my explanation away.

"No, never mind," she said. "Taking that cat along isn't any odder than Avery lugging that little naked statue or Rose carrying tea bags everywhere she goes."

Everyone had to check out the new SUV before we could head over to The Black Bear. But anything that could distract Charlotte was fine with me. I set Elvis on the front seat. He immediately stuck his head out of the top of the bag and looked around, sniffing the air.

"Stay in the bag," I reminded him.

Mac, Rose and Charlotte ended up riding with me. Liz and Avery said they'd meet us at Sam's.

"Nonna, could I drive?" I heard Avery ask as they started for the car. "I think I know a faster way."

When we got there, Sam had a table saved for us. "Have you heard anything yet?" he asked.

I shook my head. "It's going to be a while."

He gave me a reassuring smile. "It'll be all right. I asked around. Josh Evans knows his stuff."

"Good," I said, shrugging off my jacket and hanging it over the back of my chair. "Could you do me a favor?" I held out my keys. "Elvis is in the SUV—I got it today, by the way. I'm parked about three spots down on this side of the street. Could you take something out to Elvis?"

"Your cat's in your new SUV?" he said, tipping his head to one side and narrowing his gaze at me.

I crossed my arms over my chest and nodded. "Yes, I brought my cat. People drive around all the time with dogs. Why does everyone think it's weird if someone drives around with their cat?"

Okay, so I sounded more than a little defensive.

Sam looked like he was having a hard time not laughing. "I didn't mean I thought it was strange that you drive all over town with your cat. I'm just wondering if you're sure he's actually *in* the SUV."

I stared at him, a sinking feeling in my stomach. "That's where I left him. Why are you asking?" I'd definitely locked the doors and I was holding the keys, so there was no way Avery could have "rescued" Elvis. There was no way she could have coached him to unlock the door. Was there?

Sam opened his mouth and closed it again, swallowing a laugh—with difficulty—before he spoke. "Sarah, why does Rose have your gym bag? And why is it . . . moving?"

Rose and Avery were on the other side of the round table, probably still talking about the little fertility statue. My black gym bag was on the floor next to Rose's chair and Sam was right: the bag was, well, squirming.

I held up a finger to Sam. "Don't move," I said.

I walked around the table. "I know what you two are up to," I said, glaring at Rose and Avery. Avery looked guilty. Rose, on the other hand, was the picture of innocence.

"We're just trying to decide whether or not to split a fish platter," she said.

"I'm talking about that." I pointed at the nylon bag on the floor. Elvis had stopped moving, probably the moment he'd heard my voice.

Rose glanced down and then her eyes met mine again. "Oh, I guess I brought your bag in," she said. "No harm. I'll just keep it here with me."

"I know that Elvis is in that bag," I hissed.

Avery looked very uncomfortable. Her eyes kept sliding away from my face and she shifted restlessly from one foot to the other. She was an awful liar, which in a teenager was a good thing.

Rose leaned toward the bag, squinted, and then put a hand to her mouth. "Oh, my goodness, you're right. He is."

"This is a restaurant," I said sternly. "If the health inspector came in and found Elvis here they'd shut Sam down. Do you two want that to happen?" I felt a twinge of guilt about lecturing them, seeing as how Elvis and I had had breakfast in the back booth just a few hours earlier. I reminded myself that the pub had been closed then, not more than three-quarters full of people, all eating.

Rose gave me a sweet smile. "Sarah, dear, that's not going to happen. Elvis will sit right here next to me. It's not like he's going to get up and dance on the table."

Out of the corner of my eye I saw Avery smirk at the idea. She had the good sense to hide it when I looked at her again.

"Elvis is not going to dance on the table or anywhere else because he's going to be in Sam's office," I said.

Avery groaned. "That's not fair. Elvis isn't hurting anything. And . . . and it's like you're putting him in jail."

I pressed my lips together, closed my eyes for a moment and mentally counted to five before I opened them again. "Sam's office is not jail," I said. "Elvis can have some supper and stretch out on the futon until we're ready to leave." I knew Sam had an old fourteen-inch

TV in his office. Elvis could probably watch *Jeopardy!* if he wanted to, but I didn't say that.

I bent down and picked up the bag before Rose and Avery got any more ideas. I looked from one to the other. They were both trying to look innocent, but Rose was doing a much better job of it. I frowned at her although we both knew I wasn't really mad.

"You're old enough to know better," I said, sternly, raising my eyebrows at her to make my point. "And you," I said, pointing at Avery, "are clearly the more mature person, so I'm counting on you to act like it."

I walked back around the table to Sam. Mac and Charlotte had their heads together over a menu.

There was a mischievous gleam in Sam's eyes. "Could I check your cat for you?" he asked.

"Very funny," I said. "Could Elvis stay in your office?"

He laughed. "Sure."

I handed him the bag.

"I have some pretty decent halibut tonight," he said. "Okay if I give him a little?"

A meow came from the bag. Luckily it was noisy enough in the pub that no one else heard it.

I leaned sideways. "He's not talking to you," I said quietly in the general direction of the bag. "Yes, he can have a bit of fish," I said to Sam.

"I'll send a waitress over," he said, and headed in the direction of his office with Elvis.

Josh didn't call for almost another hour. Everyone's head came up when my phone rang. It was noisy in the bar. "Hang on a second," I said to Josh. "I'm just going to move somewhere where I can hear you better." I pushed my chair back from the table. "I can't hear very well," I said. I pointed. "I'm just going over by the washrooms."

I walked to the back before anyone had a chance to get up and follow me, and stepped into the small hallway to the men's and women's bathrooms. It was a lot quieter there, but I'd also wanted to be away from the table to hear what Josh had to say without so many sets of eyes watching my face.

"Okay, go ahead," I said, turning my back on the restaurant.

Josh was officially Maddie's lawyer. He'd advised her not to say anything and she'd followed that advice.

"She's going to have to spend the night in jail, Sarah," he said.

I sighed. "I kind of expected that."

"It's not a night in a five-star hotel, but it's not a hole in the ground, either. She'll be all right and she'll be arraigned first thing in the morning."

I repeated Liz's offer of bail.

"That's good. I don't think the judge will set bail too high, given her age and the circumstances." I could hear him shuffling papers.

"Can we be there in court?" I asked, wrapping my free arm around my midsection.

"Yes, you can," he said. "In fact, it would be good for the judge to see that Maddie has a support system."

We made arrangements to meet at the courthouse in the morning. I thanked Josh again and we said good night.

I thought about Mac's question to me earlier. Was I certain Maddie hadn't had anything to do with Arthur Fenety's death?

I remembered the night of my fifteenth birthday. We'd had a party in Gram's backyard and we were making s'mores in the outdoor brick fireplace when Maddie arrived. She'd hugged me and handed me a beautiful bouquet of flowers from her garden. "I have something else for you out in my car," she'd said. We'd walked out to the street and she'd taken a guitar case from the backseat. I'd looked at her, wide-eyed. "I can't," I'd started to say, knowing my parents would never let me keep a guitar. It was way too expensive a gift.

Maddie had shaken her head. "Yes, you can. Just open it. Please."

I'd carefully unsnapped the latches and lifted the lid of the black, hard-shell case. My breath stuck in my chest and my field of vision got dark from the outside in until the only thing I could see was the guitar lying in the case. It was my father's guitar. I hadn't seen it in ten years.

I looked at Maddie. "How? What . . . how?"

She cleared her throat before she answered, and even then I had to turn my head to hear what she said.

"It was thrown from the car the night . . . the night of the accident. Some, uh, someone found it a week later in the . . . in the trees." She took a breath and then swallowed. "The man who found it, he should have taken it to the state troopers, but . . . he didn't. He took it home and it just ended up stuck in the back of a closet."

I laid a hand on the smooth amber wood. I couldn't

keep my eyes on Maddie's face. It was impossible to keep them away from the guitar. My father's guitar. The words kept running over and over in my head.

"A couple of months ago I went to an estate sale over in Belfast," Maddie continued. "The moment I saw that guitar—don't ask me how—I knew it was your father's guitar. You used to sit on his lap and he'd show you chords. You probably don't remember."

I did remember. I couldn't say that, though, because I knew if I said a word I'd start to cry. I blinked a couple of times and swallowed hard.

"I hope this is okay," Maddie said.

I got to my feet and flung my arms around her. "It's the best present ever," I'd said.

It still was.

I swallowed and blinked a couple of times. Whatever secrets Maddie was keeping, I was absolutely positive that she hadn't killed Arthur Fenety. She didn't have it in her.

I put my phone away and went back to the table to share what Josh had told me.

"She's going to spend the night in jail?" Charlotte said, twisting her napkin in her hands.

"I'm sorry," I said. "Maddie will be arraigned first thing in the morning and Josh doesn't think there will be a problem with bail. We can all be there."

Liz was sitting to my right. "Maddie will be okay," she said. "She'll be in a cell by herself, unless there's some kind of a crime wave tonight. The cells are small, but they're clean."

She looked around for our waitress, and when she

caught the young woman's eye Liz gestured at her coffee cup.

"I don't even want to know how you know that," I said to Liz.

She gave me a sly smile. "No, Sarah, you probably don't." She looked across the table at Charlotte. "Maddie will be fine. We'll all be at the courthouse in the morning, and she'll be out of there long before lunch."

"I'll open up tomorrow," Mac said.

He was sitting on my left side and I shot him a smile of thanks.

"I can take the morning off school and help," Avery offered, leaning forward and propping her elbows on the table.

"No, you can't," Liz said firmly.

Avery made a face at her grandmother, who made one back at her.

"I appreciate your offer," I said, "but we're not that busy in the morning. So go to school, but I could use you in the afternoon, if you really want to help."

"I do," Avery said, tucking a strand of cranberry-colored hair behind one ear.

"Good," I said. "If you're finished, how about you go find Sam, collect Elvis and wait by the front door?"

"Are you just trying to get rid of me so you can talk about stuff you don't think I should hear?"

"Because that's worked so well in the past," Liz commented.

I picked up my coffee cup and shook my head. "I'm not. I'm just trying to get Elvis out of here without anyone noticing you brought him in here in the first place."

"Okay, then," she said, pushing back her chair and getting to her feet.

Out of the corner of my eye I saw Liz extend her arm under the cover of the tablecloth and brush Avery's hand with her own.

"Keep him out of sight, Avery," I said.

"Yeah, I know." She flapped a hand at me as she headed in the direction of the kitchen.

My coffee was cold and I was about to drink it, anyway, when our waitress came over with a fresh pot. "Could you bring our check when you have a minute, please?" I asked as she poured.

"It's already been taken care of," she said with a smile. She moved around me to top up Mac's cup.

I turned to Liz. "You didn't have to do that," I said.

She smiled and shrugged. "Sorry, kiddo. I didn't. Someone else beat me to it."

"Sam," I said, reaching for a little paper packet of sugar.

"I don't think so." Liz pointed a perfectly manicured nail toward Mac. He had one elbow leaning on the table as he talked to Charlotte and Rose.

"Mac?"

Liz added cream to her cup. "When he excused himself to wash his hands just after we got here, I saw him speak to our waitress."

I leaned back in my chair and folded my hands around my own cup. "That's really, really . . . nice."

"Mac's a pretty nice man," Liz said. "In case you hadn't noticed."

Before I could answer her I caught sight of Avery

coming from the direction of Sam's office. My gym bag was over her shoulder and at least it didn't seem to be moving. I decided the rest of us should get moving. I didn't want to push our luck.

I took one last drink of my coffee. "You ready to go?" I asked Liz.

She nodded.

I leaned over and touched Mac on the shoulder. He turned. "Ready to leave?" I asked.

"I am," he said.

I looked at Rose and Charlotte. "Ready to head home?"

Charlotte glanced at her watch. "I'm ready," she said. Was she wondering why Nick hadn't called either one of us? I was.

Rose had started putting on her coat. I heard her make a comment to Liz about Liz's faux-snakeskin shoes. They weren't at all practical, waterproof or sensible. Then again, none of Liz's shoes were. They were gorgeous, though.

Mac was pulling on his jacket. "Thank you for supper," I said.

There was just a bit of a smile playing on his lips. "How did you know?"

"I have my sources," I said with an offhand shrug.

"Could we keep it between us?" he asked, checking his pockets for his keys.

"Why don't you want the others to know you paid for dinner?"

He ducked his head and smiled. "I just don't want to make a big deal out of it."

"All right," I said, pulling on my own jacket. I understood not wanting to make a big deal about some things.

We collected Avery and Elvis and stood outside on the sidewalk to make plans for the morning. "I'm picking up Rose and Charlotte. I can pick you up, too," I told Liz.

"That'll be fine," she said. She held out her car keys to Avery, who had Rose's towel-wrapped statue under one arm. "You can drive, but no shortcuts this time."

"My way is faster," Avery said, taking the keys. "You just don't want to admit that." She stood up a little straighter. "Young people have good ideas, too, you know."

Liz rolled her eyes. "Here we go," she muttered. She leaned over, nudged my shoulder with hers and said, "I'll see you in the morning." Then she started down the sidewalk with Avery. "I didn't say your ideas were bad," I heard her say. "I said your shortcuts are bad."

Mac touched my arm. "It's a nice night, Sarah," he said. "I'm going to walk."

"Okay," I said. "Thanks for coming and . . . everything."

"You're welcome," he said with a smile. It struck me that Mac should smile more often. "Don't worry about the shop in the morning. Take as long as you need."

I tucked my hair back behind one ear. "Thanks," I said. "I don't know what I'd do without you."

He shrugged. "Well, luckily, you don't have to find out." He said good night to Charlotte and Rose and cut across the street. I was guessing he'd take a walk along the harbor front before he went home.

"Sarah, I'm not going home. I'm going to Charlotte's," Rose said as I pulled the SUV away from the curb. She was in the back, with Elvis on the seat beside her. Charlotte was in the front passenger's seat.

"You are?" Charlotte said, half turning around to look at her friend.

"I am," Rose said firmly. "I know you're worried about Maddie. So am I. We may as well worry together. Unless you'd rather come stay at Shady Pines with me?"

I glanced at Rose in the rearview mirror. I knew that look on her face. Once she made up her mind about something it was a waste of time trying to sway her.

"I don't suppose I could just say 'I'm fine, go home,'" Charlotte said.

"You can say it all you want," Rose retorted. "I'm still spending the night, unless you think Shady Pines would be more fun."

"You have to stop calling Legacy Place Shady Pines. They're going to sue you for slander."

"Ha!" Rose snorted. "It's not slander if it's true."

"Merow!" Elvis chimed in.

"See?" she said. "Elvis knows I'm right."

"Elvis is a cat, Rose," I said, taking my eyes off the road for a split second to look in the rearview mirror again.

"Doesn't mean he's not smart," she countered. "Cats pick up on things we miss. They have very keen powers of observation. He knows there's something fishy going on at that place."

Elvis meowed again, probably because he'd heard the word *fishy*.

"'Legacy Place, when you're here you're home,' my aunt Fanny," Rose grumbled.

"You can drop us both at my house," Charlotte said quietly, the corners of her mouth twitching.

"How early do you think we should be at the courthouse in the morning?" I asked as I waited to turn left at a stop sign.

"I'd like to be there early enough that we can be close to the front, so Maddie can see us," Charlotte said. "If that works for you."

"Okay. What if I picked you up at nine thirty? Is that early enough?"

"You're changing the subject," Rose said from the backseat.

"Well, I certainly am trying," I said. I wiggled my fingers at her in the rearview mirror.

She gave me her best angelic little-old-lady smile. "I can take a hint," she said.

I dropped off Rose and Charlotte, and drove home with Elvis. He stayed in the back, perched in the middle of the seat like he was royalty.

"What is this? The feline version of *Driving Miss Daisy*?" I asked as I turned onto our street.

He bobbed his head and gave a sharp meow. Okay, so he liked the idea. Why didn't that surprise me?

I kicked off my shoes and dropped onto the sofa when I got inside my apartment. It had been a long day and I was tired.

Elvis jumped up and stretched out on my chest. I eased my cell phone out of my pocket. Still no call from Nick. I hoped he'd at least called Charlotte by now.

I stroked Elvis's fur with one hand. "I still think there's something Maddie's not telling us, but she didn't kill Arthur Fenety. Not on purpose. And if she'd killed him by accident, she wouldn't lie about it."

He murped his agreement. Or maybe he just liked having his fur stroked.

I folded my other arm under my head. "So, who did kill him?"

Elvis blinked his green eyes at me. Clearly he had no idea.

Neither did I.

Chapter 10

I picked up Liz just before nine thirty in the morning. She was wearing a black suit, the jacket banded around the neck and down the front in white. Her hair and her makeup—and her nails—were perfect. She looked confident and affluent, like someone who was accustomed to having things go her way, which, now that I thought of it, she was.

"You look so elegant," I said.

"Thank you," she said as she fastened her seat belt, carefully smoothing the fabric of her suit jacket so it wouldn't wrinkle. "Avery said I looked intimidating."

"That might not be such a bad thing today." I glanced sideways in time to see her smile at me.

"You look very pretty," she said. "I like that shade of red on you. It goes with your skin tone."

I was wearing a silver-gray dress with a cranberry red blazer and my favorite spike-heeled black boots. I hadn't exactly been sure how to dress to go to court.

"Thank you," I said. "And thank you for offering to take care of Maddie's bail."

"I told you last night—we're family. Not by blood." She tapped her chest with her fingers. "But in here. And we take care of each other."

Rose and Charlotte were waiting out by the curb in front of Charlotte's house.

"Sarah, did you talk to Isabel last night?" Charlotte asked as she fastened her seat belt.

I nodded. "She wanted to come back. I told her there isn't anything she can do. She's going to call you."

"There isn't," Rose said. "Josh Evans is a very smart young man. He'll get this straightened out lickety-split."

"I don't think it's going to be that simple," Liz said.

"What do you mean?" Rose asked. Out of the corner of my eye I saw her lean forward in the seat.

"Think about it, Rose. The police have evidence—of some kind. They wouldn't have arrested Maddie without it."

"You think she killed Arthur?" Rose said, her voice tinged with surprise.

"That's not what she said," Charlotte interjected, holding up one hand.

Beside me Liz shifted in her seat, turning toward the backseat. "Thank you," she said to Charlotte. "I know Maddie didn't kill Arthur. I've already said that and I'm not saying it again. What I am saying is that the police have some reason they think she did. They must know he didn't die of natural causes. We need to find out what makes them think Maddie killed him and find some way to show them they're wrong."

"I don't know if that's a good idea," I started to say, but they talked right over me.

"You're right." Rose was nodding so vigorously she looked like a gray-haired bobble-headed doll. "I'm sure Josh must have some idea why the police arrested Maddie. They'd have to tell him, wouldn't they? We should talk to him."

"And Maddie, as well," Charlotte added.

I glanced in the rearview mirror again. I knew that look in Charlotte's eye. She was already making a mental list of things to do.

"There's no time like the present," Liz said.

"We could bring Maddie back with us," Rose said. "I don't think she should be all alone, anyway."

"I'm hoping she'll stay with me," Charlotte added.

"Josh's office probably has their own investigator, you know." I didn't like the direction the conversation was going in.

"I'm sure they do, dear," Liz said, sending me a look that seemed a little . . . condescending before she turned back to her friends.

Thankfully we were almost at the courthouse. I found a parking spot in the nearby lot and we walked down the sidewalk to the building.

"Is Christopher going to be here?" Liz asked Charlotte.

Maddie's son, Christopher, was a mining engineer who traveled all over the world.

Charlotte shook her head. "He's in northern Russia."

"Does he even know?" Liz asked, smoothing down the sleeve of her suit jacket.

Charlotte slid the strap of her purse over her shoulder. She was wearing a navy suit with a bright print scarf at her neck. She looked like the school principal she used to be. "I don't know. Maddie said she called him, but . . ." She shrugged and gave her head a little shake.

Josh Evans was waiting for us inside the courthouse. He smiled and walked over when he caught sight of us. "Sarah, I would have known you anywhere," he said, taking the hand I offered in both of his.

"Is that good or bad?" I asked, smiling back at him.

"All good," he said.

I would have recognized Josh, as well. His sandy hair was in the same short, spiked style he'd had when he was twelve, except now it was styled with a lot more expensive cut. He was tall and lanky but he'd lost his geeky awkwardness. He still wore black-framed glasses, except the frames were a designer name now and they weren't held together with duct tape at one corner. His blue eyes were keen behind his glasses, taking everything in. Even as he smiled at me I felt myself relax, just a little.

Josh said hello to Liz, Rose and Charlotte. Then he quickly explained what was going to happen. "After the charges are read the judge will ask Mrs. Hamilton how she pleads," he said. "She'll say not guilty. The prosecutor and I have already talked about bail. I'll agree with her suggestion and I don't see why the judge will have any problem with it."

He gave us an encouraging smile. "Things should go pretty quickly."

And they did.

Maddie came into the courtroom looking a little tired and very serious but she smiled when she saw us all sitting in the front row. Josh was right about the bail and very quickly we were all in the hallway outside the courtroom.

Charlotte took both of Maddie's hands in hers. "Are you all right?" she asked, her eyes searching Maddie's face.

Maddie nodded. "I'm fine. I'm just . . . glad to be here with all of you." She smiled at Charlotte, Rose and Liz in turn and then she turned to me. "Sarah, you sweet girl, I don't know how to thank you," she said. "Josh told me you sent him."

I reached out and touched her arm. "All I did was make a phone call. It was Rose's suggestion."

Maddie looked at us all again. "I don't know what I'd do without all of you," she said.

I could see the glint of unshed tears in her eyes. I remembered what Mac had said to me last night when I'd said pretty much the same thing to him. I smiled and patted Maddie's arm. "It doesn't matter," I said, "because you're not going to find out."

Josh touched my elbow and we moved a few steps away from the women. "You and Mrs. Elliot found Arthur Fenety's body," he said.

I nodded. "Yes."

"I'll need to talk to you at some point."

"Just let me know when."

"So, you've talked to Michelle." A hint of a smile played across his face.

"I have." I glanced over at Maddie again. Surrounded by her friends she didn't look quite as tired as she had in the courtroom.

"Michelle's fair, Sarah," Josh said. "And she's a good

cop. If we come up with anything, she'll investigate. She wants the truth."

"That's good," I said.

He pushed back the sleeve of his suit jacket and checked his watch. It had a wide black leather strap with a silver dial, and on the black face I saw something familiar.

"Wait a minute. Is that Darkwing Duck?" I asked, leaning in for a closer look.

Josh grinned and held up his arm so I could get a better look. It was the purple-suited cartoon superhero on the face of his watch. Josh had been obsessed with Darkwing Duck when he was a kid. The summer he was nine he'd worn a purple cape everywhere. I guess it said something good about the majority of kids in North Harbor that he didn't get beaten up once.

"It's good to see you haven't changed too much," I said, grinning back at him.

He tugged his sleeve back down. "Sarah, most people in town remember the dorky little kid I used to be. It would be pretty difficult to get too full of myself."

"You weren't a dork," I said. "You were quirky."

"Quirky," he said, nodding slowly. "Okay. I like that." He glanced over at Maddie and the other women. I hoped they weren't pumping her for information for their "investigation."

"If you saw Michelle, then I'm guessing you saw Nick, as well," Josh said.

I nodded. "I did." I slid the strap of my purse back up onto my shoulder again.

"Heck of a first week." Josh shook his head. "A murder investigation for his first case, and then he spent most of last night talking a suicidal teenager off the Memorial Bridge."

"What?" I said. It didn't sound like the kind of thing an investigator for the medical examiner's office would be doing.

"He was going somewhere and he saw this kid who had climbed up on one of the girders of the bridge. He pulled over. She started talking to him and she wouldn't talk to anyone else."

That sounded like Nick: always the hero. And it explained why he hadn't called me back. I wondered if Charlotte knew. I glanced down at my own watch. I really needed to get to the shop. I knew Mac could more than handle things, but I didn't want to dump everything on him for too long.

Josh needed to spend some time going over the case with Maddie. He offered to drop her off at the shop later.

"Are you sure?" I said.

He nodded, setting his briefcase down to pull on his navy trench coat. "I'd love to see the place. I'm assuming I've earned enough brownie points to get a tour."

"Absolutely," I said with a smile.

We said good-bye to Maddie and Josh and walked back to the parking lot.

Neither Charlotte nor Rose said much on the way across town. There was a tour bus full of leaf peepers at the shop when we got there, but Mac seemed to have everything pretty much under control, although there was a line at the cash register.

Rose peeled off her coat and handed it and her purse

to Liz, bustling over to help out. We'd stopped to pick up Elvis on the way. I set him down and he swiped a paw over his face before making his way over to a group of three women looking at the quilts.

Over by the window a woman had a teacup garden in each hand and was looking around for another set of hands. Charlotte piled her purse on top of Rose's bag in Liz's arms and headed across the floor to help.

"You might as well pile your things on, too," Liz said to me.

"Thank you," I said, hooking the strap of my purse over her shoulder.

"I suppose you're going to want tea and coffee," she said.

"You don't have to do that." I brushed a clump of cat hair off my red jacket. "Why don't you go wait in my office?"

She smiled. "This is a onetime offer, kiddo. Who knows when it will come again?" She started for the stairs, looking a little like a Nepalese packman.

"I love you, Liz," I called after her.

She waggled her elbow at me as she went up the steps. "Everybody does."

It was just a bit more than half an hour before the tour bus pulled out of our parking lot. Liz handed me a steaming cup of coffee and gave one to Mac, as well. He came to stand beside me by the front window. I was counting how many of the teacup gardens we'd sold.

"How was court?" he asked.

"Maddie's out on bail," I said, folding my fingers around the coffee mug.

"What happens next?"

I shrugged. "I'm not sure. Maddie's with her lawyer right now." I glanced over to where Charlotte, Rose and Liz were sitting around a small round table with a mosaic glass top. Rose was talking, gesturing with her hands, while the other two listened.

Mac followed my gaze. "Problem?" he asked.

I crossed my arms over my midsection, still holding on to my cup. "Umm, maybe," I said.

He raised an eyebrow and I could see genuine interest in his warm brown eyes.

I sighed. "On the way over to the courthouse they were talking about looking for evidence to prove Maddie is innocent."

"They're not serious?"

I nodded. "Oh, I think they're very serious. That's what worries me."

Mac looked over at the three women sitting around the small round table with their teacups. "Realistically, Sarah, how much trouble could the three of them get into?"

"You have no idea," I said, rolling my eyes. Before I could say anything else the door opened and Nick Elliot stepped into the store.

Charlotte immediately pushed back her chair and stood up. I handed my cup to Mac and walked over to Nick.

"I got your message," he said. "I thought it would be faster to just stop in. I hope that's okay."

"It's okay," I said.

Nick was dressed casually in khakis, a blue-striped dress

shirt and his navy Windbreaker. The ends of his sandy hair were damp and I wondered if he'd had any sleep.

"You know about Maddie." It wasn't a question.

"We do," I said. "She's out on bail."

He nodded. "Good."

Charlotte stood in front of Nick and put her hands on his shoulders. She was only a few inches shorter than he was. I should have told her what Josh had told me about how Nick had spent his night. I wondered what she was going to say. I had a couple of ideas.

"I'm so proud of you," she said, beaming at him.

Okay, not that.

"You are?" Nick said. His eyes darted to me and then back to his mother. I didn't have any answers for him.

I looked over at Liz and Rose. There was a little self-satisfied smile on Liz's face. I knew who had told Charlotte.

"I heard what you did last night," Charlotte said. "You saved that girl's life."

Nick had that *when did I fall down the rabbit hole?* look on his face. "How did you know?" he asked. He looked at me again and I gave an almost imperceptible headshake.

She shook her head. "It doesn't matter. And I'm sorry. I haven't been supportive about this new job and I should have been."

Nick put a hand over his mother's. "It's okay." They smiled at each other. I looked over at Liz again. She caught my eye and smiled, too.

Charlotte dropped her hands and Nick cleared his throat. "So, Maddie's out on bail and she has a lawyer?"

His mother nodded. "And we're already working on a plan to figure out who really killed Arthur Fenety." She made a gesture with one hand that seemed to include me.

Nick's brown eyes narrowed. "Hang on a minute, Mom," he said. "What do you mean, you're working on a plan?"

"She means we're going to investigate and find the real killer," Rose said. Liz sent her a daggers look and for a moment I thought she was going to swat Rose with her napkin.

"No, you're not," Nick said, emphatically. "This is a police investigation. He made a circular motion with one finger that, like his mother's gesture, seemed to include me. "You all need to stay out of it."

"Excuse me?" Charlotte said.

She wasn't my mother or even my grandmother; still, I knew what her tone meant. So would hundreds of her former students. Somehow Nick didn't.

"Let the police do their job," he said. He spoke slowly, enunciating each word.

"They don't seem to be very good at it." Charlotte crossed her arms defiantly over her chest. "Or they wouldn't have arrested an innocent woman."

Nick took a deep breath and let it out slowly. The set of his jaw showed that he was grinding his teeth together.

Suddenly Mac was at Nick's elbow, holding out a mug. "Have a cup of coffee," he said.

Nick turned to look at him. "What?" he said.

"Have a cup of coffee," Mac repeated. "There isn't anything stronger." One eyebrow went up.

A little of the tension in the air seemed to dissipate. Nick took the cup and I mouthed a thank-you at Mac.

I touched Nick's elbow. "Let's go for a walk." I smiled at him. It was a little fake but a smile nonetheless.

"I know what you're doing, Sarah," he said, shaking off my hand.

"Good," I said. "I need to stretch my legs. Get the blood circulating." I looked at him, thinking, *Don't be a dipwad.* And hoped somehow he would get the message.

"We're fine, Sarah," Charlotte said without looking at me.

"I know you are," I said, keeping my voice light. "I just want to take a little walk and I don't want to go by myself."

Nick pressed his lips together for a moment. "I'll be right back," he said. "Sarah wants to take me outside because she wants to give me a little lecture."

"Yes, everyone knows that," Liz said dryly. "So, why don't you just get on with it?"

I looked at Nick. "So could we get on with it?" I asked.

He looked at Charlotte. "We're not done, Mom." It was a good thing he'd decided to move at that point, because I was ready to give him a nudge with the perfectly pointed toe of my black boot.

Nick didn't say a word until we were outside, standing in the small side lot. He took a sip of his coffee, nodded his approval and then held out his free hand. "Okay, start lecturing me." His sense of humor seemed to have returned.

"I'm not going to lecture you," I said, keeping my voice and face as neutral as possible and holding up my hands like I was about to surrender. "I just want to ask you a question without everybody listening."

"What's the question?"

I took a step closer to him. "What the heck are you thinking?" I said. "Do you really think telling your mother, Rose and Liz to stay out of Maddie's case is going to work?"

He made a face. "You think they should just start poking around in a murder investigation?"

I fought my first impulse, which was to roll my eyes at him. I took a deep breath and then a second one when the first one didn't get rid of much of my aggravation. "Of course I don't. But they aren't going to sit around and do nothing. They're three of the most loyal people I know. You're lucky my grandmother isn't here. There'd be four of them to deal with."

He had the same stubborn look I'd seen dozens of times on his mother's face.

"Nick, let me see what I can do."

He took another sip from his coffee. "You think you can talk them out of this ridiculous idea?" He sounded skeptical.

"Maybe. Or at least convince them there's really nothing they can do."

He looked past me for a moment and I stayed silent while he weighed my words. "Okay," he said, finally.

"But they're your responsibility, Sarah. My mother, Liz, and Rose."

I nodded. "That's fine." Surely I could find a way to talk them out of the idea of playing detective.

"So, was this a long enough walk for you?" Nick asked teasingly.

We started back toward the building across the bit of lawn in the front. "You should come running with me sometime," I said.

"Running? You mean like jogging around the block?"

I laughed. "No. I mean putting in some miles and getting sweaty and stronger."

"I don't know," Nick said, grinning and shaking his head. "I think I'm busy."

"I haven't named a time," I said.

"I know," he said. "I'm still busy."

I mock frowned at him. "I have a feeling that if I were suggesting lunch, suddenly you wouldn't be so busy."

Still smiling, he held up a hand. "I'm not going to answer that, on the grounds that it will probably get me in trouble."

There were two customers in the store. Mac and Liz had both disappeared. I was guessing they were in the storage room and upstairs, respectively. Rose was at the cash register and Charlotte was arranging a set of wineglasses and an ice bucket on the table that she and Rose and Liz had been sitting at earlier.

She walked over to us. "How was your walk?" she asked.

"It was . . . helpful," Nick said, glancing sideways at me. "But I need to get to work."

"No lecture?" Charlotte asked, raising an eyebrow.

He smiled. "No lecture." Then he leaned forward and kissed his mother on the cheek. "I'll talk to you soon." He turned to me. "Thank you for the walk, Sarah," he said. Then he handed me his empty coffee cup and was gone.

Charlotte leaned sideways so she was in my direct line of sight. "What did you say to Nicolas?" she asked.

I linked my arm through hers and we started for the storage room. "I just reminded him that you're a smart woman and you and Rose and Liz aren't going to do anything stupid." I leaned my cheek against her shoulder and smiled oh, so sweetly at her.

Charlotte smiled back at me. "I knew you'd understand, sweetie," she said. "And we aren't going to do anything stupid. I give you my word on that."

I felt myself relax. Problem solved.

"We're just going to find out who killed Arthur Fenety," she said.

Or not.

Chapter 11

I didn't argue with Charlotte. I'd seen how well that had worked for Nick. I bit my tongue—literally—and left her unpacking the rest of the wineglasses. I cut through the storeroom and walked out to the back to see how Mac was doing with the table. Maybe once Charlotte and the others talked a little more to Maddie, they'd realize that they needed to leave it to the police and Josh to figure out who'd killed Arthur Fenety.

I was wrong about that, too.

Josh dropped off Maddie at about eleven thirty. I'd ordered sandwiches for lunch from Lily's Bakery. There wasn't enough space for a table and chairs in the tiny cubbyhole we used as a staff room, so Mac and I set up a folding teak table that we'd gotten from our last Saturday morning yard sale run in the storage room. It had been painted an ill-advised shade of highlighter yellow. I carried over the chairs I'd mentioned to Mac earlier.

"You know, I think you're right," he said, standing back and studying them, his arms folded over his chest. "I think they would work with my table."

"Are you going to join us for lunch?" I asked.

"Thank you, but I think I'll man the cash register," Mac said.

I grinned. "Are you sure?"

He smoothed a hand back over his close-cropped dark hair and smiled. "Very."

"Oh, Sarah, you didn't have to go to so much trouble," Maddie said when she walked in with Charlotte.

"All I did was put out mismatched plates and paper napkins," I said, inclining my head in the direction of the table, which, because of the color, looked like it was glowing a little. "And don't worry; I didn't cook."

"We should teach you how to cook," Charlotte said, taking off the apron she wore in the store and draping it over the back of one of the chairs.

I reached for the teapot to pour her a cup of tea. "It's a lost cause. Just ask Gram. I set off her smoke detector so many times I ruined it."

"You're not serious," Maddie said.

"Yes, I am," I said. "Would you like a cup of tea?" I gestured at the teapot. It was sitting on top of an old sewing-machine table that I'd repurposed as a small buffet table.

She nodded.

"Rose, we need to teach Sarah how to cook," Charlotte said, as her friend bustled into the room. Rose was wearing her own store apron and carrying a large plate of sandwiches. Liz was behind her with a second one.

"That's a lovely idea," Rose said. She smiled as she moved past me and set the large blue bubble-glass plate on the table. "When do you want to start, dear?"

"Rose, I'm a terrible cook," I said, as I handed Maddie her cup of tea. "I made a cake once and it was so awful I buried it in Gram's backyard."

Rose laughed. "No, you didn't," she said, coming around the table and picking up a cup for herself.

"Sadly, I did." I reached for the teapot. "Mom tried to teach me and Gram tried to teach me and I just can't cook. I'm hopeless."

"Nonsense," she said, turning around to hand the cup of tea I'd just poured to Liz. "You just haven't had the right teacher."

I reached for another cup, poured and handed it to her. "Julia Child couldn't make me into a cook," I said. "The only thing I know how to make is scrambled eggs."

She pushed her glasses up her nose. "Julia Child couldn't make anyone into a cook. She's dead. You'll do just fine." She moved around the table and took the chair at the far end. Liz was on her right and Charlotte on her left, next to Maddie.

Rose reached up and touched my arm as I went by her. "You'll be hosting dinner parties before you know it."

"As long as they're not for the fire department," I said, grinning at her and taking the chair next to Liz.

"As soon as we figure out who killed Arthur we'll start your lessons," Rose said, adding milk to her cup.

I opened my mouth to explain to her that tracking down a murderer wasn't quite the same as teaching me how to make meat loaf, but Maddie spoke before I could.

"Rose, the police think I killed Arthur."

"We know something the police don't," she said, spreading her napkin on her lap.

Maddie looked confused. "What?" she asked.

"We know you didn't do it," Charlotte said.

Maddie smiled, and her eyes welled with unshed tears. She blinked them away and laid a hand on top of Charlotte's hand. "You have no idea what it means to me to have your support," she said. "All of you. Josh's law office has an investigator—he's a former police officer from Portland. Josh says he's very good. I guess I'm just going to have to have faith that he can find out who really killed Arthur."

Rose looked up the table at Charlotte, who shook her head so slightly. I would have missed it if I hadn't been looking in her direction.

"Why don't we eat?" I said, reaching for my own napkin. I was happy the idea of Rose and the others playing detective had been put to rest for the moment, but I'd seen the look exchanged between Rose and Charlotte, and I knew they hadn't given up on the idea.

I picked up one of the platters of sandwiches and offered it to Maddie. She took half a ham and Swiss and smiled at me. "Sarah, I love your shop," she said. "Where do you get everything?"

"Yard sales and flea markets," I said, taking half a roast beef, tomato and dill pickle sandwich for myself. "We buy things from people who are moving to a smaller house or into assisted living, or just clearing out the old to bring in the new." I gestured with one hand. "Pretty much everywhere."

Avery blew through the door then. She was wearing skinny black jeans and a gray-and-black-checked jacket, and she had her backpack slung over one shoulder. "Most boring morning ever, and I'm starving," she said. "I forgot my lunch but Mac said there's food back here." She caught sight of Maddie and skidded to a stop on the concrete floor. She looked at me. "Sorry, Sarah. I didn't know you were busy."

"It's all right," I said.

"Hello, Mrs. H.," she said. "I heard what happened. I'm sorry. It bites."

"Yes, it does," Maddie said. She gestured at Avery's left wrist. "I like your bracelets. Where did you get them?"

Avery held up her arm. She had four brightly colored fabric bracelets around her wrist. "I made them."

"How did you get the material to hold its shape after you twisted it?" Maddie asked, leaning forward for a closer look.

Avery stretched her arm across the table. "It took a few tries," she said. She pushed the top bracelet of the stack up her arm a little. "See, this one isn't as tight. But I figured out that if I wet the fabric and let it dry all twisted, the bracelet held together better."

She was leaning over my plate as Maddie studied the red-and-black fabric. I grabbed my cup and plate and nudged my chair back.

"Take my seat, Avery," I said.

She turned her head for a second to look at me. "Oh, hey, thanks," she said, pushing her hair out of her eyes with one hand. I moved over and slid an empty plate across the tabletop to Avery.

"Nonna says you have a big flower garden," Avery said to Maddie.

She nodded. "Yes, I do."

"Have you ever used marigold petals to dye fabric?" Avery asked. She slipped her backpack off her shoulder onto the floor.

"No," Maddie said, reaching for her cup. "But I have used turmeric to dye cotton fabric. It gave me a lovely yellow color."

"Seriously?" Avery said, reaching for a sandwich. "How long did it take?"

Avery and Maddie spent the next five minutes talking about dyeing fabric. Avery ate a sandwich and a half while peppering Maddie with questions. Finally I leaned over and touched her arm. "Go give Mac a hand," I said. "I can hear customers."

"Okay," she said, jumping to her feet and swinging the backpack up on her shoulder again. "I'm so glad I got to see you," she said to Maddie. "Maybe I could come over and see your garden sometime."

Maddie smiled. "I'd like that," she said. "I'm glad I got to see you, too."

Avery headed for the front of the store as Elvis wandered in, stopping to rub against my leg before walking around the table and jumping up onto Maddie's lap. He tucked his front paws underneath himself and started to purr.

"I was thinking about getting a cat," she said as she stroked Elvis's fur, "but Arthur was a dog person."

"How did you and Arthur meet?" I asked.

Rose had slipped out and made a fresh pot of tea. She was moving around the table, filling everyone's cups, and I smiled a thank-you at her as she got to me.

"We met at a fund-raiser for the Botanic Garden. We were at the same table." Her free hand traced the edge of her plate. "He told me later he switched his place card with someone else's because he wanted to meet me." She had been staring down at the table, but now she looked up at me. "Of course, now I know he wasn't really interested in me at all." The color was high in her cheeks. "There's no fool like an old fool," she said softly. She looked away again.

"You're not an old fool," Charlotte said at once.

"Aren't I?" Maddie said. "I wasn't some love-struck teenager. I'm a grown woman who should have known better."

"Don't be so hard on yourself," Liz said. "It looks like Arthur Fenety had been charming women out of their money for a long time. He'd had a lot of practice."

"Maddie, did you give him any money?" I asked. I felt a little awkward asking the question, but I wanted to make sure she wasn't in any kind of financial trouble. And I still had the feeling she wasn't being totally frank. She seemed to have trouble looking me in the eye for very long.

She reached for her tea, still stroking Elvis's fur with her other hand. His eyes were closed in kitty bliss. "No, Sarah, I didn't," she said. "The only thing Arthur ever said about money to me was on the day he . . . died."

"What did he say?" I asked.

"Just that he was going out of town for a couple of days because he had some investments he had to see to."

"Did he say what kind of investments?" Liz asked.

Maddie shook her head. "No. He was singing when

he got to my house. I asked him what had him in such a good mood and he said he'd finally figured out what was important in life." She looked down at the table once more. "He said he had to go out of town to take care of some investments, but after that he was moving to North Harbor for good."

"Did he get any phone calls while he was with you?" I asked.

She looked up at me. "Not as far as I know, but I was inside cooking, so I guess he could have. I told you that it took longer than I'd expected to make the omelets. First, the burner on my stove wasn't working properly, and then the phone rang."

She was still petting Elvis, but he'd stopped purring, I realized. He'd stayed stretched out on Maddie's lap, but something had clearly annoyed him. His face was scrunched up in a sour expression like he'd just caught of whiff of something he didn't like. And maybe he had, for all I knew. He could smell a rodent a good forty feet away.

I got to my feet, gathered my dishes and set them on the old sewing table. Then I walked around the table and lifted Elvis off of Maddie's lap. "Go help Avery in the store," I said, setting him on the floor. I made a shooing motion with one hand. He made a face back at me, shook his head and headed across the concrete floor toward the door.

Maddie looked tired. There were pinched lines around her mouth and dark circles like smudges of ash under her eyes. "I didn't poison Arthur, Sarah," she said.

"He was poisoned?"

She nodded. "The police said it was in his coffee, some kind of pesticide that was banned a couple of years ago."

I heard Charlotte catch her breath, and at the end of the table Rose was shaking her head. Charlotte cleared her throat. "What kind of pesticide?" she asked.

Maddie played with the strap of her watch. "I don't know," she said, looking at her friend. "Something they used to sell to keep slugs off roses, I think." She shook her head. "They think because of the garden that I had whatever chemical it was, even though you can't buy it anymore. But I didn't. I've never used any chemicals on my plants and I didn't put anything in Arthur's coffee."

I bent down, put my arms around her shoulders and gave her a hug. "Everyone here knows that," I said. "And when Josh shows that you don't have any connection to that pesticide, whatever it is, that will go a long way to proving your innocence."

I finished clearing the table and carried everything up to the staff room. When I came down, Maddie had her jacket on and she and Liz were standing by the front door with Charlotte.

"We're going now," Liz said. "I'm going to walk Maddie to Charlotte's house."

"I'll drive you," I said. "Just let me run upstairs and get my purse and my keys."

Maddie caught my arm. "Thank you," she said, "but I really want to walk after being . . . inside all night."

"Okay," I said.

"Thank you for everything, Sarah," she said, folding me into a hug.

"You'd do the same for me," I whispered against her cheek.

Maddie and Liz headed off down the sidewalk, and I was about to go back up to my office to deal with a morning's worth of messages, when I caught sight of another tour bus pulling into the parking lot.

Charlotte was already showing a man and woman a washstand I'd painted black and stenciled with silver stars. Avery and Rose were with a young woman with spiky lime green hair, looking at a pretty decent beginner-level guitar. Elvis was sitting in the tub chair, washing his face. The messages would have to wait.

The second bunch of leaf peepers spent even more than the first had and I wished I'd planted more teacup gardens. They'd all sold and I probably could have sold half a dozen more if I'd had them. Once the store cleared Mac went out to work on the table a little more. I sent Avery to plant some more cups, and left Rose dusting.

"Yell if you need me," I told her. She waved her dust cloth at me and I headed up the stairs.

When I came back down about an hour and a half later Liz was back. She'd changed into black trousers and a loose white shirt with a denim jacket. She and Rose were sitting in the tub chair with Elvis between them. Avery was cross-legged on the floor at their feet, and Charlotte was leaning against the cash desk.

"What's going on?" I asked, even though I was pretty sure I knew what the topic of conversation was.

"We were just talking about Maddie," Rose said. She folded her hands primly in her lap.

"Okay," I said.

Her eyes darted to Charlotte and then Liz before she looked at me again. "Whoever killed Arthur Fenety has to be connected to those women he scammed."

"That makes sense," I said. The coatrack in the window display was crooked. I turned it so the vintage baby bonnets on its hooks could be seen from outside. When I turned back around I noticed that Charlotte had Tuesday's paper on the counter next to her.

I took a deep breath and let it out slowly. "You heard what Maddie said. Josh has an investigator. He'll look at everything."

"One investigator," Charlotte said. "How many clients does that office have?"

I closed my eyes for a moment. It didn't matter how many deep breaths I took; I still felt frustrated.

"I know that you all want to help Maddie," I said. "But you're not detectives. You don't have the skills to do this."

"But we do," Rose said. There was a determined gleam in her eyes that I knew was trouble. "Together we have more expertise that any retired police officer." She stuck out her chin and stared defiantly at me. Charlotte folded her arms. Liz leaned against the back of the oversize tub chair and a small smile played on her lips. Avery nodded, and even Elvis got into the act, resting one black paw on Rose's leg.

I shook my head and narrowed my eyes at them. "Okay, explain this expertise to me," I said.

Rose pointed at Charlotte. "Charlotte was a school principal and I was a teacher. Between the two of us we've heard every excuse and made-up story there is, and we can see through all of them." She looked at Liz. "Liz ran the Emmerson Foundation for years. She can follow the money trail."

Avery raised her hand then. "And I'm a master at underhanded and sneaky." She said the words with a certain amount of pride. "I can spot a fake a mile away." She pulled herself up a little straighter. "And, by the way, when that Arthur Fenety guy came in here last week I said he was off, and you all said I was rude."

Liz gave her head a tiny shake. "Next time we'll pay more attention to your judgment."

Avery inclined her head in her grandmother's direction like she was royalty. "Thank you, Nonna," she said. She glanced at Rose, who gave her an encouraging smile.

They'd practiced this, I realized. I sighed and pulled a hand over the back of my neck.

"We have life experience, Sarah," Rose said.

They were going to do this whether I liked it or not. And whether Nick liked it or not. Maybe I could at least keep them out of trouble. I seemed to be the only responsible adult in the room.

"There's no way I can talk you out of this, is there?" I said.

Liz and Avery shook their heads.

"No," Charlotte said.

Elvis chimed in with a loud meow while Rose watched my face.

I sighed. "Just don't do anything illegal," I warned. "There isn't enough in petty cash to bail anyone out."

Rose beamed at me. She got to her feet and wrapped me in a hug. "You are the dearest, dearest girl," she said.

"I'm the craziest girl," I said.

She pulled back and smiled. "I think you should tell Nicolas. He'll just try to give his mother orders and you know how that will turn out."

"In other words, you're sticking me with the job no one else wants."

Rose put a hand to her chest and looked offended. I knew it was an act. "Of course not," she said. "It's just that I think Nicolas will respond a lot better to your charm than he would, say, to mine."

I leaned forward and kissed her cheek. "I'm glad you use your powers for the good guys and not for the evil empire," I said.

We closed the shop, and Liz gave everyone a drive home. Actually, Avery drove, sitting exaggeratedly upright with her hands at ten and two on the steering wheel as she pulled out of the parking lot, her latest act of rebellion over her grandmother's comments about her driving.

I collected Elvis and we headed home. The first thing I did was change into the gray sweatpants I used for running and a long-sleeved orange T-shirt so I was easy to see.

"Want to come running?" I said to the cat as I tied my shoes. He yawned, flopped to the floor and rolled onto his back. "So not funny," I said.

I stretched and turned south so I could run around the water tower. I hoped the running would help me figure out how I was going to explain to Nick that I hadn't exactly talked his mother out of nosing around in Arthur Fenety's murder.

I took a shower when I got back, pulled on jeans and a sweater and sat down to make the promised phone call to my grandmother. I could hear the relief in her voice when I told her Maddie was out on bail and staying with Charlotte. After I talked to Gram I tried my mom and dad but the call went to voice mail. The same thing happened when I tried my brother, Liam. I knew Jess was on a date, although I couldn't remember who with. Elvis was watching *Jeopardy!* I was restless, wired, with no one to talk to, and when I looked in the refrigerator I remembered that I still hadn't gotten to the grocery store. *Maybe I should take Rose up on her offer of cooking lessons,* I thought. I was getting tired of scrambled eggs and toast. I grabbed my jacket and purse. "I'm going out," I called. I felt a little silly letting a cat know I was leaving. Then I heard an answering meow and it didn't seem quite so ridiculous.

I was hungry, thinking more about Sam's chili over a bowl of rice than I was paying attention to where I was walking, which was probably why I turned the corner and walked smack into Nick Elliot.

Chapter 12

Both of my hands landed on Nick's broad chest. "Are you okay?" he asked, putting a hand on my shoulder.

"I'm fine," I said. "I'm sorry. I wasn't watching where I was going." I realized I still had my hands on his chest. I dropped them and took a step backward, almost tripping over a crack in the sidewalk. I reached out, just out of reflex, grabbing his arm.

"I've got you," Nick said, tightening his grip on my shoulder.

I caught my balance, giving him a sheepish smile. I let go of his arm, but I couldn't help noticing the bulge of muscle under the sleeve of his jacket.

"Thinking deep thoughts?" Nick asked, dropping his hand from my shoulder.

"Only if you consider daydreaming about a bowl of Sam's chili to be thinking deep thoughts," I said, brushing a stray strand of hair off my cheek.

He frowned. "So, you haven't had supper yet?"

I shook my head. "I went for a run. You know, something that you couldn't do because you were so busy."

"Oh yes, I was busy," he said solemnly. "Very, very busy."

I laughed. I couldn't help it. He reminded me of a teenage Nick.

"I haven't eaten, either," he said with an easy smile. "Have supper with me. We said we were going to have dinner and catch up. I'm assuming you weren't going to just eat and run." He waggled his eyebrows at me when he said *run*.

"You are so, so not funny," I said shaking my head. "So, I'm going to take pity on you and have supper with you."

We fell into step and walked maybe ten feet before I stopped. Nick got a couple of steps ahead of me before he noticed I wasn't beside him.

He turned to look at me. "Sarah, is something wrong?"

"I couldn't talk them out of it."

It took a second for what I meant to register. He looked skyward for a second, shaking his head. Then he looked at me. "What happened to your powers of persuasion?"

"Rose's logic," I said.

"Which is?"

I stuffed my hands in my pockets and shifted from one foot to the other. "That their combined life experience makes them better at investigating Arthur Fenety's murder than anyone else."

Nick put both hands behind his head, lacing his fingers together. "They've lost their minds," he said. "All three of them—my mother, Rose and even Liz. They have some kind of age-related cognitive impairment."

"No, they don't," I said. "They're trying to help a friend. They haven't gone senile."

"My mother and her friends seem to think they're some kind of geriatric version of Nancy Drew." He exhaled loudly. "How exactly is their life experience going to help them investigate a murder? That's a job for the police."

I didn't like the way he was selling his mother and Rose and Liz short. "Of course," I said. "Because the police have done such a good job so far." I tried to keep my voice even and nonjudgmental, but a little snark still snuck in.

His mouth moved as though he were trying out the feel of what he wanted to say before he said it. "They've somehow convinced you that this is a good idea," he finally said. "Are you out . . . ?" He had the good sense not to finish the sentence.

I waited, arms folded, to see what he'd say next.

He let out a breath and studied the stars overhead for a moment. "I should just stop talking, shouldn't I?" he said, when his gaze finally dropped to my face.

"I'm thinking it would probably be a good idea," I said. My momentary anger was gone, like a match that had been struck and immediately blown out. I didn't want Charlotte and the others investigating Arthur Fenety's murder any more than Nick did.

"Still want to have supper with me?" he asked.

"As long as we talk about anything except Maddie's case."

He nodded. "Deal."

We fell back in step again.

"Nice weather we've been having lately," Nick said after a too-long awkward silence.

I stopped walking again. Nick stopped as well. "Sarah, at the rate you're walking we're going to be having breakfast instead of dinner."

"Do you really want to spend the next hour talking about the weather?" I asked.

He stuffed his hands in his pockets. "Well, I don't want to argue with you."

"So what do you suggest?" I said, smiling so he'd know I didn't want to argue with him, either.

He laughed, pulling a hand down over his chin. "I don't know."

I laughed, too, because the whole situation was kind of funny when you thought about it. Or maybe I was just tired and hungry. "Look, Nick," I said, "There isn't anything either one of us can do about your mom and Rose and Liz. They've decided they're going to investigate and it doesn't matter what either one of us says. I'll do what I can to keep them out of trouble. And you try not to huff and puff when you talk to your mother."

"I don't huff and puff," he said, a little indignantly, it seemed to me, until I saw a glint of humor in his eyes. "Maybe I growl a little."

I tried not to laugh, but I couldn't help it. "So, do we have a deal?" I asked.

He nodded. "We have a deal."

We started walking again. "What exactly are they planning to do?" Nick asked after a moment.

"I don't know," I said with a sigh. "Not for sure. They

think Fenety's death has to be connected to all those women he scammed. Which makes sense to me."

Nick turned to look at me, narrowing his eyes. "What do you mean?"

"Arthur Fenety was poisoned. That takes planning. It's personal. It's hard to poison someone without thinking it through."

"You're right," he said, stepping behind me for a moment to let some people pass us. "A death like Fenety's—just one person being poisoned—he was targeted. It was very personal. But Fenety's victims are spread all over New England."

"Nick, you don't think Maddie killed him, do you?"

This time it was Nick who stopped walking. "Good Lord, no," he said. "I've known Maddie my whole life. She couldn't hurt anyone or anything." He raked a hand through his hair. "When I was five she paid me a nickel a bug to pick aphids off of her rosebushes. I don't see her poisoning a person when she wouldn't poison a bug."

We were in front of The Black Bear and Nick held the door open for me. "What I meant was that a lot of Fenety's victims that we know about are in other states. Maybe there's at least one we don't know about who's a lot closer."

"Maybe," I agreed as we stepped inside. I was remembering being at the pub with Jess and seeing one of the women who had been married to Arthur Fenety. Maybe his other victims weren't so far away after all.

Sam was standing by the bar when Nick and I walked in. He turned around as if somehow he'd known we were there and smiled as he walked across the room to us.

"Nick Elliot! How the heck are you?" Sam said. They shook hands and grinned at each other.

Nick exhaled loudly and looked around. "I haven't been here in years," he exclaimed.

"I'm glad you decided to change that," Sam said.

"Please tell me you still have live music," Nick said.

Sam gestured at the corner stage.

"The good stuff?" Nick asked raising an eyebrow.

Sam held out his hands. "I like that old-time rock and roll."

Nick laughed. "You know," he said. "It's good to be home."

"Did you bring a guitar home with you?" Sam asked. "Tomorrow's Thursday."

"You still have Thursday-night jam?" Nick glanced over at the stage again. I wondered if he was remembering the first time he took his guitar up on the stage in here and sat in with the band. "I haven't played much lately."

"It'll come back," Sam said. "Or you can do what the rest of us do: make it up as you go along."

Nick laughed. "Wouldn't be the first time I've done that."

Sam showed us to a table near the front window, grabbing a couple of menus as we passed the bar. "I'll send Adam over."

I slipped off my jacket and hung it on the back of my chair.

"I'll be up in the morning to pick up the Rickenbacker," Sam said.

"Okay," I said. "I put it in my office. Mac knows, in case I happen to be out."

Nick looked at me. "Sam bought the Rickenbacker? The one I played?"

I nodded.

"Nice," he said, nodding, and I wondered if Nick was sorry he hadn't bought the guitar.

"Think about tomorrow night," Sam said. "Sarah and Jess are coming, and I'll probably have the Rickenbacker." He laid a hand on my shoulder for a moment and headed for the kitchen.

Nick pulled out his chair and sat down. "You and Jess are still friends."

I smiled. "I think we're like Gram, your mom, Rose and Liz. I think we're friends forever." I traced the edge of my menu with a finger. "She makes me laugh. She nags me about working too much, and I still can't get her to come running with me."

"She's probably busy," he said, completely deadpan.

I narrowed my eyes at him. "Uh-huh. There's a lot of that going around."

"You and Michelle didn't reconnect?" he said, opening the menu.

I shook my head. All these years later I still didn't know why Michelle had stopped being my friend, all but stopped talking to me.

Out of the corner of my eye I saw our waiter on the way over. "What about you?" I said. "Did you keep in touch with anyone?"

He closed the menu and pushed it aside. "No," he

said, picking up his knife and setting it back down again. "I kept saying I'd get back for a visit but it didn't happen that often." He shrugged. "Time would just get away from me. You know how it is.'

I nodded.

"Mom kept me more or less up-to-date, though."

"Yeah, so did Gram when I was away." I didn't say that listening to my grandmother talk about what people were doing in town—and sometimes who they were doing—after I'd lost my job kept me from falling down a rabbit hole of depression.

Nick ordered a Bear Burger, Sam's take on a cheeseburger made with fresh mozzarella cheese, a tangle of sweet fried onions and a spicy mayo-mustard blend that was Sam's own creation. I ordered what I'd been craving: chili over rice.

We talked about the town while we waited for our food, and then as we ate.

Neither one of us felt like dessert. Nick picked up both checks when Adam brought them to the table.

He smiled at me. "Don't waste your breath, Sarah," he said. "I asked you to join me and I'm my mother's son. That means I'm paying."

"Which way are you headed?" I asked when we were outside on the sidewalk again.

"I'm walking you home," he said, zipping his jacket. It had gotten a little cooler and there was a breeze coming in off the water.

"You don't have to do that."

He smiled down at me. "I know, but, like I told you, I am my mother's son."

I tipped my head to one side and studied him for a moment. "You are, you know," I said. "You both get that same look when you've made up your mind about something."

He winced. "Is that good or bad?"

I bumped him gently with my hip. "From my experience it depends on whether someone's on the same side or the opposite one."

We walked along, talking about some of the differences of opinion Nick and his mother had had over the years.

"You know, the most humbling thing is when I look back I see that most of the time she was right." He shook his head ruefully.

"Keep that in mind," I said.

We were in front of my house. "This is home," I said.

"Oh, you're living in Isabel's place while she's on her honeymoon."

I shook my head. "No. I'm not in Gram's place. The main-floor apartment is mine. Actually the whole house is mine. Gram was living here to keep an eye on things for me when I was away."

Nick took a step backward and looked up at the house. "It's beautiful," he said. "How did you end up owning a house here?"

I brushed my hair back off my face. "It's a long story, but basically I cleaned out a barn."

His eyes darted uncertainly from side to side. "And what?" He gestured with his hands. "You found this in an old cardboard box?"

I shook my head. "No, I found a Volkswagen bug that

hadn't been driven in twenty-five years—maybe longer. The woman who owned the barn said if I could get it out of the building I could have it. So I did."

Nick glanced at the house once more and then his gaze came back to me. "And then the car magically turned into this house? What? Were there magic beans in the glove compartment or something?"

"You're not that far off," I said with a smile. "I did a little work on the car—well, I bribed Liam to do a little work on the car. Then I traded it for an old MG." I ticked off the trades on my fingers. "I traded the MG for a camper van, which I lived in for six months. I traded the camper for a one-room cabin"—I shook my head—"and when I say *cabin*, I mean 'shack'—that Jess and I lived in for our last year of college. I used the cabin as a down payment on this house." I held out my hands. "Ta-da!"

"Wow," Nick said, shaking his head in amazement. "Why didn't I know any of this?"

I shrugged. "Well it didn't happen overnight."

"I guess I should have come home more often."

I smiled up at him. "You're here now. You can catch up." I looked at the stars overhead. It was a clear night, and away from the water there wasn't any breeze. "Thank you for walking me home," I said.

Nick smiled. "You're welcome. I'm not on call tomorrow night. Maybe I'll see you at Sam's."

I nodded. "Maybe you will."

He took a step toward me and I thought he was going to kiss me, but all he did was lay a hand on my shoulder for a moment.

"Good night, Sarah," he said, and then he headed

down the sidewalk. I stood there for a moment, feeling oddly disappointed that he hadn't at least tried to kiss me. Not that I wanted him to. At least that was what I told myself.

I opened the store in the morning, and once Rose arrived I printed out a copy of the offer for the pieces I wanted to buy from the Harrington property and got Mac to take a look at it. He leaned against the counter by the cash register, rapidly scanning everything I'd printed, Elvis at his elbow. The cat's furry black head was bent over the pages like he was reading, too.

"It's fine," Mac said, after a few minutes.

Elvis put one paw on the pages and meowed his approval, as well.

"Thanks," I said. I reached over and scratched the top of Elvis's head. "And thanks to you, too." He bobbed his head as if to say "You're welcome"; then he jumped down and headed toward the storage room. "I'm going to drop this off and go to the bank," I said to Mac.

"Take your time," he said. "I'm going to finish sanding that table."

"And I'm going to change that window display," Rose said as she came bustling down the stairs. Halfway to the storage room she stopped and turned around. "You don't mind, do you, dear?"

I shook my head. "No. Do whatever seems right to you."

She beamed at me. "Thank you," she said.

Once Rose had disappeared into the back, Mac looked at me, a smile pulling at his lips. "You know you just gave Rose carte blanche to do whatever she wants."

I shrugged. "It'll be interesting."

By the time I got back there were just a few clouds overhead and the sun was shining. Mac was sanding the top of the long table. I could see the fine grain of the wood now that the layers of paint were gone.

"You're right," I said, walking over to where he was working. "It should be stained. At least the top."

He pulled the dust mask down off his face. "That's the plan," he said, running his hand over the dusty table-top.

"You want me to paint the legs?" I said, leaning over to see what shape that wood was in. I could see some nicks and gouges but overall it looked good.

"Please," Mac said as I straightened up. "You're a lot better at detail work than I am."

"Just let me know when it's ready."

The leaves on the big maple tree next to the old garage were about four or five different shades of crimson. The air was clean, and for some reason I just felt very glad to be home.

"It's a good day," I said to Mac as I started for the back door.

He set down the sanding block he'd been using and reached for a rag. "Hold on to that thought, Sarah," he said.

What does that mean? I wondered as I opened the door. That thought was immediately followed by *Why do I smell bleach?*

The answer to that question was easy. There was a bucket of hot, soapy water that smelled like bleach in the middle of the small sunporch. Rose was on a stepladder, a hammer in one hand.

"Rose, what on earth are you doing?" I said.

She turned sideways to look at me, which made her perch on the ladder look a little precarious. "Oh, hello, dear," she said. "I'm trying to get a nail into this bracket."

"How about you come down?"

She shook her head, which made the ladder wobble just a bit. "I can't," she said. "I can't reach without the ladder." She made a face. "Sometimes I don't like being short." She looked at me. "My mother used to say I was the little package good things come in, but sometimes I wish the package was just a bit longer."

I crossed over to her and put a hand on the side of the aluminum stepladder to brace it.

"Come down," I said. "I'll do that for you."

"I almost have it," she said, and I caught the stubborn edge to her voice.

"Please," I said, fighting the urge to lean over and snatch the screwdriver from her hand. "I'm taller. It's easier for me to reach."

"Fine," she said. She climbed down off the ladder and handed me the screwdriver. I was tall enough to reach without having to climb on anything, and it took only a few turns to tighten the screw.

"What are you doing?" I asked. Rose had moved down to the end of the porch and was looking up at the single window.

"Well, bless me," she said. "There are already brackets up here." My words registered then and she turned to look at me. "I'm hanging blinds, dear. The sun can be pretty strong in here in the afternoon."

I didn't know where to start. I was still holding on to the screwdriver. *The blinds,* I decided. "Rose, I don't have any blinds to hang in here," I said.

"You do now." She turned and walked back to me, stopping to take the screwdriver from my hand before she headed into the storeroom.

I stood there stupidly for a moment, and then I went after her. She was standing by the workbench. "What do you mean, I do now?" I said.

She brushed off the front of her apron. "Do you remember those old tea chests we brought over from Will Hathaway's place?" she asked.

"Yes," I said slowly, wondering where exactly the conversation was going.

"There were some nice roller blinds in one of them."

"I know that," I said, "But those blinds are way too wide for the windows in the sunporch."

Rose beamed at me. "Not anymore. I cut them to fit."

"You cut them to fit?" I rubbed the space between my eyes with the heel of my hand.

Rose picked a bit of cat hair from my arm. "Don't worry, dear," she said. "I measured every one of them twice."

"Good for you," I said.

The blinds were spread out on the workbench behind her. She started to gather them up.

"Let me get those." I took them from her.

"They're all numbered," she said. "One is the window by the door, and they go from there."

I smiled at her. "Pretty resourceful."

She fluffed her gray hair and started for the porch again. "I'm not just another pretty face, you know."

That made me laugh. "No, you certainly aren't," I said.

I set the blinds down on the floor just inside the porch and closed the stepladder, leaning it against the wall. "Rose, what did you use to cut the blinds?" I asked.

She was bent over, looking for number one in the pile, I guessed.

"Well, first I used pliers to pull off that little metal end thingy," she said. "After that I just used that little saw of Mac's to cut them, and then I glued the metal thingy back on." She found what she was looking for and straightened up. "I do like that little saw," she said. "It's just the right size for someone who's tiny like I am."

I had to fake a cough to cover the laugh I couldn't quite swallow. Now I knew why Mac had said "hold on to that thought" when I'd gone on about what a great day it was.

Rose had measured carefully, I discovered. The first blind fit perfectly into the slots in the hanger. So did number two.

She found the third one and handed it to me.

"Rose, why did you decide to put these blinds up now?" I asked, pushing on the bottom of one of the brackets so I could slide the slotted end piece into place.

She pushed her glasses up her nose. "I think an office needs a little privacy, don't you?"

"I already have an office upstairs," I said.

"Of course you do." She pulled the blind all the way

down and raised it again to make sure it was working. "But you need your office, so I thought we could work here."

I couldn't believe it had taken me this long to get it. Even so, I asked her to make sure. "Who's *we*?"

"Charlotte and Liz and I," she said. "We can't do any kind of an investigation without an office."

"No, I don't suppose you can," I said.

I finished hanging the blinds, and then the two of us dragged a small wood-and-metal drafting table out to the porch along with a couple of chairs. Mac came in from outside while Rose was shifting the chairs around.

"Is it getting interesting yet?" he asked, working to keep from grinning at me.

I glared at him. "You knew," I said, keeping my voice low.

"I was just letting Rose do what seemed right to her," he said. He looked around. "And she did manage to find a use for those old blinds. At least they won't end up at the landfill. That's good."

I laid a hand on his arm and crinkled my nose at him. "Hold that thought, Mac," I said. "She used your miter saw to cut them."

The rest of the morning was busier than I'd expected. We didn't have any tour buses, but several tourists taking a relaxed few days to drive around and enjoy the changing leaves stopped in.

Mabel Harrington's son called late morning to accept the offer I'd put together for the furniture and other items from his mother's house. I told him I'd get back to him at the first of the week with a timeline for picking things up. I hung up the phone and smiled at Elvis, who had been sitting smack-dab in the middle of my small desk, seemingly listening to my side of the conversation.

"He took my offer," I said. It seemed to me he smiled before licking his lips. I leaned over and gave the top of his head a little scratch. "Oh, c'mon, you know you're not really going to eat anything you find out there," I said.

He stared unblinkingly at me. I stared back at him, and I have no idea how long that would have gone on, except all of a sudden his whiskers twitched. His furry black head swiveled toward the door and he lifted his chin and sniffed the air.

"I don't smell anything," I said.

His green eyes focused on me for a moment. He gave me a look that could best be described as dismissive and then he jumped down and went over to the door. When I didn't immediately jump up he looked back at me and meowed loudly.

"I'm coming," I said. I got up, squeezed around the desk and opened the door for him. He went about half a dozen steps into the hallway; then he stopped and looked back at me.

"Give me a second," I said, pulling my keys out of my pocket. "I need to lock the door."

He sat down and began thumping his tail against the floor, not unlike someone impatiently drumming his fingers.

"That's not making me move any faster, you know," I said.

The tail thumping stopped. It occurred to me that not

only was I turning into one of those people who talked to their animals, but now I was also expecting an answer.

Elvis led the way downstairs. Liz was standing just inside the front door. A brown paper shopping bag was at the floor by her feet. Mr. Peterson was on her other side.

"Good morning," I said to Liz. I leaned sideways to smile at Mr. P. "Hello, Mr. Peterson."

He smiled back at me. "Hello, Sarah," he said. "I like your store. It's a trip down memory lane for me."

"Thank you," I said.

I was shooting *what is he doing here* looks at Liz, who was studiously avoiding meeting my eye.

Mr. P. was carrying a small black nylon briefcase, but Elvis's attention was completely focused on Liz's shopping bag. He sniffed at it and then pawed at the brown paper.

"Don't do that," I ordered, bending down to pick him up.

"He probably smells lunch," Liz said, finally meeting my gaze. "I brought Chinese chicken salad for everyone from McNamara's."

Elvis twisted in my arms and the look he gave me was totally triumphant.

"That was very . . . thoughtful of you," I said. Now I knew something was up. I knew a bribe when it was sitting on the floor of my store in a paper shopping bag.

I was about to grab Liz by the arm, pull her away from Mr. P. and ask her what the heck was going on, when Rose came from the storage room. She caught sight of us and a smile stretched across her face. She hurried across the floor, stopping for a moment to speak to a man and woman who were looking at a large rectangular mirror that was hanging on the wall near the cash register.

"Alfred, thank you for coming," she said, taking Mr. P.'s free hand in both of hers.

"I'm happy to help in any way I can, Rose," he said, smiling back at her.

She let go of his hand and turned to Liz. "You brought lunch," she said. "Thank you."

Liz handed her the shopping bag and Rose peeked inside. "I thought you were going to cook," she said, looking up at her friend.

"I said I'd bring lunch," Liz said. "I didn't say anything about cooking,"

Rose gave me a quick smile and turned back to Liz. "I'm going to give Sarah cooking lessons when all this upset with Maddie is over."

"Won't that be fun?" Liz said dryly.

"You can come if you need to brush up on your skills."

"As long as I can call for takeout I'm fine."

I could see where this was going. Time to change the subject. "So, what's happening?" I said to Rose.

She shot Mr. P. another quick smile and then focused on me. "Alfred is going to help us figure out who really killed Arthur Fenety. He's a computer genius."

I looked at Mr. P.

"I don't know if I'd say *genius*," he said, ducking his head modestly.

"You didn't say *genius*. I did," Rose said. "And you

are." She took Mr. P.'s arm with her free hand. "The office is all set up. Come take a look and see if there's anything else you need."

"I'm sure everything's fine," he said. He couldn't stop looking at Rose, and there was something about the expression on his face that made me think of a love-struck sixteen-year-old boy. It occurred to me that he would have happily followed her off the edge of a cliff.

Mr. P. had a thing for Rose. Oh, great.

I turned to look at Liz, raising my eyebrows.

Liz held up her hands. "Don't look at me," she said. "All I did was pick up lunch—and Alfred."

I leaned over, put my arm around her shoulders and kissed her cheek. "I will get you for this," I whispered. Then I headed for the cash register, where a customer was waiting.

Mac came in a few minutes later. "Table's all sanded," he said. "Do you want to see what I'm thinking about for stain?"

I nodded. "I do. Let me get Charlotte and I'll come out and take a look."

"Okay," Mac said.

I headed for the storeroom door. "By the way, Liz brought lunch," I said.

"That's not all she brought, I see." He tipped his head in the direction of the sunporch. "That's Mr. Peterson, isn't it?"

"Yes, it is."

"Interesting."

I shook a finger at him. "Oh no. We are not using that

word in here for the rest of the day. It's already gotten me in enough trouble."

He laughed and made a shooing motion with one hand. "Go find Charlotte."

Charlotte and Rose were with Mr. P. in their new "office." Liz was unpacking lunch, dividing the food between two metal TV trays. Someone had brought in a black wicker chair and Elvis was perched on it, watching Liz's every move. "Charlotte, could you keep an eye on the cash for a few minutes?" I asked. "I just need to look at some stain samples with Mac. You can take your lunch right after that."

"Of course," she said. She looked at Rose. "I'll be right back."

I linked my arm through Charlotte's as we walked back to the front of the building. "Mr. P. likes Rose," I said.

She smiled. "You noticed."

"It's kind of hard not to. He's like a love-struck teenager."

"Alfred is a nice man," Charlotte said, glancing back over her shoulder. "That whole incident over at Legacy Place aside. He's very popular with the ladies."

I leaned my head against her. "You know that if he hurts Rose in any way I'll have to have a serious talk with him."

"I know," she said. She reached over and laid a hand against my cheek. "And speaking of talks, thank you for whatever you said to Nicolas."

"I didn't have to say much," I said. "Nick loves you."

"I know." She shook her head. "He also thinks I'm a hundred and two and should be home, in a rocking chair, with a shawl around my shoulders."

I laughed. "C'mon, Charlotte. He's not that bad."

She smiled. "All right. He's not. But he doesn't understand why we need to help Maddie. I'm glad you do. I'm glad you're on our side."

As far back as I could remember, Charlotte and Rose and Liz had been in my life. They were a cross between Cinderella's Fairy Godmother and Mother Teresa. I'd never for a moment doubted how much they loved me.

I laid my head on her shoulder for a moment. "I'm always, always on your side," I said.

Mac took me out to the workshop to show me his choices for the table stain. "That one," I said immediately, pointing to the darkest of the four choices.

"That was my choice, too," he said.

We talked about paint colors for the table legs and then I headed back to the shop.

"I'll be there in a minute," Mac called after me.

I lifted a hand in the air to show I'd heard him.

Liz was waiting for me by the door to the sunporch. She handed me two cardboard takeout containers.

"Thank you," I said. "What do I owe you?"

"Nothing," she said. She glanced over her shoulder. Mr. P. was showing Rose something on his computer screen.

Rose looked up from the computer then and beckoned to me. I handed the food containers back to Liz and walked over to her.

"Alfred needs the—" She looked at Mr. P.

"Password for the Wi-Fi," he said.

"Are you going to be doing anything illegal?" I joked, smiling so he'd know I was kidding.

"Not that could be traced back here," he said. His expression was completely serious and for a moment I wondered if he was, too.

I gestured at the keyboard. "May I?" I asked.

Mr. P. nodded and I leaned over and typed in the long combination of letters and symbols that made up the password. "There you go," I said.

Rose smiled. "Thank you, Sarah." She caught my hand and gave it a squeeze.

I retrieved lunch from Liz just as Mac came in the back door. "I'll be out front if you need me," I told her.

I sent Charlotte back to eat with the others. Mac pulled out the low stool we kept behind the counter and I sat in the tub chair.

"We should make another one of those," Mac said, gesturing at my seat with his chopsticks. "How many times has someone wanted to buy that one?"

"At least half a dozen," I said, taking the lid off my container of Chinese chicken salad. Second Chance wasn't usually busy at lunchtime. Today wasn't any different. Mac and I ate our lunch and talked about when we could pick up the furniture from Mabel Harrington's house.

"It's awfully quiet back there," I said, as he collected our containers to be rinsed and recycled.

"Go see what they're doing," Mac said. "You know you want to."

I stood up and stretched my arms up over my head. "I

do," I said. "I'm just kind of afraid of what I might find them doing. What if Mr. P. has hacked into the police-department computer?"

Mac smiled. "Then you'd better hope he's as good as he says he is."

"You're not helpful," I said over my shoulder as I headed for the back of the building.

I could hear him laughing behind me. "I wasn't trying to be," he said.

In the sunroom Mr. P. was still working on his laptop. I decided that if I didn't look at what he was doing I had plausible deniability if I needed it. Liz, Charlotte and Rose were sitting by the windows, talking.

I stuck my head around the doorframe. "Hi. Do you need anything before I head up to my office?"

Rose looked up. "Sarah, do you still have Tuesday's newspaper?" she asked.

"I think it's in the recycling bin."

"It's all right," Mr. P. piped up. "I already retrieved it from their Web site."

Rose smiled and Mr. P. glowed. "I guess we don't need anything, then," she said. She looked at her watch. "Is there anything special you'd like me to do this afternoon?"

"Would you unpack the last of those quilts?" I asked. "They seem to be popular with the leaf peepers."

"I will. Would you like me to put out more of the Depression-glass plates, as well?"

I nodded. "That's a good idea."

Avery blew in the back door then, her cranberry-hued hair windblown and her gray-and-black jacket hanging open. She stood in the doorway, held up a piece of paper and grinned from ear to ear. "I am a mathematical genius!" she proclaimed.

I leaned over to look at her math test—that was what she was holding up. Then I grinned back at her. "Avery! That's a ninety-two. Wonderful!"

"Yes, it is," she said, squaring her shoulders with pride. She held up her hand and I high-fived her.

Charlotte and Rose were both smiling. Rose clapped.

Liz got out of her seat and came over to Avery. "Good work," she said. "I'm proud of you."

"Really?" Avery asked.

"Really," Liz said, wrapping her in a hug. She turned her head to look over her shoulder at Rose. "Rose, we're going to need a cake."

"Well, yes," Rose said. She leaned forward in her chair and looked at Avery. "What kind of cake would you like?"

"Chocolate with that topping stuff that has brown sugar and coconut," Avery said, as Liz let go of her and took the test from her hand.

"German chocolate," Rose said.

Avery nodded enthusiastically. "That's it." Then, like a little kid, she added, "Please and thank you." She noticed Alfred Peterson then. "Hey, Mr. P.," she said.

He looked up from the keyboard. "Hello, Avery," he said. "Good job on the math test."

She grinned again. "Thanks. I bet you were good at math because you're good with computers."

How did she know that? I'd found out about his alleged computer skills only about an hour ago.

Mr. Peterson smoothed a veiny hand back over the top of his mostly smooth head. "I'm afraid not," he said. "I was a bit of a bad boy in my high school days."

Liz suddenly had a coughing fit. I thumped her on the back. "Avery, get your grandmother's tea," I said. "It's dry in here." I'd caught a glimpse of Liz's face and I knew her sudden coughing spell had nothing to do with dry air and everything to do with Alfred Peterson's declaration that he'd been a bad boy back in his high school days.

Liz took a sip of her probably cold tea and sat down again. I noticed she avoided looking me in the eye—just as well because I was a bit afraid that if she did I'd be the one having a sudden coughing jag.

"What are you all doing out here, anyway?" Avery asked.

"It's our office," Rose said.

"You mean for helping Mrs. H."

Charlotte nodded. "Mr. Peterson is helping us."

"Very cool, Mr. P.," Avery said. She held up her hand and the old man high-fived her, which made me like him just a little bit more. "Hey, Nonna, you know what you are?" Avery asked.

"The world's best grandmother?" Liz said.

Avery rolled her eyes. "You're so funny," she said. "You guys are Charlie's Angels." She looked at Charlotte. "You're Lucy Liu. Nonna is Cameron Diaz and Rose is Drew Barrymore."

Liz looked over at me. "Not a word, Sarah," she warned, but her eyes were sparkling with amusement.

I mimicked zipping my mouth, locking it and putting the key in my shirt pocket.

"Does that mean I'm Bernie Mac?" Mr. P. asked.

"Uh, yeah," Avery said, as though that was obvious.

"I'd like to be Farrah," Liz said, patting her blond hair.

Avery shook her head. "Well, whoever that is, she's not one of Charlie's Angels, so you can't."

Charlotte smiled. "Farrah Fawcett was one of the original Charlie's Angels," she said. "On TV."

"Are you serious?" Avery asked. She glanced over at me.

I nodded.

"I have to see that. Can we download it?" she said to Liz.

"When your homework is done," Liz said, reaching for her tea and frowning at the empty cup.

"You should be Jaclyn Smith," Rose said to Liz.

"Why?" Liz asked.

"She had the nicest clothes."

"So that would make you Farrah."

Rose nodded. "I know. I have the best hair so I should be Farrah." She tossed her gray curls.

"Maybe I should be Farrah," Charlotte said.

Rose and Liz both turned to look at her.

"You're Kate Jackson," Liz said.

Rose nodded her agreement. "No doubt about it. You're the smartest of all of us."

I waved a hand at them. "What about me?" I asked. "Who am I?"

"Napthathion," Mr. P. said.

I looked at him. "Excuse me?"

"I'm sorry, Sarah," he said. "That's the name of the poison that killed Arthur Fenety."

"Naptha what?" Liz asked.

"Napthathion. It's a pesticide. It was banned just over two years ago."

"This helps, doesn't it?" Rose said. "How on earth could Maddie have gotten her hands on a chemical that was banned two years ago? What was it used for?"

Mr. P. glanced at the computer screen again. "Before it was banned it was used to control—"

"Earwigs," Charlotte said, slowly. "Not slugs. Earwigs." All the color had drained from her face.

"How did you know that?" I asked. This was the second time I'd seen Charlotte react to a conversation about what had killed Arthur Fenety.

She had to swallow a couple of times before she answered me. "I have a bottle of it in my garage," she said.

Chapter 13

"I thought you cleaned everything out of the garage last year," Rose said.

"I did," Charlotte said. "All I kept was the naptha-thion and something to get rid of the ants. But Maddie didn't know I had it. Nobody knew."

I turned to Avery. "Go help Mac, please. Now."

"You don't want me to hear stuff," she said.

"No, I don't."

She nodded, her expression serious. "Okay." She leaned down and gave Liz a hug and then left.

I looked at Mr. P. and gestured toward his laptop. "What can you tell me about napthathion?"

His fingers moved over the keyboard. "It was on a long list of herbicides and pesticides that the state banned two years ago," Mr. P. said after a moment. He scrolled down the screen. "Where is that?" he muttered.

I waited.

"Here it is," he said. He looked up at me. "Sarah, it wasn't until napthathion was taken off the shelves that anyone figured out that it had any effect on people. It messes up electrical signals in the heart, but only in someone who already has some kind of heart problem and who's taking a couple of different medications."

"The perfect storm," I said, softly.

Mr. P. nodded. "Exactly."

"Whoever poisoned Arthur would have to have known that," Liz said. "And they would have to have known that he had a heart condition and what drugs he was taking."

"Maddie didn't know," Charlotte said. Her color was better now. "She told me that she liked the fact that he didn't talk about his ailments, and then she said because he was so healthy he didn't actually have any."

"Well, that's good, isn't it?" Rose said.

"It's not bad," I said.

"But that pesticide in my garage is." Charlotte fiddled with her teacup.

I nodded. "Yes, it is. The police will say Maddie had motive. They'll say she found out that Arthur was scamming her."

"But she said that she hadn't given him any money," Rose said. "So she doesn't have a motive after all."

Liz shook her head. "Even if she can prove that, it doesn't mean Maddie didn't have a motive. The man had what? Four wives and at least that many girlfriends. That kind of humiliation is a pretty good motive."

"So, who could have known that Arthur Fenety had a heart condition and also known what medications he was taking?"

"It sounds like the kind of things a wife would know," Mr. P. said.

"Alfred's right," Liz said. "It's a lot harder to hide something like that when you're living in the same house."

"I'll see what I can dig up on Fenety's wives." Mr. P.'s fingers were already moving over the keyboard.

I nodded. I didn't want to know how he planned to do that so I didn't ask. Just the way I hadn't asked how he'd gotten the name of the pesticide that had killed Arthur Fenety. I was beginning to suspect Mr. P. had a little more of the bad boy in him than I'd thought.

"Is there anything I can do to help?" Liz asked.

"Do you have a phone?" Mr. P. said.

"Yes." She pulled her cell phone out of her pocket.

"Can you sound like an old lady?" he asked.

"What? You'll have to speak up," Liz said. Her voice was shaky and pitched a little higher. She sounded a good ten years older.

Mr. P. smiled approvingly. "You can help," he said.

Rose looked at her watch. "I need to get to work." She got to her feet.

"And I should go home and see how Maddie's doing," Charlotte said.

Rose laid a hand on Mr. Peterson's shoulder as she passed behind him. "Thank you so much for your help, Alfred," she said. "I don't know how to thank you. Could I at least get you another cup of tea?"

He smiled broadly. "Maybe in a little while," he said.

I remembered the woman Jess and I had seen at The Black Bear the same day that Arthur Fenety died. I raked my fingers back through my hair. "Start with Grace MacIntyre," I said. "Jess and I saw a woman who looked just like her photograph at Sam's on Monday night."

"One of Arthur's wives was in town?" Rose paused in the doorway.

"Maybe."

"Don't worry. I'll find her," Mr. P. said.

"I'll talk to you later," Liz said to Charlotte. She pulled her chair a little closer to Mr. P. "So, where do we start?" I heard her ask him.

I walked out to the front of the store with Charlotte. "Can I ask you something?" I said.

She smiled. "I don't know. Can you?" she said.

It was an old joke between us and I was glad to see it could still make her smile.

"Do you think Maddie killed Arthur Fenety?"

She looked at me like I'd suddenly sprouted an apple tree on the top of my head. "Why on earth would you ask that? Of course I don't."

"Then don't beat yourself up because you have an old bottle of bug killer in your garage."

Charlotte smoothed the front of her yellow shirt. "Maddie thought I'd gotten rid of all those chemicals. She'd been after me for years about using them." She took a deep breath and exhaled slowly. "But what if the person who actually did kill Arthur used the naptha-thion in my garage?"

I looked at her. "Seriously?"

She looked back at me a bit sheepishly. "It sounds silly, doesn't it?"

"Maybe a little," I said.

She reached over and tucked a loose strand of hair behind my ear. "You remind me of your grandmother."

I smiled. "Thank you. I take that as a compliment."

"It's meant as one."

Mac had carried in a large box with the rest of the quilts that Jess had repaired and I'd managed to remove the musty smell from with vinegar and Woolite. I'd made a display stand out of an old folding clothes rack and painted it creamy white. Rose was sorting the quilts by color. She clearly had everything under control, and I left her to it.

"I'm going to do those dishes before I go," Charlotte said. "I just remembered that Maddie had another meeting with Josh so she isn't home right now."

"Thanks," I said.

She smiled. "Liz and Alfred Peterson are out in the sunporch, trying to find Arthur Fenety's wives. I think I'm the one who should be thanking you."

I shrugged. "I like Mr. P., especially when he has his clothes on."

Charlotte laughed and headed for the steps. Mac walked over to me, carrying a couple of message slips. He handed me the pieces of paper. "Everything okay?" he asked.

"There's a geriatric computer hacker using my Wi-Fi and doing things I don't want to think about, but, otherwise, things are fine."

"I've got things covered here," he said. "Rose and I can handle the shop. Avery's outside, washing those plastic chairs you wanted to put in the window. Why don't you go up to your office to take a break?"

I pulled a hand over my neck and looked at the messages Mac had given me. "I suppose I could return these," I said.

"Or you could put your feet up and let the world turn without you for five minutes."

"Okay, that too," I said.

As I started up the steps Elvis came from the small storage area underneath the stairs. There was a dust ball stuck to one of his ears and a bit of tape on his front left paw.

"What were you doing down there?" I said as he came level with me.

He seemed to shrug and then moved past me on up the steps.

"You'd better not have been poking around in any boxes," I warned.

He flicked his tail at me. I was pretty sure I knew what that meant.

I unlocked my office door, sank onto my chair and propped my feet on the edge of the desk. Elvis jumped onto my lap and nuzzled my cheek. I reached over and scratched underneath his chin.

"I wish Gram was here," I said.

My cell phone rang. I reached for it, smiling when I saw who was calling. "Hi, Mom," I said.

I leaned back, shifting Elvis on my lap.

"Hi, sweetheart," she said. "How's everything?"

"You talked to Gram," I said. I pictured her smiling and nodding.

"I did. I can't believe Maddie Hamilton was arrested. She wouldn't kill anyone."

Elvis had stretched out in my lap and was lazily washing his face with a paw.

"Do you remember Josh Evans, Mom?" I asked.

"Was he the little guy in the purple cape who could argue your ear off?"

I laughed. "That's Josh. The purple cape is gone, and he's a lawyer now. He's representing Maddie."

"Good," she said. "Is there anything I can do?"

"There might be," I said. Elvis took one last swipe at his face, then laid his head on my leg and closed his eyes. "Does Dad still have any contacts at the paper?"

My stepfather had been a journalist for many years. Now he taught journalism and writing at Keating State College in New Hampshire.

"He does," Mom said. "A bunch of them got together a few weeks ago to talk about their glory days."

"I bet that was fun."

She laughed. I pictured her sitting out on the patio overlooking the backyard, watching the squirrels defeat Dad's latest contraption to keep them out of the bird feeder. "Actually it was," she said. "I finally got the real story about how he got that little scar on his forehead."

"I have a feeling I'm going to like it," I said.

She laughed again. "I know you are." I heard her shift in her seat, probably reaching for a cup of tea.

"So, what do you need to know?" she asked. "I'm assuming that's why you asked about the paper."

"Yeah," I said, picking a clump of black cat hair off my shirt and dropping it onto the floor. Elvis didn't stir. "It's a little complicated. Rose and Charlotte and Liz are kind of investigating."

"You mean the murder?" Mom said.

I sighed. "Yes."

"I'm not so sure that's a good idea."

"I know," I said. "Try convincing them of that. I'm just trying to keep them from getting in too much trouble."

"What do you need to know?"

I shifted in my seat again and this time Elvis lifted his head and glared at me. I stroked his fur and after a moment he put his head down again.

"Arthur Fenety spent some time in New Hampshire," I said. "At least one of his wives is there. Anything about Fenety's background might be useful. And I'll pass everything on to Josh."

"I'll ask your dad when he gets home," Mom said.

"Tell him thank you," I said.

"I will," she said. "I'll let you get back to work. I love you, pretty girl."

"Love you, too," I said.

I ended the call and set the phone next to me on the loveseat. Someone knocked softly on my door.

"Come in," I called.

Mac stuck his head around the door. "You're not on the phone," he said. "That's good."

I smiled. "I was, but I was talking to my mom."

"I brought you a cup of coffee," he said, coming into the room. He had a cup in each hand.

I took the mug he held out. "Thank you," I said. "I could use a little kick start of caffeine."

He leaned against my desk, folding his hands around his own cup.

"Have Charlie's Angels come up with anything yet?"

I asked. I took a long drink from my coffee. It was hot and strong, just the way I liked it.

"Charlie's Angels?" Mac said, narrowing his gaze at me.

I nodded. "Yeah. Avery kind of gave them the name."

"New Charlie's Angels or classic?" he asked.

Elvis sat up and shook himself.

"That's still up for debate. Although Rose sees herself as Farrah Fawcett."

"Because?" Mac prompted.

"She has the best hair."

He laughed. "So that must mean Mr. Peterson is Bosley?"

"He is."

"And what about you?"

Elvis sniffed the air; then he jumped down and went out into the hallway.

I picked more cat fur off my lap. "I think I'm Charlie."

He nodded. "I can see that."

"This isn't exactly what I envisioned when I hired Rose and Charlotte, you know," I said.

"I seem to remember you telling me nothing ever happened around here," he said, raising an eyebrow.

"Mac, do you ever wish you were back in your old life?" I asked, leaning back in my chair.

"What? And give up all this?"

"I'm serious," I said.

He smiled. "So am I." He set his coffee on the edge of the desk, tenting his fingers over the top of the cup. "I can sail for close to half the year. I get to work with my hands. And, c'mon, it's never boring around here."

I laughed.

"I don't want to wear a suit and a tie. And I don't want to sell stocks and bonds. I want to sell things I can touch. I don't want to worry about what the Dow is doing. I'd rather see what Rose or Avery are doing." He made a face. "Sorry. I didn't mean to give a speech." He pushed away from the desk and straightened up. "I'd better go see how Avery *is* doing."

I held up my mug. "Thank you for the coffee," I said.

Mac smiled. "Anytime," he said.

I stretched my legs out in front of me. Then I reached for the phone. I really did need to return those messages.

Charlotte came out of the staff room just as I was about to head back downstairs. "Would you like more coffee?" she asked.

I shook my head. "No, thanks. I'm good."

We walked downstairs together. "I talked to my mom," I said. "Dad's going to use his contacts to see if he can get any information about Arthur Fenety."

"Thank you," she said. "I just know his death has to be connected to all the women he scammed. Nothing else makes any sense."

Mac was standing in the middle of the store, talking to two women. When he caught sight of me he beckoned me over. "Sarah, these women are looking for a rectangular table that folds for storage," he said.

"The only thing we have is the Big Bird table," I said, referring to the long canary yellow table that we'd had lunch at the day before. "And that hasn't been restored yet."

"Could I see it?" the younger of the two women said.

She was dressed casually in jeans, boots and a fisherman-knit sweater. She looked enough like the older woman that I guessed they were mother and daughter.

"Of course," I said. "It's in the storage room. Come have a look."

I took them into the back room and showed them the table. It really did seem to glow even under the bright overhead lights.

"That's what I want," the woman in the fisherman-knit sweater said. "Can you refinish it for me?"

I nodded. Behind her Mac held up two fingers, which I knew meant two weeks. "It'll be about three weeks," I said, adding an extra week so we'd have some wiggle room. I did a quick calculation in my head and added twenty-five percent to the cost. She didn't quibble at all when I named the price.

"You have a deal," I said, thinking maybe I should have added thirty percent instead.

We went out to the front counter and did the paperwork.

"Very nice," Mac said once they were gone.

"I didn't think anyone would want that table. I looked back toward the storeroom door. "It's a very plain design. Not to mention it glows in the dark right now and most people can't see beyond that."

Mac just smiled his Cheshire cat smile at me.

I hadn't seen any potential in that table but he had. "You can say 'I told you so,'" I said.

The smile got wider. "No. That would be petty."

I laughed. "You were right about that table."

"Always good to have my genius recognized."

I heard a noise behind me and turned to see Mr. P. standing there with his laptop. He had a pleased look on his face.

"Did you find something?" Rose asked. She'd been dusting a collection of tiny china animals.

"I think I might have," he said. "I've been looking through the archives of the *Burlington Free Press*." He carried the computer over and set it on the counter. There was a photo of a man who looked like he was in his late forties on the screen. His head was shaved smooth but he had a neatly trimmed goatee that seemed to be about half graying. He was tall and heavyset, and in the photo he was wearing rimless glasses.

"Who's that?" Charlotte asked.

"His name is Jim Grant," Mr. P. said. "His mother is one of Arthur Fenety's wives. Jim Grant threatened to kill him." He pushed his own glasses up his nose. "Actually he threatened to drive his truck over Arthur and turn him into roadkill, which I think is pretty much the same thing."

"Maybe he decided that poison would be a little neater," Rose said. She smiled at Mr. P. "We should talk to this Jim Grant. How do we get hold of him?"

"That's going to take a little more digging," Mr. P. said.

I heard the front door open and I looked over to see if there was more than one customer.

"Maybe it's not," I said, slowly.

Jim Grant had just walked into the store

Chapter 14

I looked at Mr. P. and shifted my eyes to the storeroom door. He was very quick on the uptake.

He touched my arm and smiled. "Thank you dear," he said. "Facebook can be so confusing." Then he picked up his laptop and headed back—I hoped—to the sun-porch.

I smoothed the front of my shirt and met Jim Grant in the middle of the room in front of the tub chair. It was him, I realized, the man in Mr. P.'s photo. It wasn't wishful thinking on my part or a trick of the light. I gave him a businesslike smile. "Hello," I said, "Welcome to Second Chance."

He was wearing khakis and a navy Windbreaker, and since I didn't see his glasses I was guessing he was also wearing contacts.

"I'm looking for Sarah Grayson," he said. "Would you be her?"

I nodded. "Yes, I am. How can I help you?"

"My name is Jim Grant." He offered his hand and I shook it. His left arm was covered with a gauze bandage that disappeared up his sleeve and there was an angry rash on the back of his hand. "Detective Andrews said that Arthur Fenety sold my mother's tea set to you. Did he sell you anything else?"

Well, now I knew where the tea set had come from. And I'd been right that Arthur's selling it wasn't on the up-and-up.

"I'm sorry," I said, shaking my head. "The tea set was the only thing he brought in and the police have that now."

He shrugged. "That's what Detective Andrews said, but I wanted to see for myself. I hope I haven't offended you."

"You haven't," I said. "You're welcome to prowl around the store. Maybe that will put your mind at ease."

He looked around the open space. "Thank you, but I don't see anything that looks like hers. You don't sell jewelry, do you?"

"No, we don't," I said. Out of the corner of my eye I could see Rose and Charlotte folding a quilt and trying not to be obvious as they eavesdropped. "There is a pawn shop just one street up from the harbor front, though."

He ran his fingers over his bearded chin. "I've already been there."

"I'm sorry Arthur Fenety took advantage of your mother," I said, hoping I could somehow get him talking so he'd stay for a few minutes. "Madeline Hamilton is a family friend."

"The woman they charged."

I nodded. "She didn't kill him."

Jim Grant shrugged. "There are some people who

wouldn't blame her if she had. Fenety left some of those women he scammed penniless." His face tightened with anger. "He took my mother's silver and her good jewelry, which was bad enough because those things have memories for her. But she has her house and most of her money. Some of his so-called wives weren't that lucky."

Rose was making her way over to us. She was moving slowly, limping. Why hadn't I noticed that earlier?

"Excuse me for interrupting," she said, directing her attention to Jim Grant, "but I heard you mention Arthur Fenety's name. Was he a friend of yours?"

Grant shook his head. "No. Arthur Fenety was certainly not a friend of mine."

"He was a despicable man," Rose said.

Jim Grant nodded. "You knew him, then?"

She nodded. "He was seeing my friend, Maddie Hamilton." She held out her hand. "I'm Rose Jackson."

"Jim Grant," he said, taking her hand and shaking it, gently. "I heard your friend was arrested. I'm sorry."

Rose patted his hand before she let go of it. "A man like that had to have known some very unsavory people. I'm sure the police will find out that it was one of them who killed him."

Elvis had come down the stairs. He came across the floor and wound around Jim Grant's legs. "Hello, puss," he said, reaching down to stroke the top of the cat's head. I was beginning to think there wasn't anyone that the cat couldn't charm. Just like the original Elvis, this one had charisma.

"I wish I'd gotten here a day sooner," Grant said. "Then it would have been Fenety in a jail cell."

"He took advantage of your mother," Rose said. "The man was a heel and a reprobate."

I looked down at Elvis. Something was annoying him. He had the same pissed-off look he'd gotten when we'd all had lunch together and Maddie had been petting him.

"I admit when I found out what he'd done there was a moment when I thought I could have killed him." He shook his head. "It's not a very good thing to admit to, is it?"

Rose reached out and touched his sleeve. "I understand completely. I've had a few dark impulses about the man myself."

"Now that he's dead I don't have much hope of getting my mother's jewelry back." He blew out a breath and shook his head. "When I got here Tuesday morning and checked into my hotel, the newspaper was on the desk by the phone. I'd been looking for Fenety for months. I admit it felt like some cosmic joke that he was dead just when I'd finally tracked him down." He straightened up and brushed off his hands. "Thank you, Ms. Grayson," he said, "for giving the police the tea set. At least we'll get that back eventually."

"I'm sorry we didn't have any of your mother's jewelry," I said. I glanced down at Elvis. Whatever the aggravation was, it had passed.

Grant shrugged. "It was probably gone before Fenety even got here."

He turned to Rose and smiled. "I hope things work out for your friend."

Rose smiled sweetly back at him. She was playing the

slightly befuddled little old lady to the hilt. "I hope you find your mother's things." She touched her watch. "I know how I'd feel if someone stole my memories."

I bit my tongue so I wouldn't laugh. I knew Rose's watch had come from a Target store in Portland.

"Oh, my goodness," she said, still looking at her watch. "Look at the time. I need to get home."

She looked at me for the briefest moment. I knew I was supposed to do or say something. I just had no clue what.

"Umm, if you can wait a few minutes, I'll drive you," I said.

Rose shook her head. "No, no, dear. You have work to do. It's not far. I'll be fine." She started to hobble toward the front door.

"Mrs. Jackson, I'm on my way back to my hotel," Grant said. "Could I drop you somewhere?"

Rose hesitated. "I don't want to put you out."

He smiled. "You wouldn't."

She hesitated just a moment longer. I was shooting warning glances at her but she was pointedly ignoring them. Then she turned that smile on. "All right. Thank you. I don't move as fast as I used to."

He offered his arm and Rose took it.

"Thanks again," he said to me, and the two of them went out the door.

Charlotte walked over to me. I pulled a hand back through my hair. "What the heck was that?" I said. "Who does Rose think she is? Meryl Streep?"

Charlotte smiled. "She's detecting. Let her go."

"That could be Arthur Fenety's killer."

"He couldn't have killed Arthur. You heard what he said. He didn't get here until Tuesday morning."

"And of course murderers never lie," I said. "I shouldn't have let her go with him."

"Rosie's fine." Mr. P. was standing in the storeroom doorway. He held up his cell phone. "She called my phone. I'm on speed dial. It's a little muffled but I can hear what they're saying." He smiled proudly. "She's pumping him for information."

I raked my hand back though my hair again and watched some long strands float down to the floor. "I'm going to be bald," I said to Charlotte.

She smiled and reached over to brush a strand of hair off my cheek. "Don't worry. We'll knit you some very nice hats."

But I did worry until Jim Grant had dropped Rose off at the medical clinic. I held out my hand. "Give me the phone," I said to Mr. P.

"Sarah wants to talk to you," he said, and then he handed it over.

"Hello, dear," she said.

"Promise me you won't do that again," I said.

"Do what?"

"Go off with a man you don't even know, who could be a murderer."

She laughed. "Don't be silly. James doesn't have the grip strength to kill someone. Didn't you notice what a limp handshake he has?"

I took a deep breath and exhaled slowly through my nose. It didn't help. "Rose, Arthur Fenety was poisoned, not strangled."

"Well, I know that," she said with just a touch of exasperation in her voice. "But that limp handshake shows weakness of character. He's a bit of a mama's boy. Not a killer."

"Okay," I said, realizing that I wasn't getting anywhere. "Just don't take any more rides from people you don't know. Please."

"All right, dear. If it will make you feel better." She was humoring me but that was okay. "Oh, and Charlotte's taking the rest of my shift."

"I noticed," I said.

"Tell her she doesn't need to cook. I'm bringing dinner."

"I will," I said. I handed the phone back to Mr. P. and relayed the message to Charlotte. When I turned back around he was tucking the phone in his pocket. "Good job finding Jim Grant's picture," I said. "And cooking up that phone business with Rose."

He smiled. "Thank you." He turned to head back to the sunporch. "Oh, and I found that woman."

"What woman?" I said.

He stopped and turned back around. "The woman you saw at Sam's."

"One of Arthur's wives?" Charlotte asked.

"Her name is Grace MacIntyre. And she was a girlfriend. Not a wife."

Charlotte looked at me. "We should talk to her before she leaves town."

Mr. P. made a face. "I'm afraid you're too late," he said. He looked at his watch. "She checked out of her hotel about fifteen minutes ago. She's on her way to the airport."

"We have to go to the airport," Charlotte said immediately. "We have to talk to her before she leaves town." She looked around. "Where's Liz?"

"I'm right here," Liz said. She was coming down the stairs. "I was making tea." She looked at me. "By the way, you're almost out of tea bags."

I was probably out of my mind, too, given what I was just about to do.

"Forget about the tea," Charlotte said.

Liz narrowed her eyes at us. "Why?"

"Because we're going to the airport."

"The airport?" Liz looked even more confused. "Why?"

"Because it's what Charlie's Angels would do," I said.

Chapter 15

"I'll turn off the kettle," Liz said, heading for the stairs.

"Would you bring my purse down, please?" Charlotte called after her.

Liz nodded and lifted a hand to show she'd heard.

"I'll go tell Mac where we're going," I said. I found him outside, carrying a box full of old bottles over to the planting table by the back door, where Avery was set up with potting soil, moss and some small plants.

"What's up?" he said, setting the box on the end of the table.

I exhaled loudly. "Rose drove off with a possible murderer who she's certain couldn't be one because he has a floppy handshake. She's fine, by the way."

"Okay," Mac said slowly.

"Charlotte and Liz and I are going to the airport to try to catch one of Arthur Fenety's girlfriends before she leaves town." I shook my head. "I'm crazy, aren't I?"

Mac smiled. "You're kindhearted and loyal and a good friend." He held up his thumb and index finger about a quarter of an inch apart. "And maybe just a little bit crazy."

I laughed. "How did I get myself into this, Mac?"

"They're family," he said with a shrug. "Don't worry. I'll take care of things here."

"Seriously, how would I manage without you?"

"I'm not going anywhere," he said.

I ran up to my office and grabbed my purse. When I came back down, I found Charlotte and Liz waiting by my SUV, along with Mr. P. and Elvis.

"I'm coming," Mr. P. said. "I don't mean to be sexist, but you three need some muscle."

He was completely serious. I didn't dare look at Liz because I knew I'd laugh. Mr. P. wasn't exactly the bodyguard type. On the other hand, he'd already surprised me with his computer skills so maybe I shouldn't judge.

I looked down at Elvis. "Why do you need to come?" The cat looked at Mr. P., then back at me.

"He's part of my security team," Mr. P. said. I gave the two of them a once-over—Mr. P. with his trousers up under his armpits and the cat with the scar slicing across his nose. They were the most unlikely security team I'd ever seen. And I didn't have time to get into a long discussion about it. "Get in," I said.

Liz rode shotgun. Charlotte, Mr. P. and Elvis climbed in the back with Elvis in the middle.

The Knox County Airport is about twenty minutes outside North Harbor. I looked at my watch when we hit the highway; if we were lucky, we might catch Grace MacIntyre before she went through security. I didn't speed, but I kept it right at the limit all the way to the airport turnoff.

The universe or someone was smiling on us because we found a parking spot. We piled out and I pointed a finger at Elvis. "Guard the truck," I said.

He gave an answering meow and sat up a little straighter.

We couldn't exactly run for the terminal buildings. Liz was wearing heels and I wasn't sure about making Mr. P. move that fast, so we more or less speed-walked from the parking area.

"Which way?" I asked once we stepped inside. Mr. P. did a quick survey and pointed. "That way. She's probably in the security line." He spoke with such assurance that I decided to head in that direction, mentally crossing my fingers that he was right.

When Jess and I had seen Grace MacIntyre she'd been wearing a baseball cap and sunglasses, so I scanned the terminal for someone with the same dyed red hair as I'd noticed peeking out from under her cap. It was like looking for a needle in a haystack. And then I spotted her—or a person I hoped was her—in the middle of a line snaking toward the security check.

"I think I see her," I said.

"Where?" Charlotte asked at my elbow.

I pointed. "The redhead behind the woman in the green jacket. I think that might be her."

"Go," Liz said. "This is as fast as I move in these shoes."

Charlotte and I hurried across the tile floor as the line moved forward.

"What are you going to say to her?" Charlotte asked.

I kept my eyes on what I sincerely hoped was the back of Grace MacIntyre's head. "I don't know," I said. "I can't exactly start out by saying, 'Hello. Did you by any chance kill Arthur Fenety?'"

We were almost level with the woman by then. She glanced in our direction and I recognized her face. It *was* the woman Jess and I had seen at Sam's. Before I could say anything Charlotte took a step in from of me and touched her on the shoulder.

"Excuse me," she said. "Are you Grace MacIntyre?"

"Yes," she said frowning a little at us.

"My name is Charlotte Elliot," Charlotte said. "And this is my friend, Sarah Grayson. Could we talk to you about Arthur Fenety?"

Grace pressed her lips together and looked down at the floor for a moment. When she met Charlotte's eyes again all she said was, "He's dead."

"I know," Charlotte said. "We're trying to find out who killed him."

"A woman named Madeline Hamilton."

I shook my head. "No, she didn't."

Grace shrugged. "She was arrested."

"The police are wrong," Charlotte said firmly.

"You think I killed him?" Grace asked.

"No," I said. "But how did you locate him here? From what I understand there were a lot of people looking for Arthur Fenety."

She laughed, but there really wasn't any humor in the sound. "I hired a private detective."

"When you found him, why didn't you just call the police?" Charlotte asked.

"It wasn't because I was planning on killing him."

"Arthur was a very charming man," Charlotte said.

I hadn't been expecting her to say that but I figured she had to have a plan, so I kept my mouth shut and my expression neutral.

"Yes, he was," Grace said and a smile flitted across her face. "He was a bit of a scoundrel, but he had his good points." She was carrying a leather tote bag and she shifted it from one hand to the other as the line moved forward again. We were running out of time. She shrugged. "There's no harm in telling you, I guess. I didn't come here to get back at Arthur. I came to get him back."

Charlotte actually looked sympathetic. I was trying just not to look surprised.

"I have more than enough money," Grace said. "What I don't have is anyone to share my life with."

"I understand," Charlotte said, nodding slowly. I glanced over at Liz and Mr. P., who were standing a few steps away. "Did you see Arthur?" she asked. We were only half a dozen people away from the security check.

"The morning he . . . died." Grace looked away for a moment and then her gaze came back to Charlotte's face. "He turned me down. He said the money didn't matter; he was in love for real this time. He kissed me on the cheek and wish me well."

"I'm sorry," Charlotte said.

Grace nodded. "Me too. Maybe if he'd given us another chance he's still be alive." She took a deep breath and let it out. "My mother always said it's just as easy to love a rich man as it is a poor one. I think it's the same for a rich woman. But Arthur didn't see it that way." She cleared her throat. "And since I'm confessing my weaknesses to you I may as well tell you that I spent the rest of the day with my private detective going over all the information on Arthur that he had."

I'd wondered how the newspaper had dug up so much on Arthur Fenety so fast. "You sent it all to the paper," I said.

She nodded. "I did. My mother also said revenge is a dish best served cold."

"In my experience, revenge is a dish best not served at all," Charlotte said softly.

Grace turned and pointed to a man several people back in the line behind her. "The man in the brown leather jacket, he's the detective I hired. You can ask him where I was on Monday."

"Thank you," I said.

"I hope things work out for you friend," she said. The line moved again and she was at security.

Grace MacIntyre's detective, Malcolm Kent, had a strong handshake, deep blue eyes, and iron gray hair in a brush cut. I introduced Charlotte and myself and explained who we were.

"Mrs. MacIntyre just sent me a text," he said. "What would you like to know?"

"She was with you on Monday?" I asked.

He nodded. "She was. From about eleven thirty until

close to three o'clock at the Fairgate Hotel. We ordered room service, if that helps."

"It does," I said.

"Mrs. MacIntrye asked me to give you a copy of everything I learned about Arthur Fenety. If you give me your e-mail address I'll send it to you."

I gave Malcolm Kent the store's e-mail, thanked him and Charlotte and I walked over to Liz and Mr. P.

"Any luck?" Liz asked.

Charlotte shook her head. "She has an alibi."

We headed back out to the parking lot. "There has to be an easier way to do this," I said, fishing the keys to the SUV out of my pocket. "There has to be some way to find out which one of the women in Arthur Fenety's life wanted him dead."

"Wasn't that pretty much all of them?" Liz said dryly.

Charlotte shook her head. "No. Grace MacIntyre actually wanted him back."

Liz rolled her eyes.

"Don't you think the woman who knew him best would know that?" Mr. P. said.

We all looked at him.

"Who would that be?" I asked.

Mr. P. looked at the three of us, a slightly baffled expression on his face. "His sister, Daisy. Has anyone gone and talked to her?"

Chapter 16

"No," Charlotte said. "None of us know her very well. She only got here a couple of months ago and she's kept pretty much to herself."

"I've never met her," I said, sliding onto the driver's seat. Elvis had climbed into the front while we were gone and he nuzzled my arm. "Good job on keeping the SUV safe," I said, giving him a quick scratch behind one ear. He licked my hand and sat up just a little straighter.

"Actually, you have," Charlotte said. "Do you remember the woman who came in—let's see—maybe three weeks ago and bought that forget-me-not cream pitcher?"

I shifted so I could see Charlotte in the backseat. "That was Daisy?"

She nodded.

I pictured the woman in my mind. Daisy Fenety was tall and elegant with blond hair waved back from her face in a smooth bob. She'd come across as a little aloof but very knowledgeable about the china.

"I'll go talk to her," Charlotte said. "I've at least spent

a little time with her. She and Arthur came with Maddie to help sort books for the book sale for the playground fund-raiser." She pulled out her phone.

"I'm calling Rose," she said. "I don't have time to make anything and I can't go to see Daisy empty-handed."

"Charlotte, we can stop at Lily's and get a cake or something."

She looked at me like I'd suggested we all go skinny-dipping in the fountain in front of the library. "I'm going to express my condolences," she said. "I can't show up with a store-bought cake."

Mr. P. caught my eye and gave a tiny shrug. Obviously he hadn't heard of that rule.

"Do you have any blueberry muffins in your freezer?" Charlotte said into the phone. Rose must have said yes because Charlotte smiled. "Okay, then. Take them out to thaw. I'm going to see Daisy and I need something to take with me." There was another pause and then they started debating the merits of blueberry muffins versus rhubarb muffins. At least I assumed they were debating it, since I could hear only Charlotte's side of the conversation.

I started to back out of the parking spot. "I wouldn't have a problem taking a store-bought cake," Liz said quietly beside me.

I shot her a quick smile. "That's why I love you," I said.

We got back to the store just in time to catch a bus-load of Canadians on their way to a football weekend in Boston. Mr. P. disappeared into the sunporch with his laptop.

"I'll go make the tea," Liz said. She headed upstairs,

Elvis at her heels. I made a mental note to get tea bags. It seemed like this version of Charlie's Angels pretty much ran on tea.

The bus tour kept us busy until after four thirty. Liz brought us all tea and I was happy to sit down for a minute and drink it. The teacup gardens had sold out again, along with three of Avery's four wine-carafe gardens. One woman had bought a small corner table that we were going to pack and ship all the way to Newfoundland for the ridiculously large fee Mac had quoted to her. Without prompting, Avery got the vacuum out and started on the stairs.

"Where does Daisy live?" I asked Charlotte. She was straightening up the bookcase.

"She and Arthur were renting a house just down from the stone church." The stone church was actually the Church of the Good Shepherd, but around town it was known as the stone church. It was close to two hundred years old, made from Maine limestone.

"I'll go with you," I said. "It's too far for you to walk down to Legacy Place and then all the way to Daisy's." I seemed to be getting way more involved in this investigation than I'd planned to—than I'd wanted to, but it didn't seem right to let Charlotte walk all that way and talk to Daisy by herself.

Charlotte smiled. "Okay. I wouldn't mind having some company. I'm not exactly sure what to say to her."

"We'll just play it by ear," I said. I didn't really know what to say, either. I called Rose to let her know we'd be down soon to get the muffins. "We should be there in about fifteen minutes," I said.

"I'll be out in front of Shady Pines, waiting for you," she said.

Rose was standing on the sidewalk when we pulled up in front of her apartment building. She handed a small pansy-patterned tin to Charlotte through the passenger's window.

"I put them in a tin because she'll have to give it back to you and that will give you another chance to talk to her," Rose said.

I leaned over and smiled at her. "Pretty crafty."

"I try." She smiled, not at all modestly. "I'll save you some supper," she said to Charlotte. She looked at me again. "What about you, Sarah? Could you join us? I'm making potato scallop."

"I'd love to," I said. "But I'm meeting Jess later."

"I'd better get back upstairs and check on things," she said.

We waved and I headed across town for Daisy Fenety's house.

"What do you know about Daisy?" I asked Charlotte.

"Not very much," she said, smoothing a wrinkle out of her skirt. "I know she's a few years younger than Arthur. She worked in the registrar's office of a small private college but I don't know where. And as far as I know she never married." She folded her hands over the tin of muffins in her lap. "And the only reason I know any of that is because Maddie tried so hard to draw her out while we were sorting the books."

"She may not tell us anything," I said, looking both ways before I turned left.

"Do you think she knew about all Arthur's shady dealings?" Charlotte said.

"Maybe," I said. "But maybe not. You said she's only been here a few weeks. And if she was working before that, it's possible she didn't know a thing."

"See the white bungalow with the yellow door?" Charlotte leaned forward and pointed.

"That's it?" I said.

She nodded.

I pulled to the curb in front of the house and shut off the engine. I turned to Charlotte. "We don't have to give Daisy the third degree," I said. "I can see it makes you uncomfortable. We'll give her the muffins and express our sympathy. If we learn anything, fine. If not, that's all right, too."

Charlotte smiled. "Thank you," she said. "Maybe I'm too soft, but I feel sorry for Daisy. Her brother's dead. Whether she knew anything about what he'd been doing or not, he was still her brother—the last of her family. She doesn't have anybody now."

I reached over and laid my hand on hers for a moment.

"You're one of the kindest people I know," I said. "And I wouldn't want you to be any other way."

We walked up the stone pathway to the front door and rang the bell. Beside me I heard Charlotte take a deep breath. I understood how she felt. It didn't seem right to ambush Daisy Fenety. But on the other hand, it didn't seem right for Maddie to go to jail for something she didn't do.

Daisy opened the door and seemed surprised to see us standing there.

"Charlotte. Hello." She said. "What are you doing here?"

"I'm sorry about Arthur," Charlotte said. She held out the tin of muffins. "These are for you. I just wanted to make sure you were all right."

"Thank you," Daisy said, taking the small round can from Charlotte's hands. "That's so thoughtful of you." She hesitated for a moment. "Would you like to come in?"

"For a minute," Charlotte said. She turned to me. "Daisy, this is Sarah Grayson, my friend Isabel's granddaughter. She drove me here."

I held out my hand and the older woman took it. "I think we met at my shop, Second Chance," I said.

Daisy nodded. "Yes, we did."

"I'm sorry about your brother."

"Thank you," she said. I couldn't help noticing how guarded her expression was. Then again, if my brother had been murdered I'd be guarded around people, too.

We followed Daisy inside. We stepped into a small entryway, which led to the living room. The house was beautifully decorated. Someone had excellent taste. Daisy, I suspected.

Charlotte and I sat on the sofa. It was leather, the color of a bar of dark chocolate and very comfortable. Daisy took a wing chair opposite us. She set the muffins on the round table by the front window and folded her hands in her lap. Then she looked at Charlotte and cleared her throat.

"I know you and Madeline are friends," she began. She pressed her lips together for a moment. "I'm not condoning what she did, but I want you to know I'm not condoning what my brother did, either."

"You didn't know," Charlotte said, gently. "I'm sorry. It must have been an awful shock."

"I opened the paper and I couldn't believe it. That wasn't the brother I grew up with." She looked away for a moment. "I wish I could apologize to all the women he took advantage of. I wish I could do something for them." She sat very straight, her shoulders rigid, and in her lap her hands were tightly clenched together. "As far as I can tell, just looking through Arthur's papers, the money is gone." She paused for a moment. "There were some pieces of jewelry I found in a box in his closet. I can give those to the police. But there don't seem to be any secret bank accounts."

"It's very thoughtful of you to try to help," I said. I wondered if that jewelry would turn out to belong to Jim Grant's mother.

She looked at me. "I believed Arthur when he told me that he had a pension and had saved a lot of money. I didn't really know my brother."

I thought about Liam and wondered how I'd feel if I were in Daisy's place.

She looked at Charlotte. "I really believed he cared about Madeline," she said. "He called me right after he met her and he seemed genuinely happy." She pointed to the vase of lilies on the coffee table. "He bought those flowers for me the day he died. He was in such a good mood that morning."

"Did your brother do any gardening?" I asked.

Daisy shook her head. "He didn't know a thing about plants. We grew up in Meridian, Florida, with a tiny backyard. He met Madeline at some event for the Botanic Garden but he was only there because he won the ticket." The bottom hand on her lap kept pulling the fabric of her trousers into little folds. "Madeline talked about gardening and plants all the time. Arthur listened because . . . because he liked her."

I gestured to the vase holding the flowers. It was china with a raised flower design; white daisies with yellow centers and deep green leaves. "That's very pretty," I said. "It's the Daisy May pattern, isn't it?"

Daisy looked surprised. "Yes, it is. Arthur bought it for my last birthday. She looked down at the gleaming hardwood floor, then met our eyes again. "It's my fault he's dead," she said.

Charlotte shook her head. "No, Daisy, it's not your fault. There wasn't anything you could have done."

"She invited me, too."

"You mean Maddie?" I said. Charlotte and I exchanged glances. Why hadn't Maddie told us that?

Daisy nodded. "I declined because I had an emergency dentist appointment. I can't help thinking if I'd gone to lunch, as well, Arthur would still be alive."

"There was no way you could have known what was going to happen," I said.

She gave me a faint smile. "Thank you for saying that," she said. "It's hard not to keep second-guessing myself. I took the car because I was going to the dentist. I dropped Arthur at the park. It was such a nice day he'd decided to walk. The last time I saw him he was standing by the park gates, talking to the mailman." She lifted a hand to her throat. "What he did was wrong. I understand that. But Madeline shouldn't have killed him for it."

"We don't think she did," Charlotte said. "Maddie couldn't kill anyone."

"Arthur was at her house. She made the coffee," Daisy said, two bright spots of color appearing on her cheeks. "I don't see who else could have done it. I understand your loyalty, but I'm sorry. I think you're wrong."

There really wasn't anything else to say. We told Daisy again how sorry we were for what she was going through and then we were back out in the SUV.

"I don't know why I thought Daisy would be any help," Charlotte said. "Of course she blames Maddie. I would, too, in her place."

"We know where they grew up," I said, sticking the key in the ignition. "Maybe Mr. P. will be able to dig up something."

"So, what do we do now?" Charlotte said, fastening her seat belt.

What I should have said was "Nothing." I should have said "The next thing to do is leave it to Josh's investigator and the police." But even against my better judgment I was getting caught up in Maddie's case. "We need to know if anyone knew that you had that bottle of napthathion in your garage. Or if anyone else had kept a bottle."

Charlotte nodded thoughtfully. "Could we stop at Liz's house for a moment?" she asked.

"Sure," I said.

We found Liz and Avery in the kitchen. Avery was making what I guessed was a quiche, based on the pie-crust and eggs she had out on the counter. She also had a huge amount of kale.

"Any luck with Daisy?" Liz asked.

"We know where Arthur and Daisy grew up," I said. "Maybe Mr. P. can do something with that."

"We need to know if anyone knew I had that bottle of pesticide," Charlotte said.

"Or if anyone else kept a bottle after it was banned," I said.

"You want the town gossip," Liz said.

I nodded. "I guess we do."

"Done," she said. "I'll call Elspeth."

Elspeth was Liz's niece. She ran a very successful spa and salon in town, Phantasy. We had tourists who came to North Harbor several times a year just for a couple of days of pampering at the spa. Elspeth was a lot like Liz, with the same big heart and sardonic sense of humor, just in higher heels.

Liz held out her hand and studied her impeccably manicured nails. "I had my hands in too much water today. Look at my manicure." She smiled. "I'll have to go to the salon first thing in the morning for fingers, toes and what everyone knows."

Chapter 17

I dropped Charlotte off at Rose's apartment building. "Give Maddie my love," I said.

"I will," she promised.

Before I could pull away from the curb Elvis meowed from the backseat.

"What?" I said, turning around to look at him.

He craned his neck as though he were trying to see over the seat back and then he looked at me.

"You can come up if you want to," I said.

"Merow," he said somewhat plaintively, it seemed to me. Then he did the neck-craning thing again.

"You're a cat," I said. "You can jump from there."

He stood up and seemed to study the seat back.

"You can make that," I said.

He sat back down and blinked his green eyes at me.

I shrugged. "Okay. You can stay there. We're not that far from home." I looked in the rearview mirror just in time to see him flick his tail at me.

I took Elvis home, gave him his supper and made myself a scrambled egg and tomato sandwich. I had to get to the grocery store. My refrigerator had officially gone from bare to pitiful.

After a shower I sat cross-legged on the bed while Elvis watched *Jeopardy!*, letting my damp hair air-dry instead of smoothing out the waves with the hair dryer. I opened my e-mail and looked through the file Grace MacIntyre's detective had sent. I didn't learn anything new. Everything he'd dug up on Arthur had ended up on the front page of the newspaper. My dad called halfway through the program. Unfortunately he hadn't been able to get any more information, either.

"Call me if I can do anything else for you," he said. "Or if you need bail."

I laughed. "I will, Dad," I promised. "I love you."

"Love you too, baby," he said.

When I got to The Black Bear, Jess had already snagged a table close to the stage. "Hey, how was your day?" I asked as I slid onto the chair beside hers.

She was wearing her long hair smooth and sleek, parted in the middle, and her lip gloss matched her plum-colored sweater. "Great," she said. "I found some fantastic vintage denim jackets in those boxes. Are you sure you want to sell them to me?"

I nodded. "We don't have the space for them and that kind of thing really doesn't go with everything else we sell."

She smiled. "Okay, then. Thanks."

I glanced around to see if I could catch sight of Nick anywhere. All I saw was a waiter threading his way over to us through the increasing crowd. He had a basket of nachos and a bowl of salsa, along with a glass of wine for each of us.

"I ordered," Jess said. "I hope that's okay."

"Absolutely. You know I'm a sucker for Sam's home-made salsa." I grabbed a chip. They were thin, crisp and warm. "What happened to your healthier lifestyle?" I asked.

"Salsa and chips are healthy," she said. "Anyway, I've decided what I really need to work on is a healthier mind-set." She made a sweeping circle around her head.

"How was your date?" I asked before I popped a chip in my mouth.

"Short."

"Stature or duration?"

"Both," Jess said, tucking her hair behind one ear and reaching for her wineglass.

"He's a surgical resident. He got called back to the hospital before dessert." She grabbed a chip, scooped up some salsa and ate the whole thing. "Umm, that is so good." She gave a little groan of pleasure. "And he's my height, so I guess he's not that short by real-world stan-dards." Jess was five-nine in her socked feet and, like Liz, she usually wore heels, which made her closer to six feet.

I shot another look in the vicinity of the door.

"He's not here," Jess said.

I frowned at her. "Who's not here?"

She took another sip of her wine before she answered. "Nick."

I shifted in my chair so I was facing her. "How did you know I was looking for Nick?"

Jess tapped the side of her head with her right index finger. "Deductive reasoning," she said. "You told me you saw Nick. You probably told him you were going to be here tonight. So he can pretend he's coming for Thursday-night jam even though everyone in town knows he's had a thing for you since he was fifteen."

I stared at her, my mouth hanging open just a bit. "What do you mean everyone in town knows he's had a thing for me?" Okay, so Nick and I had kind of made out a little that summer we were fifteen, but I'd never thought that meant he had a thing for me. Two weeks later he'd been in music camp, drooling over one of the percussionists, who had a big pair of . . . cymbals.

Jess shrugged and scooped up more salsa. "Okay, well, everyone but you."

She was serious, I realized. For all of that teasing smile on her face, she was serious. I could see it in her eyes and hear it in her voice.

I took a sip of my wine. "Why didn't I know that?" I finally said.

"Because you don't notice those kinds of things."

"What kind of things exactly?" I said, running a finger up and down the stem of my glass.

"Men-women things." Jess dragged another chip through the salsa and ate it.

"If you're trying to say I don't notice when some man tries to flirt with me, you're wrong," I said, reaching for another chip myself. "Every time I go to Noah's for that organic cat food for Elvis, the guy who works behind the counter flirts with me. I notice that."

Jess sank back against the chair, laughing. "Tyler is all of nineteen years old and he flirts with every woman who walks into the place. He'd flirt with his own grandmother if he thought it would sell a case of dog food."

She picked up her wineglass. "I mean you don't notice when a man our age is interested in you."

"That's because there aren't any men interested in me," I said a little hotly. "Including Nick Elliot." I knew I wasn't as dense as Jess was making me out to be.

She tipped her head to one side and studied my face. "How many times have you seen Nick since the first time you saw him Monday afternoon?"

"He stopped by the store. So a couple of times."

Her eyebrows went up but she didn't say a word.

"He was worried about Charlotte. I told you that she and Rose and Liz are trying to help Maddie."

"Uh-huh," Jess said, fishing a chip out of the basket and breaking off a corner.

I made a face at her. "Nice try, but you're not sucking me in. Nick and I have been friends forever and that's all we are now." That I'd thought about maybe kissing him when he'd walked me home after dinner was just a momentary aberration brought on by the fact that I couldn't remember when I'd last had a date. And he hadn't tried to kiss me. Which meant he wasn't interested. The whole thing was meaningless, so meaningless I didn't even need to tell Jess about it, I decided.

"You know, I don't think Arthur Fenety would have been able to work his way into your life," Jess said, frowning thoughtfully. "I mean, if you'd been closer to his age."

"Thank you?" I said.

She laughed.

I thought about Gram. I couldn't quite picture her being swept off her feet by anyone like Arthur Fenety. It wasn't that she was smarter than Maddie or any of the other women Fenety had scammed. It's just that she wasn't the kind of woman that any kind of line would work on. Gram was drop-dead practical.

"Jess, why do you think Arthur Fenety was able to scam so many women? Maddie's very intelligent and I don't think of her as being particularly gullible."

Jess shifted in her chair. "I don't think any of those women were stupid or gullible. I think Fenety just made them feel like they weren't invisible." She looked around for our waiter, caught his eye and pointed at her glass, holding up two fingers. "Did you ever notice how women love Sam?" she asked.

I laughed. "Oh yeah," I said. "Women adore Sam."

"Why?"

"I don't know," I said. "He's funny. He's a good listener. He's just a nice guy."

"Exactly," Jess said. "I'm guessing that was what Fenety was doing. He probably couldn't keep the nice-guy routine up long-term, but he could do it long enough to con someone."

The waiter arrived with two more glasses of wine. He set one in front of me and I thanked him. He put the other one in front of Jess. "Hey, thank you," she said, looking up at him and giving him the full force of her smile. He grinned back and almost fell over his own feet as he left.

I shook my head. If Jess suddenly decided to start conning men out of their money I could see she'd be very successful. "Promise me you'll use your powers for good and not for evil," I said.

She just laughed.

I looked around again. "I guess Nick's not coming."

Jess flipped her hair back over her shoulder. "Oh, he'll be here." She snagged the basket of chips with one finger and slid it across the table, closer to us. Then she narrowed her eyes at me. "I bet you a basket of these that not only will Nick be here but he will have shaved."

"What does shaving have to do with anything?" I reached for the bowl of salsa before Jess ate all of it and the chips, too.

"If a guy likes you he'll shave again at the end of the day." She put a hand under the chip she'd just loaded with tomato, onion and peppers. "What did Nick wear for aftershave when he was in high school?" she asked.

"Hugo," I said.

"You got that one pretty fast."

I made a squinty face at her, which she ignored.

"Okay. Not only will Nick shave, he'll also be wearing Hugo."

"Fine," I said. "Just to prove that you're wrong I'll take your bet."

Jess stuck out one hand and shook it like she'd just gotten it wet. "Shake," she said with a grin. She'd been doing that as long as I'd known her. I held out my hand and did the same.

Sam came out first, without any announcement, carrying his favorite guitar. He slipped onto a stool and went right into the slow version of Clapton's "Layla." It took at least a minute for people who had never been to Thursday-night jam—in other words, tourists—to figure out that the set was beginning. About halfway through

Eric came out, picked up his bass and joined in. Sean and Vincent slipped into place just as Sam played the first few notes of "Sunshine of Your Love." Jess suddenly turned her head, looked toward the door and held up her arm. Then she smiled and turned back to the stage. I didn't need to look to know Nick was on his way over to join us. Jess was still smiling, her eyes locked on the small stage.

Nick dropped onto the chair Jess had snagged earlier.

"Hey, big guy. How are you?" she said, a huge smile stretching across her face.

"I'm good and it's good to see you," Nick said, grinning back at her. "How have you been?"

"I've been well." Under the table she kicked my leg. "You've been home, what? Two, three weeks? And you're just making it down for Thursday-night jam now?"

"I've been busy."

Jess rolled her eyes. "You sound like Sarah."

Nick leaned forward and smiled at me. "Hi, Sarah," he said.

I lifted a hand in hello. I was playing along in my head, already pulled away by the music. After the Clapton set Sam and the guys moved into some Joe Cocker. I glanced over on "When the Night Comes" and saw that like me Nick was mouthing the words.

The boys ended the set by playing "With a Little Help from My Friends." Jess put two fingers in her mouth and gave a piercing whistle of appreciation. The rest of us clapped and stomped our feet.

Sam lifted a hand in acknowledgment. "Thank you," he said. "We'll be back."

Jess turned to Nick and nudged him with her elbow. "See what you miss when you run off to the big city?"

He nodded. "You're right about that."

She leaned in a little closer and sniffed. "What is that you're wearing?" she asked. "It smells familiar."

"Hugo," he said.

She kicked me again. "It's nice," she said. "You clean up good."

She was right about that. He was wearing jeans and a purple shirt and he did look good.

"You too, Jess," he said.

She got to her feet and stretched. "I see someone I need to talk to." She looked at me. "And I'll see if I can find our waiter. Didn't you say you wanted another basket of chips?"

"Yes, please," I said, sending her a daggers look while she was blocking Nick's view of me.

She gave me a sweet and very fake smile and squeezed between her chair and Nick's. "Beer for you?" she asked him.

He nodded. "Please."

"I'll be back."

Nick slid over into her seat. He folded his arms over his chest and studied me for a moment. "Charlie's Angels?" he asked finally.

"I had nothing to do with the name," I said, holding up my hands as though surrendering. "That was Avery."

"And they have an office?"

"A table and some folding chairs on my sunporch."

He pulled a hand over his chin. "Please tell me they

didn't really convince Alfred Peterson to join their band of merry detectives?"

I couldn't help grinning at him. "He's their computer guru."

Nick shook his head. "Heaven help us." He exhaled loudly. "So what have they been doing?"

"Did Charlotte call you?" I asked.

"If you're asking if she told me about the bottle of banned pesticide she has in her garage, the answer is yes. I called Michelle. She's sending someone to pick it up in the morning."

I let out the breath I hadn't realized I was holding.

"What the heck was my mother thinking?"

"Probably that a little bit around her roses wouldn't hurt anything.'

He pulled a hand across his neck and sighed. "You're probably right. Anyway, I don't think it's going to be a big deal."

"You didn't leave any fingerprints, did you?" I asked as I reached for my wineglass.

He frowned. "Excuse me?"

"You didn't actually pick up the bottle and leave any fingerprints on it, did you? Because I know you went and checked on it."

He got that little-boy-who'd-been-caught-with-his-hand-in-the-cookie-jar look. "How did you know?" he said.

I raised an eyebrow at him. "Because if I'd had a key I would have gone and checked that bottle in the garage."

"The bottle is up on a shelf and it has a layer of dust on it that you could write your name in."

I felt my shoulders unknot with relief. So whoever killed Arthur Fenety hadn't used the poison in Charlotte's garage. "Did you know the son of one of Arthur Fenety's wives is in town?" I asked.

"I can't answer that, Sarah," Nick said.

"All right, that's a yes."

"I didn't say yes," he countered.

I shrugged. "If it was no you would have been asking for details."

The waiter showed up then with a large basket of chips, a big bowl of salsa and Nick's beer. Clearly since I was paying, Jess was getting her money's worth.

Nick picked up his beer. I used a chip to scoop up a mouthful of salsa. "Did you know one of Fenety's ex's was also in town?"

He drank a mouthful of beer before he answered. "Since *I can't talk about that* seems to mean *yes* to you, I'll just skip that part and say yes."

I smiled at him. "I told you I'd keep you in the loop."

"So I should consider myself looped?"

I nodded. "Yes."

Nick swiped a chip, scooped up some salsa and ate it.

"Don't even think about double dipping," I said, pointing to the half a chip he was still holding.

He put his free hand on his chest. "Me?" he asked, the picture of fake innocence.

"Yes, you," I said. "You used to do that so you could keep the salsa all to yourself."

"It never stopped you, as I remember."

I felt my face flood with color. Nick laughed. I ducked my head over my wineglass.

"Are you going to play?" I asked after a minute of awkward silence.

He shook his head. "I didn't bring a guitar and, anyway, I'm way too rusty. You heard me the other day."

"You didn't sound rusty to me," I said. "And you know Sam has more than one guitar here."

"That I do," a voice said behind me.

I turned and smiled up at Sam. "What do you say?" he asked Nick.

"The same thing I said to Sarah." He held up his left hand. "My fingers are out of practice."

Sam shrugged. "Best way to get in practice is to play." He looked at me. "The Rickenbacker is great. Thanks."

"Anytime," I said. "I'm glad someone's playing it instead of leaving it in a closet."

He pulled his fingers through his beard. "Yeah. A good guitar should be played."

Out of the corner of my eye I saw Eric coming with his bass.

Sam saw him, too. "Almost time to get started," he said. "I'll talk to you later." He pushed through the crowd toward his office.

Jess made her way back to the table. "Stay there," she said to Nick when he went to get up.

She took Nick's seat and pulled the basket of chips a little closer. "Umm, these are even better than the last batch," she said after she'd loaded a corn chip with about a third of the bowl of salsa and eaten the entire thing in one bite.

Sam and the rest of the guys made their way back on stage and started with "For Your Love." They went right into "Eve of Destruction" after that.

"Sometimes our friends join us for a song or two on Thursday nights," Sam said after the song was over. That got him a cheer from the audience. "One of those friends is here tonight. And it's been a few years since he's been up here on stage."

"He wouldn't," Nick said quietly beside me.

I just looked at him without saying anything. Because I knew Sam would.

"Ladies and gentlemen," Sam said. "Please give a warm Black Bear welcome to Nick Elliot!"

There were enough people there who knew Nick that the room got loud with people clapping and hooting. Jess whistled again and clapped, hands in the air.

I leaned toward Nick. "Welcome home," I said.

He got to his feet, raising a hand to acknowledge the applause. Then he made his way to the stage, and I saw him raise an eyebrow at Sam, who simply handed him the Rickenbacker and then gave a nod to Eric. As soon as Eric began the bass line I knew what song they were going to do. So did Nick. He had taken the empty stool next to Sam and he lifted his head from the guitar, looked right at me and flashed a quick smile.

"Peaceful Easy Feeling" by the Eagles was the first song I'd taught myself to play on my dad's guitar, the one Maddie had rescued for me. I'd played it for Nick. I swallowed a couple of times against the rush of emotion I suddenly felt.

Jess moved over into the empty chair next to me. She leaned against me as Sam and the guys started to play. "Thank you for the chips. They're so, so good," she said.

"This doesn't prove anything," I said, grateful to have something else to focus on.

"Yes, it does," she said, reaching for another chip and nodding along with the music.

Nick had picked up the melody and Sam launched into the first verse. He gave Nick an encouraging smile on the chorus and as he slid into the second verse Nick joined in singing harmony. I'd forgotten what a great voice he had. Or maybe, more truthfully, I'd pushed the memory of how much I liked listening to him sing and play out of my mind. Sam came right out of "Peaceful Easy Feeling" right into "Hotel California" and Nick followed along.

"He's good," Jess said in my ear.

I just nodded. Not only was I enjoying the music, but I was also enjoying how much fun Nick was having. It was written all over his face.

At the end of the song Sam held out a hand toward Nick and once again the whole place erupted with cheers and applause. Nick stood up, grinning, and took a bow. Jess was whistling and stomping her feet, and I had my hands up over my head, clapping. Nick handed the Rickenbacker to Sam and came back to the table. He dropped into his seat, face flushed.

Jess grinned at him. "That was great," she said, her eyes dancing.

Nick shook his head and leaned toward us. "I'm just lucky Sam picked something my fingers remembered."

Sam and the guys were playing the intro to "Pinball Wizard" and the crowd was clapping along. I shook my head. "No. You're just good," I said, and then I turned back to the stage.

The music was over too soon. Jess slumped against the back of her chair, one arm folded up over her head. "We have to do this more often," she said.

"You always say that," I said.

"And I'm always right," she countered.

I turned to Nick. "I'm so glad you sat in for a couple of songs."

"Sam didn't exactly give me a choice, but me too," he said.

I got up and stretched. Across the room I caught sight of Michelle, standing near the door. She saw me and lifted a hand. From the expression on her face it was clear she wanted to talk to me. "I'll be right back," I said. I worked my way over to Michelle, smiling at more than one person I recognized.

"Hi," she said when I got close to her.

She was wearing jeans, brown boots with chunky heels and a cropped black jacket over a green sweater. She was a little thinner than I'd first realized.

"Hi," I said. "They were good, weren't they?"

She nodded. "Some things don't change."

I thought about saying *some things do*, but decided that would probably be a bad idea.

"Was there something you wanted to ask me?" I said instead.

"Nick told me what his mother and her friends are up to."

I nodded. "I thought he would."

"If you have any influence with them at all, please tell them playing detective is a very bad idea."

"I've already tried that," I said with a sigh. "It didn't work."

"Poking around in a murder investigation isn't something they should be doing," she said. She touched the pocket of her jacket and I wondered if her phone was vibrating inside.

"I know that," I said. I sounded defensive when I didn't really mean to. I was feeling a little guilty about how much poking around I'd been doing, too. "C'mon, Michele. You've known all of them for years. You know what they're like when they get fixated on an idea. And it's not always a bad thing, by the way. We wouldn't have the bookmobile or the Botanic Garden or the new playground. Short of locking them up I don't think you can stop them."

I was expecting she'd give me an argument. Instead all she said was, "I know." She hesitated as though she was searching for the right words. "Could you do what you can to keep them out of trouble?"

"I'm trying," I said. I *was* trying. It was just that I kept getting sucked into helping. I thought about what my Gram would say about good intentions.

She smiled. "Thanks, Sarah. I appreciate that."

There was an awkward silence. "I should get back to Jess and Nick," I said. I don't really know what made me say what I said next. "Can you join us for a few minutes?"

She looked surprised. Then again, I was surprised

that I'd asked. "Umm, thanks, but I have to get back to the station."

I nodded. "Maybe another time." I turned to head back to the table.

"I'm glad you're home, Sarah," she said.

It felt like she meant it.

"Me too." I said.

Chapter 18

I had an appointment first thing in the morning to go through the storage area of a local motel to see if there was anything left after their recent renovation work that I might be interested in buying. I left Elvis at the store with Mac and drove up to the highway.

The storage room was like a time capsule from the 1970s. I started making a pile in the hallway of things I wanted, handing them to the young man the owner had sent to help me. I found two lamps; a sleek, curved-edge coffee table; a hanging wicker chair and several boxes of vibrant Fiestaware dishes.

The space was crammed with furniture, mostly bed frames, chests of drawers and boxy-looking chairs. I climbed over a couple of long, low sofas to hand a box of dishes to my helper, whose name was Brent. He had a bandage wrapped around his left hand. "Can you manage that?" I asked.

"Oh yeah, this is fine," he said, holding up his hand. I gave him the box and scrambled over the sofas. One was

piled upside down on the other. I thought I'd seen another lamp but now I couldn't find it.

"Is there something else I can get for you?" Brent
asked. He was maybe twenty years old, with spiked
blond hair and strong arms and shoulders.

I had the feeling if I'd said I wanted the faux–Danish
modern sofas he would have been able to throw one
over each shoulder and carry them out to the SUV.

"I thought I saw another lamp," I said. "Now I don't
know where it is."

Brent looked around. He was taller. "Over there," he
said, pointing to the far front corner.

All I could see was a bunch of metal-framed chairs
piled haphazardly on top of one another.

"I'll get it for you."

"Are you sure?" I asked.

He flexed his fingers in a crablike motion. "Yeah, I'm
fine. This is just poison ivy. It doesn't hurt. It just itches
like crazy."

He climbed over the chairs like a monkey making his
way up a coconut tree, grabbed the lamp, handed it out
to me and climbed over the chairs again. I got a better
look at the gauze bandage that covered most of the back
of his left hand. There was a red, itchy-looking rash on
the back of his wrist, as well. I realized I'd seen the same
rash just recently. On Jim Grant's hand. And on Arthur
Fenety's.

"Did you say that was poison ivy?" I asked.

Brent rolled his eyes. "Uh-huh. I was in the park a
couple of days ago, throwing the Frisbee around with

some buddies. Stupid thing went into the bushes and I went after it. I guess there's some kind of infestation of poison ivy all over the park." He rubbed the bandage with the palm of his other hand and made a face. "It doesn't hurt, but damn, is it itchy."

What had Daisy told Charlotte and me? She'd dropped Arthur off and he'd cut through the park to get to Maddie's house. Could he have had some kind of confrontation with Jim Grant? Grant had claimed he hadn't gotten in town until the morning after Arthur Fenety had been killed. Could he have been lying about that?

Brent was talking to me. "I'm sorry," I said. "I zoned out. What did you say?"

"Do you want me to start carrying this stuff out?"

"That would be a big help, thanks," I said.

With Brent's help I managed to get everything loaded into the SUV. Then we walked back to the office and I paid for the pieces I'd bought. With a little work I was confident that everything I'd bought would sell.

Mac helped me unload when I got to the store.

"Sam called," he said. "We're going to get two buses of leaf peepers in about twenty minutes."

"Is Charlotte here?" I asked.

He nodded. "And Rose and Mr. Peterson are on the sunporch."

I headed inside and stuck my head around the sun-porch doorway. "Good morning," I said. Mr. P. was on his laptop and Rose was sitting beside him.

"Good morning, dear," she said.

Mr. P. looked up and smiled. "Hello, Sarah," he said.

"Are you having any luck with the information Rose got out of Jim Grant?" I asked.

Mr. P. nodded. "Now that I know his mother's full name I did a records search. She was married to Arthur Fenety, not that it was legal, of course." He glanced down at a notepad on the table next to the computer. "Margaret Grant had a small yarn and fabric shop. It went out of business a couple of months after Arthur left town."

"Do you think he took money from the business?"

Rose nodded. "I hate to call someone a liar, but yes, I do."

"So why did Jim Grant lie to us?" I said.

"His mother losing her business is a lot better motive for murder than just losing a tea set," Mr. P. said.

"Rose, did you notice that bandage on his arm and that rash on the back of his hand?" I asked.

"I did," she said. "He told me it was an allergic reaction to furniture stripper he'd been using." She narrowed her eyes. "You don't think that's true?"

"I'm not sure." I looked at Mr. P. "Could you check something out for me?"

"Of course I could," he said. "What is it?"

"I heard there's a problem with an infestation of poison ivy in the park. Could you find out if that's true?"

He nodded. "I can do that."

"Sarah, do you think the rash on Jim Grant's arm was poison ivy?" Rose asked.

"Maybe," I said.

"Charlotte said that Daisy told you she dropped Arthur off by the park and he walked to Maddie's house. Do you think Jim Grant might have met him in the park?"

I twisted my watch around my arm. I wasn't sure if I should tell Rose about the possible rash I'd seen on Arthur Fenety's arm. I didn't want to lie to her, but it just seemed that I was getting pulled deeper into their investigation every day.

"I don't know," I said. "It's possible." I hesitated.

"Dear, is there something you're not telling us?"

"Yes," I said. "There was a mark on Arthur's wrist. I noticed it when I checked for . . . his pulse. I just glanced at it and I thought it was some kind of scrape."

"You think it was poison ivy?" Her blue eyes widened. "Do you think Jim Grant could have been waiting for Arthur in the park? Maybe he followed Arthur to Maddie's house and poisoned him there."

Mr. P. looked up from the keyboard. "You're right," he said to me. "The park is dealing with an infestation of poison ivy. It's in all the flower beds and along the sides of a lot of the pathways."

"Thanks," I said. I looked at Rose. "We don't know for sure that Jim Grant was even in the park, let alone that he saw Arthur. He said he didn't get here until Tuesday morning."

"And if James did follow Arthur, where did he get the poison and how did he get it into Arthur's coffee cup?" Mr. P. asked. He looked at Rose. "We can't jump to conclusions."

She nodded. "All right."

Mr. P. looked at me. "I'll see if James Grant had any connection to a source of napthathion."

Rose looked at her watch. "Liz should be on her way to Phantasy right now. Maybe she'll find out something that will help Maddie."

"I'll keep my fingers crossed," I said.

The two busloads of leaf peepers kept us busy until lunchtime.

Rose came in, looking dejected, to relieve Charlotte.

"You talked to Liz," I asked.

"I did." She shook out her apron and pulled the neck strap over her head. "There are at least half a dozen people in Maddie and Charlotte's neighborhood that have that pesticide in their garage or garden shed."

"Didn't anybody pay attention to the ban?"

Rose tied her apron at her waist. "It doesn't look that way," she said. "The police are going to say Maddie had lots of opportunity to get the poison that killed Arthur."

I leaned over and gave her a quick hug. "Maybe Alfred will come up with something."

"I'm not giving up," she said with a frown.

I smiled. "I didn't think you would."

Rose went to straighten a collection of old tin camp kettles. Mac was on the phone. I decided to go take another look at my morning's treasures before lunch. As I went past the sunporch door Mr. P. beckoned to me. "I might have found something," he said.

"What is it?" I asked.

"Do you remember what time Maddie said Arthur arrived?"

I thought for a moment. "Between quarter after and twelve thirty."

"And you said his sister dropped him off at the park?"

I nodded. "She said it was such a nice day he wanted to walk."

Mr. P. hiked his pants a little higher. Not that they were too low to begin with. "Sarah, how long do you think it would have taken him to walk to Maddie's house?"

I shrugged and tried to picture the trail that ran through the woods and out to the sidewalk on the other side. "No more than ten minutes."

"Which means his sister would have dropped him off sometime after noon."

I nodded. "That sounds right."

"Daisy Fenety was in the dentist's chair at eleven forty-five."

I frowned at him. "Do I want to know how you know that?"

He smiled. "I doubt that you do."

"So, Daisy would have dropped him off around eleven thirty or so?"

Mr. P. nodded. "I think so."

I rolled my shoulders forward to work out a kink. "Where was he for that extra time?"

Mr. P. nodded. "Exactly. I asked Royce Collins if he saw Arthur. He delivers flyers in that area Mondays and Fridays. He did."

Royce had been the mail carrier in Charlotte's neighborhood as far back as I could remember. I had no idea how old Royce was, but Gram always said you could set your watch by him.

"Did he say what time he saw Arthur?" I asked.

"Royce figures it was about eleven thirty."

"Then it was," I said. "That means there's at least a half an hour unaccounted for."

Mr. P. nodded. "Exactly."

I left Mr. P. to see if he could figure out what had happened in the missing time and hoped he wouldn't break any laws doing it.

I spent a chunk of the afternoon updating the store's inventory list. Avery and I washed and dried all the dishes I'd brought from the motel, and Rose arranged some of the pieces on a long, low seventies-style buffet that Mac helped me set up in the window.

"Do you have any plans for dinner?" Rose asked.

I remembered then that I hadn't gotten to the grocery store. Again.

"No," I said.

"We're going to McNamara's for clam chowder and cheese biscuits. Why don't you join us?"

"That sounds good," I said. "Yes." After the middle of September I'd decided not to keep the store open on Friday nights. There wasn't enough business. "I have to take Elvis home first. What time should I meet you?"

"Six thirty," she said.

I pulled the elastic out of my hair. "I'll see you there," I said.

Rose and Avery decided to walk to Liz's and set out together. Mac wanted to put another coat of varnish on the top of the table. I was carrying a box of old sheet music to the car when Nick pulled into the lot.

He smiled when he caught sight of me.

"Hi," he said, walking over to me and taking the box out of my hands.

"Hi," I said. "What are you doing here?"

"I wanted to give you a heads-up that the police found a safe-deposit box belonging to Arthur Fenety. In Rockport."

I exhaled loudly and shook my head. "Was there anything of Maddie's in the box?" I asked.

"I can't answer that, Sarah," he said. "I probably shouldn't be telling you about the safe-deposit box as it is, but I figured news would get around town pretty quickly, anyway."

It was as close to a yes as I was going to get.

I stuffed my hands in my pockets. "Thanks," I said.

He smiled. "You're welcome. I had fun last night."

"It's been a long time since you were up on that stage."

He shifted—self-consciously it seemed to me—from one foot to the other. "It felt good."

I smiled. "It sounded good, too."

His smile got wider. "I'm going to pretend you're not just trying to flatter me."

"I wasn't."

Nick pulled his keys out of the pocket of his Windbreaker. "I'll let you get back to work," he said. "Tell Jess next time the chips are on me."

"I'll do that," I said. I couldn't exactly tell him he was the reason they'd actually been on me last night.

Nick headed for his SUV and I walked over to Mac. Behind him I could see Elvis prowling around the shed.

Mac was wiping down the top of the table. "Was Nick looking for his mother?" he asked.

I shook my head. "The police found Arthur Fenety's safe-deposit box."

"Is that good or bad?"

"I have a feeling it might be bad."

Chapter 19

I took Elvis home, fed him his supper and turned on the TV, setting the sleep timer so it would shut off when *Jeopardy!* was over. I felt a little silly but I told myself setting up the television so my cat could watch a game show wasn't any weirder than sticking a Santa hat on his head at Christmas, and people did that all the time.

I managed to fit in a run and a shower and still get to McNamara's on time. The ladies were sitting by the window. Rose waved when she caught sight of me. It was busy inside—a typical Friday night—and the line went all the way back to the door. I squeezed my way inside. Charlotte stood up and gestured to the empty chair at the table. She mouthed something but the only word I caught was *food*. That was enough for me. I headed over to them, dodging elbows and oversize coffee cups.

"There was no clam chowder left," she said. "So I got you broccoli-cheese soup, and roast beef on a whole-wheat roll."

"You're an angel," I said, hugging her. "I need to talk to you about something," I whispered against her ear.

She nodded almost imperceptibly as she let me go.

I pulled out my chair and sat down, smiling across the table at everyone. "How are you?" I asked Maddie.

"I'm all right," she said. "I heard about your trip to the airport. Thank you."

"Anytime," I said. I studied her face, looking for any sign that she was lying, but I couldn't see one. And she was lying. I was sure of it. Not about killing Arthur Fenety, but about something. The timeline just didn't work out. But I needed to talk to Charlotte before I said anything. The broccoli-cheese soup was steaming with crisp croutons and slivers of Swiss cheese on top. Charlotte had also gotten me a cup of coffee, and for a few minutes I ate and let the conversation swirl around me.

I'd eaten about half my soup when Jess walked in. She waved and walked over to us.

"Hi," she said, reaching down to swipe the pickle off my plate.

"What are you doing here?" I asked.

"I was hungry. I kind of lost time sewing."

"Get something to eat and come and sit with us," Rose urged.

Jess shifted her gaze to me.

I nodded.

"I'll be back," she said.

I ate a little more of my soup. Charlotte reached for the teapot. "We need more hot water," she said.

"I'll go," Rose offered.

Charlotte shook her head. "Sit. You were on your feet all day."

"So were you," Rose said.

I pushed my chair back. "She wants an excuse to look at the cupcakes, Rose," I said, picking up my cup. I looked at Charlotte. "I'll come with you. I need more coffee."

"Bring enough cupcakes to share with the class," Liz said.

Charlotte and I joined the end of the line, which had gotten shorter in the previous five minutes. Jess was already at the counter, ordering.

"What is it?" Charlotte asked.

I made a face. "I don't exactly know how to say this."

"It has to do with Maddie, doesn't it?"

I nodded. "Nick stopped by for a minute after you'd all left. He wanted to give us a heads-up that the police had found Arthur's safe-deposit box."

She pressed her lips together for a moment. "What was in it?"

I folded my hands around my empty coffee mug. "He couldn't tell me, but I got the feeling they found something that belonged to Maddie."

Charlotte's gaze immediately went to the table. "But Maddie said she didn't give Arthur anything."

"I don't think she's being completely honest about that. Or about how long she was in the kitchen."

Charlotte looked at me again. I could see the worry etched into her face. "I've been wondering about that myself. You don't think she . . . ?"

"No. Maddie didn't kill Arthur, but she is hiding something." I exhaled slowly. "I think it's time we found out what it is."

Charlotte glanced over at the table where Rose was

making room for Jess and another chair. Then she looked at me and nodded slowly. "Okay," she said.

We went back to the table with a fresh pot of tea, half a dozen dark-chocolate cupcakes with mint green icing, and coffee for me.

I waited until they all had a fresh cup of tea before I spoke.

"I saw Nick just before I got here," I said.

"Did he tell you anything about the investigation?" Rose asked, pausing with her cup halfway to the table.

"The police found Arthur's safe-deposit box in a bank in Rockport." I was watching Maddie out of the corner of my eye and I saw the color drain from her face.

Rose set down her cup "Did they find any of the jewelry that belongs to Jim Grant's mother?"

"I don't know what they found. Nick couldn't tell me," I said. I looked across the table. "Do you think there was anything of yours in that box?" I said to Maddie.

She shook her head. "No. I told you. I didn't give Arthur anything." Her face was very pale.

Charlotte reached across the table and laid her hand on Maddie's. "The police are going to find out."

Rose looked flabbergasted. "Charlotte!" she exclaimed.

Liz frowned. "What are you talking about?" she said.

Charlotte just looked at her friend and the color flooded back into Maddie's face. Maddie's gaze met mine across the table at me. "They'll probably find my father's railway watch in that box. At least I hope they do."

"Oh, Maddie," Rose said.

"How much money did you give him?" I asked.

"Twenty-five thousand dollars." She looked away. "It's true. There's no fool like an old fool."

"Balderdash!" Liz said. "You should be able to trust the people you love."

"Liz is right," I said, leaning forward and propping my forearms on the table. "You're not a fool. You trusted the wrong person, who took advantage of that."

"You could have told us," Charlotte said gently.

Maddie looked up at us all again. "I was humiliated. I didn't want anyone to know, and then once I lied I had to keep telling the same story." She took a deep breath and let it out. "There's something else I have to tell you, about the day Arthur died."

"Go ahead," Liz said. "We're not going to judge you."

Maddie managed a half smile. "Thank you. This is a little complicated because it involves someone else."

"Just start at the beginning," I said.

She nodded and took a deep breath. "I knew," she said.

"Knew what?" Charlotte asked, although I think we knew the answer.

"I knew that Arthur was a con artist."

"How did you find out?" I asked.

"It was after I gave him the twenty-five thousand to invest. I kept waiting for the latest financial statement to arrive and it didn't. So I did some research into the fund." She swallowed hard. "I should have done that in the beginning. The entire thing was a house of cards, and the more I thought about it, the more I didn't see how Arthur could have been duped. So I did some research on him, too."

"What did you find?" Rose asked. I could see the concern in her blue eyes.

"At first, nothing," Maddie said. She was picking at a loose bit of skin on her index finger with her thumb. "He used different names, and most of the women he conned were too embarrassed to tell anyone. You saw the article in the paper. Then I was talking to one of the organizers of the fund-raising dinner where Arthur and I met. She asked me his name. She said she was talking to a friend of hers who thought she recognized him. And I knew. I just knew. I called the woman. Her name is Aleida Scott." She paused, pressed her lips together and swallowed again. "I invited Arthur for lunch and the two of us were going to confront him. Together. We planned to tell him that we'd go to the police with our stories if he didn't give the money back—not just ours, but everyone's."

"What went wrong?" I asked, reaching for my coffee.

Maddie continued to pick at her thumb. "At first nothing. Aleida arrived early. She seemed a little nervous but I didn't think there was a problem. She stayed inside and I got Arthur settled on the patio. When I went back in she was gone. Her car was gone and she wasn't answering her phone."

Charlotte glanced at me. "That's why it took so long to make lunch."

Maddie nodded. "Yes. I was phoning every number I had for Aleida and checking the window to see if she'd come back."

"She lost her nerve," Liz said.

Maddie looked at her. "She doesn't want her family

to find out. She's afraid they'll make her give up her home and management of her money."

Liz shook her head sympathetically.

"You have an alibi," Rose said.

Maddie shook her head. "No."

"Yes," Rose insisted. "Did this other woman, Aleida, see you make the coffee?"

Maddie thought for a moment. "Yes. I poured her a cup and then I poured one for Arthur."

"What did she do when you took it out to him?"

"She stood by the window and watched me. She wanted to see Arthur before she came out to the patio."

Rose was smiling. "So, she drank the coffee after you made it and she saw you take it to Arthur—without making a detour into your garage for any pesticide. Maddie, you have an alibi." Rose looked at me. "Sarah, am I wrong?"

"It's not perfect," I said, tracing the rim of my cup with one finger. "The police could argue that Arthur had a second cup of coffee after Aleida left and Maddie put the napthathion in that. But I think it's more than enough reasonable doubt." I turned to Maddie. "You need to tell all of this to Josh right away."

Charlotte put both of her hands over Maddie's. Liz pulled her cell phone out of her pocket. "You can use my phone," she said.

Maddie shook her head. "You don't understand. I talked to Aleida. She still doesn't want her family to find out." Her voice was edged with anxiety. "She won't vouch for me. I have an alibi that won't be one."

Chapter 20

"Then we'll go talk to her and change her mind," Rose said.

Liz looked at her across the table. "It's not that simple, Rose."

"It's not that complicated, either," she said. "This woman knows Maddie didn't kill Arthur but she's keeping quiet because she doesn't want to look foolish. If she really understood what's at stake she'd go to the police. So it's up to us to explain it to her."

I leaned against my chair. Rose did make it sound simple.

"Maddie, is it possible that Aleida put something in Arthur's coffee?" I asked.

Maddie shook her head. "No. She didn't touch it, and when I came back in, her car was gone."

Rose pushed back her chair and stood up. "Who's coming with me?" she asked.

Charlotte reached a hand across the table. "Sit down, Rose. You don't even know where the woman lives."

In some perverse cosmic coincidence, the door to the

sandwich shop opened then and Alfred Peterson walked in. A look of triumph gleamed in Rose's blue eyes.

"Alfred will find her," she said.

Maddie reached out and caught her arm. "You can't do this, Rose," she said. "You can't make Aleida talk to the police. She's afraid of what her family will do."

Rose brushed off Maddie's hand. "I understand what you're saying," she said. "But that doesn't change anything. You going to prison for something you didn't do is a lot worse than your friend looking like an old fool to her family." She looked around the table at the rest of us. "Maybe the rest of you are willing to stand back and do nothing but I'm not."

I knew that determined look in her eye and that shoulders-squared stance.

"Drew Barrymore wouldn't sit around and do nothing," she said. And then she tossed her hair, or she would have if she'd actually had enough hair to toss.

Jess leaned sideways. "Drew Barrymore?" she whispered in my ear.

"Charlie's Angels. It's a long story," I said, rubbing the knot that had suddenly tightened in my left shoulder.

Rose made her way around the table and headed for the door of the sandwich shop. Mr. P. smiled when he caught sight of her. She grabbed his arm. "Alfred, I need your help," she said without stopping, pulling him along toward the door.

Jess twisted in her seat, one hand on the back of my chair, to watch the little drama being played out behind us. "What's she doing?" she asked.

I picked up my coffee cup. "Wait for it," I said softly.

Mr. P. looked a little startled but he was nothing if not game—and totally smitten with Rose. "All right," he said.

A few feet from the entrance Rose slowed down. "In case you're not paying attention—and none of you seem to be—this is where you all come after me."

I pushed back my chair and stood up. "And there you go," I said to Jess.

She grinned back at me. "This is better than HBO."

Liz lifted a hand. "Rose, don't get your panties in a bunch," she said. She turned to Maddie. "She's like a dog with a bone. She *will* find this woman and end up on her doorstep. It's worth asking her one more time to help you. So let us go with you."

Charlotte nodded.

Maddie looked up at me.

I pointed over my shoulder with one finger. "Do you really think she's going to give up?" I asked.

"I'm not," Rose said. She wouldn't turn around.

I could almost see Maddie's thoughts as she weighed her loyalty to Aleida Scott against the possibility that she could spend the rest of her life in jail, mixed with Rose's monumental stubborn streak.

"All right," she said.

I smiled at her, and Liz and Charlotte exchanged satisfied looks. Even Jess looked pleased.

"Well, let's get this show on the road," Rose said.

I turned to look at her, "Hang on, Drew Barrymore," I said. I looked back at Maddie. "Do you want to call Aleida first?"

She traced the edge of the table with one finger. "She won't talk to me."

"Then I guess we're going to see her," I said.

"Oh, goody. Road trip," Jess said. She stood up, stretched and started gathering our dishes.

"You're coming with us?" I asked.

She grinned and handed me my cup so I could drink the last mouthful of coffee. "There's no way I'm staying behind."

I drained my coffee and handed the mug back to her. "Maddie, where are we going?" I asked.

"Rockport," she said.

Half an hour, maybe forty minutes, depending on where Aleida lived in the small resort town.

Jess headed for the counter with the loaded tray. Rose and Mr. P. had their heads together. I was guessing that she was filling him in.

Maddie had gotten to her feet, but she still looked very uncertain. I was a little worried that her kind heart was getting in the way.

"Maddie, I think you should stay here," I said.

She looked surprised. "Why?"

"Because you already tried to convince Aleida to help you. I don't want her to feel like she's being ambushed. If we go without you we're just concerned friends."

Charlotte put her arm around Maddie's shoulders. "I think that's a good idea," she said. She looked at me. "I'm going to stay here, too."

I nodded. "I'll keep Rose in check," I said.

Maddie reached out and caught my hand. "I don't

know how to thank you," she said. There was a glint of unshed tears in her eyes.

"You don't have to thank me," I said quietly. Our eyes met and after a moment she nodded.

Charlotte came around the table and hugged me. "I love you, sweetie," she said.

"Love you, too," I said, giving her an extra squeeze. "I'll call you when there's anything to share."

I walked over to Rose and Mr. P. "Are you coming with us?" I asked him.

"Absolutely, my dear," he said. "You may need tech support—or muscle."

Rose gave him an encouraging smile.

"Good to have you along," I said.

Liz rode shotgun. "Are you sure you want to sit back there?" she turned to ask Jess.

"Oh yeah," Jess said. "I have a feeling the backseat is where all the fun conversation is going to happen." She looked from Liz to me. "No offense."

"None taken," Liz said.

Maddie had written down Aleida's address. I showed it to Liz. "Highway?" I asked.

She nodded. "I know where it is. I'll give you directions once we get to the turnoff."

The conversation in the backseat certainly was . . . interesting. Rose explained how Avery had dubbed them Charlie's Angels and they debated who was who. Then Mr. P. shared some of his more colorful computer hacking stories.

"The police are going to arrive at the shop one of

these days, cut off my Wi-Fi and throw me in jail, aren't they?" I said quietly to Liz.

She shot a quick glance over her shoulder. "There's a good chance of it," she said. Then she grinned. "Don't worry. We'll take your case. We'll even give you the family rate."

"That's so comforting," I said dryly.

Liz gave clear, concise directions and we turned onto Aleida Scott's street about forty minutes after we'd left McNamara's. She lived in a medium-size gray bungalow with black shutters and a deep purple front door. There was a maple tree with buttery yellow leaves near the edge of the driveway.

"How are we going to do this?" Liz asked, shifting in her seat to look into the backseat. "We can't all go. That really would be an ambush."

"Sarah and I will go talk to her," Rose said.

Liz gave her a look.

"Don't look at me like that," Rose said, frowning at her friend. "I'm not going to attack the woman. I just want her to understand what's at stake." She turned to me. "Please."

"Let Rose and me give it a try," I said.

Now I was the one getting a look from Liz. I waited.

"All right," she said. "Go ahead."

Good luck, Jess mouthed. I saw Mr. P. give Rose's arm a quick pat.

Rose and I got out of the SUV and started up Aleida Scott's driveway.

"So, what's the plan?" I asked.

"You know Maddie didn't kill Arthur," Rose said. "You know she's not capable of anything like that."

"Of course I do," I said.

Her eyes met mine. For once there was no sign of her stubborn streak or her mischievous sense of humor. For the first time I saw fear. "I think you should talk to this woman. I think you, better than any of us, can convince her to help Maddie."

I wanted to say no. I wanted to tell Rose that she would be a lot better at convincing Aleida Scott to help Maddie. But I didn't. I could see a hint of fear in her gaze, but I could also see her complete faith in me. All of them—Rose, Liz, Charlotte, my grandmother—they had always been my cheering section. If Rose thought I could do this, then I would.

We rang the doorbell and waited. I hoped the fact that there were no cars in the driveway meant Aleida Scott was home alone.

She opened the door and gave us a polite smile. Before either Rose or I could speak she held up a hand. "I'm sorry," she said. "I'm not interested in changing my religion."

"We're not trying to convert you," Rose said. "We're friends of Madeline Hamilton."

She blanched.

"Please give us two minutes," I said. "That's all. Then we'll go."

I kept my eyes fixed on her face. "All right," she said. "You'd better come inside." She stepped back and we stepped inside.

Her living room was a warm, welcoming space with a

caramel-colored sofa and two black leather chairs. The floors were oak and there was some beautiful artwork on the walls. Aleida didn't invite us to sit down.

"I can't help Madeline," she said. "I'm sorry. There's nothing I can say that will make a difference with the police."

I felt Rose stiffen beside me. I swallowed, hoping the words I was about to say would be enough. "Mrs. Scott, when I was five years old my father was hit on his way home by a car that crossed the center line. His car went down an embankment and a tree sliced through the windshield. He died before my mother, my grandmother and I got to the hospital."

"I'm so sorry," she said.

"He didn't die alone, surrounded by strangers and machines, because Maddie was there. She was a nurse in that hospital. It was the end of her shift but when she heard about the accident she went down to the emergency room and she stayed with my father."

Rose reached over and took my hand and the warmth of hers reminded me that I could do this.

"She held his hand and he didn't die all alone. He died knowing that somebody cared about him." I worked to keep my voice steady. "That's the kind of person Maddie Hamilton is. That's how *I* know she didn't kill Arthur Fenety. *You* know because you were in her house. What I know doesn't mean anything to the police. What you know will."

The silence seemed to go on forever, even though it was maybe half a minute.

"You don't know what you're asking," she said at last.

"Yes, we do," Rose said. "That's why Maddie hasn't told the police or even her lawyer about you. I know exactly what we're asking. Please think about what you're asking her to do if she keeps your secret."

Aleida looked around her living room. "I've spent forty-one years in this house," she said. She turned her gaze to Rose. "Do you have a house?"

Rose shook her head. "Not anymore. I live in an apartment at Legacy Place. It was my daughter's idea."

"Do you like it?" Aleida asked.

Rose shook her head. "No, I don't. All my neighbors do is talk about their ailments and what store has prune juice on sale this week. But I love my daughter and I know she loves me."

Aleida sighed. She looked at me. "You're right. Madeline is a good person."

I nodded.

"If it's not too late and you can get her lawyer on the phone, I'll talk to him."

I had to swallow a couple of times before I could answer her because I could suddenly feel the press of tears at the back of my throat. "Thank you," I finally managed to get out.

Rose and Aleida had stepped into the living room. I pulled out my phone and punched in Josh's cell number.

"Hi, Sarah," he said when he answered.

I explained quickly about Aleida and then I put her on the phone. She repeated pretty much the same story that Maddie had told us at the sandwich shop.

Rose took both of my hands in hers and grinned at me. "You did it, my darling girl," she said.

I smiled back at her. "I think you did it," I said.

She tossed her head, because she couldn't really toss her hair. "Drew Barrymore would be so proud," she said.

Josh arranged to meet Aleida in person the next morning at eleven o'clock. She handed my phone back to me. "I'll be there. I give you my word."

"We know that," Rose said. "Would you have time for lunch afterward?"

"I think I'd like that," she said.

I smiled at her. "*Thank you* doesn't seem like enough."

"Thank you for showing me that I needed to do the right thing," she said.

We said good night and headed for the SUV. Once we were on the sidewalk, Rose grinned and gave the car a big thumbs-up. Jess and Mr. P. high-fived and Liz nodded approvingly.

"She's going to talk to the police?" Liz asked as I slid onto the seat.

"She's already talked to Josh," I said.

"What did you say?" Jess asked.

"We just reminded her what a good person Maddie is," Rose said.

We headed back to North Harbor, with Rose making plans for a party to celebrate the charges being dropped against Maddie.

"Slow down a little," I warned. "It may not happen right away."

"Horse pucks," she said. "They don't have a case now."

I left Liz at her house and headed for Legacy Place to drop off Rose and Mr. P.

"Are you headed home or do you want to come have a cup of coffee?" I asked Jess.

"Coffee sounds good," she said. "Do you have any cookies?"

Cookies. This was getting embarrassing. I'd forgotten to get groceries again. I made a face. "Sorry."

Jess grinned. "Not a problem," she said, holding up a bag from the sandwich shop.

"When did you get those?" I asked.

"When you were telling everyone to use the washroom before we hit the road."

"She always does that," Rose said, unfastening her seat belt. "I'll see you in the morning," she said to me.

"Next time you guys go on a road trip I want to come," Jess said.

"You're welcome anytime, dear," Rose told her. "Thank you for the cookies."

"Are you coming up front?" I asked.

Jess shook her head. "I'm fine here."

"You're as bad as Elvis," I said, shaking my head.

When we got to the house I stepped into the kitchen, turned on the light and found myself face-to-face, or, more accurately, face-to-whiskers with Elvis. He was sitting on the stool at the counter.

I jumped and sucked in a breath and Jess banged into my back. "You scared the bejeebers out of me," I said. I put my face close to his and he licked my chin. "Cute does not work on me," I warned. He licked my chin again, tipped his head to one side and blinked at me. "Nobody likes a smart-ass," I said.

Jess leaned around me. "Hey, Elvis! How's it shakin'?" Much to her delight he meowed and shook his head.

"You're as bad as Liam," I said.

Jess just laughed and picked up the cat.

Liz had called Charlotte and Maddie from the road, but I wasn't sure if Charlotte had called Nick, and he deserved to know what was going on.

"I should call Nick," I said.

"Okay," Jess said. She headed for the sofa with the cat. "C'mon," I heard her say to him. "We can sit over here and pretend we're not listening."

I took out my phone.

"Hi, Sarah. What's up?" Nick asked when he answered.

"Maddie has an alibi," I said.

"What do you mean, an alibi?"

I gave Nick just the facts, leaving out the details of our road trip. "She's meeting with Josh in the morning and then they're going to the police station," I said. "This could be over by lunchtime."

"I don't think so," Nick said. His voice was flat.

I frowned at the phone even though he couldn't see me. "What do you mean?"

"Maddie doesn't have an alibi," Nick said. "This doesn't prove anything."

Chapter 21

"Yes, it does," I said. "Aleida Scott drank the coffee and she saw Maddie take a cup to Arthur—without a detour to the garage to pour in a little pesticide."

"It's not that simple." Nick exhaled loudly.

"I'm starting to really dislike that expression," I said.

"Sarah, from what you're telling me, Maddie and this woman could have been working together to kill Arthur."

"Except that Maddie didn't kill anyone," I said tightly.

"I'm sorry," Nick said. "I know that. I'm just telling you what Michelle will say."

Anger flared in my chest. Maybe it wasn't fair to Nick, but from my perspective all I could see was that he may have been an investigator for the medical examiner's office, but that didn't mean he knew for certain what the police would do. "And you know that how, Nick?" I asked. "You work for the medical examiner. Not the police. Have you talked to Maddie for more than a couple of minutes? No. Have you talked to any of the other women Arthur Fenety conned? No. Have you seen all the evidence? *No again*. You told me your job was to figure out how Arthur Fenety died and you've done that. It's not your job to build a case against whoever killed him, so you don't know what Michelle is going to say."

"I understand that you're frustrated," Nick began. "But, like I said, it's not that simple."

I thought about Rose standing up at the table at the sandwich shop and marching indignantly for the front door to make a point.

"I'm not frustrated," I said. "And it's really simple: I'm angry." Then I hung up. Well, actually I just ended the call. That was one of the frustrations of a cell phone: no receiver to hang up in righteous indignation.

I leaned back against the counter. Jess and Elvis were watching me. "I told you she'd hang up on him," Jess said to the cat.

Elvis narrowed his green eyes at me, then looked at Jess and meowed.

"We'll see," she said.

My cell phone rang. I knew it was Nick before I checked. I let it go to voice mail.

"You were right," Jess said to Elvis, stroking the top of his head.

He gave her a blissful kitty smile and leaned against her chest.

I dropped onto the couch beside the two of them.

"What did Nick say?" Jess asked.

"He said this doesn't prove anything. Maddie and Aleida Scott could have planned to kill Arthur Fenety together."

Jess shook her head. "What happened to his common sense?" she said. "And Michelle's, for that matter."

I looked at her. "What do you mean?"

"Well, first of all, Maddie was a nurse. If she was going to kill someone I think she'd be able to come up with something better than a banned pesticide she would have had to steal from one of her friends. And she certainly wouldn't be stupid enough to kill the man at her own house or ask a complete stranger to help." She put Elvis on my lap, got up and started for the kitchen. "Was I the only kid who watched *Murder, She Wrote*?" She held out her hands as though she were appealing to a higher power.

I shifted sideways a bit and Elvis stretched out on my lap. "A, what the heck are you talking about? And B, what are you doing?" I asked.

"I'm talking about a setup," she said. "And what I'm doing is making coffee."

"You think someone set up Maddie so she'd be blamed for Arthur's murder?"

"C'mon, it's the only thing that makes sense," Jess said, scooping coffee into the top of the machine. "You're almost out of coffee, by the way."

"So, why Maddie?"

Jess shrugged. "Convenience, probably. She was seeing the guy. That would make a her likely suspect."

It made sense. "So who would do something like that?"

"Hey, I can't figure out everything for you," she said. "Why don't you call Nick back and see if he has any theories?" She was filling the carafe with water.

"Sorry," I said. "I can't hear you."

She made a face at me and turned to pour the water

into the coffeemaker. Once the machine was doing its thing she got out a couple of mugs and a plate for the cookies she'd brought.

"Cut Nick a little slack, if you can," Jess said, propping her elbows on the counter. "This new job of his can't be easy."

I closed my eyes and shook my head. "Don't make me feel sympathy for him. I want to stay mad a little bit longer."

"And then there's the fact that he's got a . . . thing for you."

"Just because Nick shaved the other night doesn't mean he has a thing for me," I said. I opened my eyes.

Jess laced her fingers together and propped her chin on top of them. "Admit it," she said, a teasing grin on her face. "You kind of like the idea. You should have a fling with him."

I stroked Elvis's fur and he put his head down on his front paws. "I'd like to fling him," I said.

"I think you kind of like Nick."

"I absolutely do not kind of like Nick!"

"Yes, you do," Jess said, turning back to the counter to get the coffee, which was ready now. "Even Elvis knows you're not being honest when you say that. Look at his face."

I leaned forward and looked at the cat. His ears were down and he had an *oh, come on* look in his half-lidded green eyes. I'd seen that look twice recently. I'd seen it when we'd all had lunch at the shop. Maddie had been petting Elvis while she told us what happened the day Arthur Fenety was killed. A story I knew now wasn't true. I'd seen the same expression on the cat's face when Jim Grant had stopped to pet him while he was telling me when he'd arrived in North Harbor.

Had he been less than honest, as well?

Jess was coming from the kitchen, carrying two mugs with the plate of cookies balanced on top of one of the cups. "You might have just helped me figure out who killed Arthur Fenety," I said.

She handed me my cup and dropped down next to me on the sofa, setting the cookies between us. "Well, here's to me," she said, raising her mug in a toast. We clinked cups. Jess leaned against the back of the sofa, folding one arm over her head. "So, who is it?" she asked, reaching for a cookie.

"I think it might be Jim Grant."

"Who's he?"

"His mother was one of Fenety's victims—one of his so-called wives, actually." I broke a cookie in half and took a bite. Elvis sniffed my hand and then put his head down again. If it wasn't fish or meat he wasn't generally interested.

"So, what did I say to inspire this epiphany?" Jess asked.

I started to scratch behind the cat's ear and he laid his head on my leg and stared to purr.

"You said that even Elvis knew I wasn't exactly being honest about Nick. I realized I'd seen that look on his furry little face a couple of times before."

"And I'm guessing one of those times this Jim Grant was petting him."

"Exactly." I took a sip of my coffee. "Am I crazy? Or

is it possible that he can somehow sense when someone is lying?"

She shrugged. "If dogs can be trained to sniff out bombs or drugs, why couldn't Elvis be able to tell if someone is lying? He's a pretty smart cat."

Elvis lifted his head, looked at Jess and meowed, as if in acknowledgment. She smiled at him. "Okay, so you think this guy set up Maddie. How are you going to prove it?"

I slumped against the back of the couch. "I haven't exactly figured that part out yet," I said.

Chapter 22

I didn't call Charlotte or any of the others to tell them about my new theory or what Nick had told me. There wasn't anything I could do tonight as far as Jim Grant went, and I didn't want to upset everyone with what Nick had said. Maybe he'd be wrong.

I picked up Charlotte in the morning. She smiled when she got in the SUV and I felt a pang of guilt knowing I was going to shoot down her happy mood.

"I talked to Nicolas last night," she said as she set her bag at her feet and fastened her seat belt.

"What did he say?" I asked carefully.

"I told him what we'd found out and he said he'd do whatever he could to persuade Detective Andrews and the prosecutor to drop the charges against Maddie."

It wasn't what I was expecting to hear.

"You're surprised," she said.

I smiled, which was easy because Charlotte was happy. "Only a little bit," I admitted, keeping my eyes on the road. "But I shouldn't be, because Nick loves you and he's a good guy."

"Yes, he is," Charlotte said, nodding slowly. "I hope he finds a woman who appreciates him." I could feel her eyes on me.

"Are you trying to play matchmaker?" I asked.

"No, dear, I'm just making conversation," she said.

I decided it was time to change the topic of the conversation. "Charlotte, do you remember when Jim Grant came in?"

Out of the corner of my eye I saw her nod. "Did you notice that he made a point of telling us that he didn't get into town until Tuesday morning?"

"I hadn't," she said slowly. "But now that you mention it, yes, he did make sure we all heard that."

I glanced over at her again.

"Sarah, do you think he killed Arthur?"

"I think it's possible," I hedged.

"So how are we going to prove it?"

"I have an idea," I said slowly. "I don't know if it'll work." The idea that had seemed brilliant at two a.m. felt a lot shakier over coffee with Elvis at six thirty.

"You haven't let us down yet," Charlotte said, pulling down the sleeve of her jacket. "Tell me your idea."

"Poisoning Arthur at Maddie's house was a crime of opportunity. No one knew he was going to be there because Maddie didn't invite him until that morning."

"So how did Jim Grant know?" Charlotte asked.

"I think he was following Arthur. Maybe he was hoping Arthur would lead him to the missing money and jewelry. Mr. P. said that Royce Collins saw Arthur in the park on the way to Maddie's house."

"Maybe he saw someone following Arthur."

"Exactly." I put on my blinker and turned into the small parking lot beside the store.

"We need to go talk to Royce," Charlotte said.

"That's what I was thinking," I said. I backed into my parking spot and Charlotte and I got out of the SUV.

"Sarah, if it was Jim Grant, where did he get a bottle of that pesticide?" she asked as we walked toward the back door.

"I'm hoping Mr. P.'s going to be able to tell me that," I said.

My favorite hacker arrived about five minutes after we'd opened the store. I knew from the smile on his face that he'd hit pay dirt.

"You were right, my dear," he said. "Jim Grant's uncle—his mother's brother—had a landscaping business. Jim worked for him during the summers."

"So, we have motive and means," I said. "All we need is opportunity."

"Royce delivers flyers on Saturdays," Mr. P. said. "You can meet him at the park at eleven thirty."

I hesitated. Then I decided, *Why not?* I threw my arms around the little old man and hugged him. "Thank you," I said.

His brown eyes sparkled. "It's my pleasure to serve, Sarah," he said. "I'm going to see if I can prove young Mr. Grant was, in fact, here in North Harbor before he said he was."

He took his nylon briefcase and headed for the sunporch.

Mac walked over to me and dipped his head in the

direction of the back of the shop. "New developments?" he asked.

I filled him in on Aleida Scott and my eureka moment about Jim Grant. Elvis was watching Charlotte dust the guitars. It looked as though she was talking to him.

"Do you think it's possible that Elvis can tell when someone is lying?" I said to Mac.

He crossed his arms over his chest. "Why not? A lie-detector test measures changes in respiration, heart rate, blood pressure and how much someone sweats. Maybe Elvis is reacting to the same things."

I glanced over at Elvis and Charlotte. "So you're saying he's a feline lie detector?"

"There are more things in heaven and earth than are dreamt of in your philosophy," Mac said.

"Did you just quote Shakespeare?" I said.

Mac gave me an enigmatic smile not unlike the cat's. "I hope you find what you need." He gestured toward the stairs. "The delivery guy from Lily's brought something for you a few minutes ago."

I frowned. "I didn't order anything. What is it?"

He shook his head. "I don't know."

I called Liz and explained what was going on. She said she could meet me at the park. I crossed my fingers we'd get the answers we were looking for.

Upstairs in my office, a small cardboard box sat on my desk. I opened the lid and laughed when I saw what was inside—a muffin with a tiny flag stuck in the middle. On the front of the flag were the words *I'm sorry. Nick.*

I broke the muffin in half and took a bite. It was bran with fat raisins and a taste of cinnamon. Okay, so it wasn't chocolate, but it was still a pretty sweet apology.

I was standing by the stone steps that led down to the duck pond just before eleven thirty when Liz came up the sidewalk. She was wearing a burnt orange sweater with gray pants and gray suede heels I wasn't sure I'd be able to walk in.

"Hello, sweetie," she said, leaning over to kiss my cheek. She looked at the gold watch on her wrist. "Royce should be along in a minute. What's the plan?"

"I don't really have one," I said, shifting restlessly from one foot to the other. "We know Royce saw Arthur Fenety the morning he was killed. What we need to know is, did he see Jim Grant?"

"I thought he didn't come to town until after Arthur was dead," she said.

I tucked my keys in my jacket pocket. "Technically he didn't," I said. "He checked into the Rosemont Inn just before lunch on Tuesday, but before that he spent two nights in a motel out on the highway." How Mr. P. had gotten that information was another thing I didn't want to know.

"Do you have a picture of the man?" Liz asked.

I nodded and held out my phone. "Mr. Peterson found one online and I downloaded it to my phone."

"You know, if Rose doesn't give the man some encouragement soon, I may have to make a move on him," she said, studying the picture. "He's smart and most of his teeth are original. All I'd need to do would be to get him out of those pants."

I looked wide-eyed at her. "Excuse me?" I said.

"I didn't mean it that way," she said, waving a hand at me. "I just meant get him into some pants that aren't way up here." She stuck her thumbs into her armpits.

"He is a little fashion challenged," I said. "But I love the way he looks at Rose."

Liz smiled. "Yes, even an old cynic like me can appreciate that."

I put my arm around her shoulder. "I don't think you're quite as much of a cynic as you pretend to be."

Royce Collins was coming up the sidewalk. He was a small man with intense blue eyes under his dark blue newsboy hat, and a bushy mustache. "Good morning, ladies," he said. "I hope you don't mind walking and talking. I have a schedule to keep." He shifted the large canvas bag half-full of advertising circulars that was slung over his shoulder.

Liz cleared her throat. "Well, then, we'll get right to the point." She fell into step beside Royce and I walked beside her. "You saw Arthur Fenety the morning he was killed?"

Royce nodded. "Yes, I did."

"What time?"

"Eleven thirty."

We turned right on the path.

"Did you see anyone else?"

He shrugged. "There were other people around. It was a beautiful day."

Liz held out her left hand. I knew she wanted the phone. I handed it to her and she showed Royce the photo.

"Did you see this man?"

Royce looked at the picture without missing a step. "I saw him."

Liz shot me a look. "Are you certain?"

"Of course I'm certain," he said. "I wouldn't say I'd seen him if I hadn't."

Liz gave the phone back to me and I tucked it in my purse. "Do you remember what he was doing?" she asked.

Royce shot her a look of annoyance. "Of course I remember."

Liz blew a breath out between her teeth. She tightened her hand on the strap of her pumpkin-colored purse and for a moment I thought she was going to swing it at him. "And what was that?" she asked, making a hurry-up motion with her free hand.

"He was following that Fenety guy."

Chapter 23

"That man I just showed you a picture of was following Arthur Fenety the day he was killed?" Liz said.

Royce looked at her, two frown lines forming between his eyes. "I just said that, didn't I?"

"Yes, you did," she said. "Did you say it to the police?"

He shook his head. "No."

"Why?" I asked.

He leaned behind Liz to look at me. "They didn't ask," he said with a shrug.

I had a little bubble of excitement in my chest. "How far did the man follow Mr. Fenety?" I asked. It struck me that the key to getting answers out of the older man was all in how the question was worded.

He pointed down the path. "Right until the path goes off through the trees just up there."

"Did Arthur know he was being followed?" Liz asked.

He nodded. "Oh, I'd say he did."

A soccer ball came bouncing over the grass toward us

and I kicked it back to the bunch of preschoolers who were playing with it just beyond the raised flower beds. A chorus of little voices yelled, "Thank you!"

"Why would you say that?" Liz asked. Her jaw was tense and it was pretty clear she was running out of patience.

Royce took off his cap, smoothed down the tufts of gray hair that rimmed his head, and put it back on again. "Because Fenety just turned around all of a sudden and knocked that fella into the bushes right there." He pointed to the spot where the path forked just ahead.

Liz and I exchanged looks. As we came level with the bushes I noticed that the side of the path sloped down at an angle there. It would have been fairly easy to catch someone by surprise and trip them into the bushes.

"Don't climb down there, girl," the former mail carrier said, raising a hand in warning.

"Why?" I asked.

"Lotta poison ivy down there."

Poison ivy. "Bingo!" I said to Liz.

I looked at Royce Collins. "What did Arthur Fenety do after he knocked the man following him to the bushes?"

"He said something—I couldn't hear what. Then he helped the guy up. They stood there talking for a bit and then Fenety went down that way." He pointed to the trail through the woods and hiked up his pants. "Other guy headed back to the main entrance."

Liz took a deep breath and smiled. "Thank you, Royce," she said. "You've been a big help."

"You're welcome, Elizabeth," he said. He tipped his

cap to her. "If there's anything else you need to know, feel free to stop by my place anytime." He gave her a big smile and a wink and continued on down the path.

Liz took my arm. "Was that enough?" she asked. "Because I'm not going to his house to ask him any more questions. You *will* be on your own."

I nudged Liz's shoulder with my own. "You know, his teeth looked very nice and he doesn't have any hair growing out of his nose. You could do a lot worse."

She glared at me. "There are sixteen-year-old boys walking around with half their underwear showing and their pants aren't as droopy as Royce Collins's are." She shook her head. "Honestly, what is it with men my age? Their pants are either up under their armpits or hanging so low we can almost see the crack—"

"Liz!" I exclaimed.

"Of dawn," she finished.

We were back at the SUV and I walked around to get into the driver's side. "You're being a little hard on the poor man. His pants weren't that bad."

"Oh, really?" Liz said. She pointed across the park. Royce Collins was almost out of sight where the path curved again. His khaki pants slumped on his hips, the seat a good eight inches below his . . . real seat.

I slid behind the wheel. "All he needs is a good woman to teach him a little fashion sense," I said, grinning at her.

She smiled back at me as she reached for her seat belt. "Would you like to talk about how both Charlotte and Rose think you and Nicolas would make an absolutely adorable couple now that he's staying in town?"

"No," I said.

She clicked the seat belt into place. "Let's just drive."

"We need to talk to Jim Grant again."

"No time like the present," she said.

We drove across town to the Rosemont Inn, where Jim Grant had been staying. The inn was a former sea captain's home, built in 1822. It was only a couple of blocks from the waterfront.

Jim Grant had gone out for lunch. We found him at McNamara's, about to start in on a pastrami sandwich.

"Ms. Grayson, hello," he said, smiling as Liz and I approached the table.

"Hello," I said, smiling in return. "And please call me Sarah."

"If you'll call me Jim," he said.

"This is my friend, Liz French."

Liz smiled. "Hello," she said.

"Jim, do you have a minute?" I asked. "There's something I wanted to ask you."

"Uh, sure," he said. "Please sit down."

I pulled another chair over to the table, and Liz and I sat down.

Jim wiped his fingers on his napkin. I could still see a bit of a bandage peeking out from below his shirt cuff. "What can I do for you?" he asked.

"You could explain why you made a point of telling me you got into town Tuesday morning when you actually arrived here on Sunday."

Jim Grant would have been a lousy poker player. A tiny muscle started to twitch on his left eyelid. He twisted his napkin into a tight ball in his right hand.

I shrugged. "It's a small place. It's hard to keep anything secret for very long."

"I didn't want you to think I'd done anything to Fenety."

"Did you?" Liz asked.

His gaze flicked over to her for a moment. "No. I didn't."

I pointed at his arm. "You followed Arthur and he caught you."

His mouth pulled into a thin line. "Twice my age and he got the jump on me. And to top it off I landed in a damn patch of poison ivy. My whole arm came up in welts that itched like a bugger. I'm really allergic to the stuff."

"Why were you following Arthur?" Liz asked.

Jim pushed his plate back. "I thought maybe he'd lead me to wherever he stashed my mother's jewelry." He reached for his coffee. "You probably heard. The police found his safe-deposit box. Most of my mother's things were in it. As for the money, I don't care what he said; it's long gone."

I leaned forward, putting both hands on the table. "Wait a minute. What do you mean, you don't care what he said?"

"He told me he'd changed. He said he'd call me in the morning and he'd give me the money he took from my mother." He looked at me. "Yeah, I didn't tell you the truth about that, either."

"What did you do after you talked to Arthur?"

"I went back to the place where I was staying and got in the bathtub with a bunch of oatmeal. It was supposed to help." He rubbed his hand over his left arm. "I told you, the damn thing itched like a bugger. I spent the afternoon getting drunk and half the night heaving my guts out."

I looked at Liz.

"Ask them at the inn," he said. "They'll tell you. I didn't kill Fenety. I wanted to get back everything he took from my mother. I couldn't do that if he was dead."

Liz and I left Jim Grant to his lunch and walked back to the SUV.

"We should go back to the Rosemont, just in case he's still not telling the truth," Liz said.

I nodded. Even without my feline lie detector I was certain Jim Grant had been honest. And it turned out I was right. The staff at the Rosemont confirmed that Jim Grant had returned to the inn just after noon on Monday, his left arm swollen and covered in welts from the poison ivy. He'd spent a half an hour in an oatmeal bath the housekeeper had gotten ready for him, and then proceeded to get standing-up-falling-down drunk in the lounge.

"I was so sure I was right," I said to Liz as we stood on the sidewalk outside the inn.

"So, now what?" she said.

I shook my head. I was at a loss. "I don't know."

Chapter 24

When we got back to the shop I pulled into my parking spot, shut off the engine and leaned my head back against the headrest. "I'm sorry," I said to Liz.

"What for?" she asked.

"For being wrong about Jim Grant. For getting everyone's hopes up that we could prove Maddie is innocent."

"I thought it was him, too," she said.

I opened my eyes and looked at her.

"We'll figure something out." She reached over to pat my arm. "We always do."

"We may as well go in," I said. "I can't hide out here all day."

Liz already had her door open. "Well, of course not," she said. "I don't think that windshield has a UV coating. All the sun would give you wrinkles."

I smiled at her. "I love you," I said.

She was already starting across the parking lot and she waved a hand at me. "Yeah. Everybody does," she said.

Rose had gotten back just before we did. Michelle

and the prosecutor had agreed to consider Aleida's statement, but for now the charges against Maddie were still in place.

"It's better than what I have," I said. I filled them in on what Liz and I had learned.

"So, if Jim Grant didn't kill Arthur, who did?" Rose asked, brushing bits of paper off the front of her apron.

"It had to be one of his other wives or someone from their families," Charlotte said.

"So how do we figure out who?" Liz asked.

I raked both hands through my hair. "For now I guess we just get Mr. P. to keep on digging."

I headed up to my office to check my messages. After about ten minutes there was a knock on my door.

"Come in," I called.

It was Mac. "Rose brought soup back with her. I heated some up for you."

"Thanks," I said, moving around the desk to take the oversize mug he'd brought me.

"Don't be so hard on yourself, Sarah," he said. "You'll figure something out. Or maybe the police will."

"I encouraged them," I said, leaning back against the desk. "I got involved in their 'investigation' and then I let them down."

"No, you didn't," he said. Elvis had wandered in behind him and the cat meowed loudly as if in agreement. "See?" Mac said. "He agrees with me.'

I laughed and stirred the soup with my spoon. "You two aren't exactly unbiased."

"And neither are you," he said, leaning against the doorframe. "Nobody else would have taken those three seriously. Nobody else would have driven all over town, trying to prove Maddie Hamilton didn't kill Arthur Fenety." He smiled. "They love you. They're not disappointed."

Right on cue Elvis meowed again. "Thanks, Mac," I said. I looked down at the cat. "You too."

I ate the soup Mac had brought me and then I returned some phone calls while Elvis sat in the middle of my desk, washing his face. When I finished I leaned back in my chair.

"I wish we knew a little more about Arthur's past," I said to the cat.

He climbed down onto my lap, walked his front paws up my chest and rubbed his face against the side of mine. I reached up to scratch behind his ear and he laid his head against my shoulder.

"I'd like to talk to Daisy again," I said. "She's the best source of information we have. She's the only one we have."

He murped in agreement. At least that's what I decided the sound meant.

I gave him one last scratch, set him on the floor and stood up. "So, what am I going to use for an excuse to talk to the woman again?"

Elvis walked across the small space to a stack of boxes packed with an eight-piece set of china that was going to auction in a week. He scrapped at the bottom box with one paw and then looked at me.

China. Daisy Fenety was looking for pieces of that daisy-patterned china. If I could find a piece or two I felt certain she'd come to the shop to see it.

"You're a genius," I said. Elvis straightened up and swiped a paw across his face, almost as though he were saying, "Of course I am."

I went downstairs and out onto the sunporch. Mr. P. was on his laptop, eyes glued to the screen, fingers flying over the keys. Rose was in a chair beside him.

"Mr. P., do you have a moment to look for something for me?" I asked.

"Certainly I do," he said. "What is it?"

"I'm looking for a piece of china. The pattern is called Daisy May."

"Isn't that the china Arthur's sister collects?" Rose asked.

I nodded. "I want to talk to her again, and I don't think she's going to want to help us prove Maddie's innocence. She thinks Maddie is guilty. I thought if I had a piece of the china maybe I could get her into the shop."

"It's a little old-fashioned, you know," Rose said.

"You've seen the china?" I said.

"Heavens, yes," she said. "My next-door neighbor has a china cabinet full of it. And she never uses it."

The lightbulb went on for both of us at the same time.

"Do you think she'd loan you a couple of pieces?" I asked.

"The woman has a wicked sweet tooth," she said. "For a cake she'd probably loan me a kidney."

"A cup and saucer or a gravy boat will be just fine," I said. "Tell me what you want from the grocery store and I'll get it. Butter, chocolate, baking . . . stuff. Give me a list."

Rose reached over and tucked a loose strand of hair

behind my ear. "I have all the baking stuff I need. I think I'll make my devil's food cake with whipped chocolate frosting. Don't worry. I'll have a cup and saucer or a gravy boat for Monday morning."

"Thanks," I said. "Maybe I can find out something from Daisy that will at least point us in the right direction."

"Alfred is looking into all of Arthur's wives that we know about," Rose said. "I'm not giving up, Sarah."

"Neither am I," I said.

She held up her hand, palm facing out, and I realized she wanted to high-five me. So I did. I figured why not? Maybe it would bring me some good luck. We could use it.

It was a busy day. The fall foliage was at its peak and we had tourists in and out all day. By five o'clock my feet hurt, but I remembered to stop at the grocery store. I carried two canvas shopping bags into the house, trailed by Elvis.

"We have coffee, bacon, chocolate and Fancy Feast," I told the cat, who had waited patiently in the back of the SUV while I shopped. "I think that covers the major food groups: sugar, salt, fat, caffeine and cat."

He licked his whiskers and then went over and sat beside his bowl.

"You're not exactly subtle, you know," I said. I put the groceries away, fed Elvis and made myself a scrambled egg and tomato sandwich. I jazzed it up a little with a dill pickle and some black olives. It was a nice night, so I took my supper out on the small verandah. I sat in my favorite wicker chair and put my feet up on the railing.

Elvis prowled around sniffing things, probably checking to see if there had been any squirrels in his territory.

It was a quiet Saturday night. Not that Saturday nights ever got rowdy in my neighborhood, or anywhere else in town. I'd finished my sandwich and was trying to decide if I wanted the brownie I'd bought badly enough to get up and get it, when a dark blue car pulled in at the curb. It took a moment for me to remember where I'd seen it before and by then the driver was getting out. It was Michelle. I dropped my feet and stood up. "Hi," I said as she walked across the grass.

"Hi, Sarah," she said. She stopped at the top of the steps and leaned against the railing post.

"Is everything all right?" I asked. I was very aware that she was a police officer—even though she was dressed in jeans and a hoodie, which suggested she was off duty—and we weren't exactly friends anymore.

She smiled, although it looked a little tentative to me. "I wanted to tell you that the charges haven't been dropped against Maddie but we are expanding the investigation."

I nodded. "Thank you. It wasn't what I was hoping for, but it's something."

She looked around. "I like your house. You've done a lot of work on it."

"I couldn't have done it without Liam and Gram," I said.

"How is Liam?" she asked, tucking her hands into the kangaroo pocket of her hoodie.

I smiled. "He's good. He's at a solar-energy conference in Montreal right now." My brother designed solar houses. His specialty was small houses that used passive solar technology.

Elvis came up the steps, stopped in front of Michelle and studied her for a moment. Then he meowed softly, his way of saying, "I remember you."

She bent down to pet him. "He looks like he's probably used up at least one of his nine lives," she said.

I nodded. "Sometimes I wonder what the other guy looks like."

Michelle straightened up. Elvis looked around as if he were confused about why anyone would want to stop stroking his fur or scratching behind his right ear.

"I didn't come here to tell you about the investigation," she said. "At least not just about that."

"So why did you come?" I asked. Elvis came to sit beside me, leaning against my leg.

She took a deep breath. "I came to say I'm sorry."

"You don't have to apologize," I said, folding my arms over my chest. "Arresting Maddie is part of doing your job."

She tucked her auburn hair behind one ear. "That's not what I came to apologize for. I came to tell you I'm sorry for cutting you out of my life."

It was the last thing I was expecting her to say. For a moment I just looked at her. Then I found my voice. "What did I do?" I asked. "One day you were my friend and the next day you wouldn't speak to me. I didn't understand then and I don't understand now."

"Do you remember that summer?" She looked down at her feet. "My father went to jail."

I tried to swallow down the lump that had suddenly

formed in my throat but it wouldn't go. I remembered that summer like it had just happened. It was the summer I'd gotten my dad's guitar from Maddie and lost my best friend. Michelle had been a summer kid, just like I was, coming to spend two months with her grandparents, long dead now. Then her dad had gotten a job as director for the Sunshine Camp. The camp, for kids with seriously ill parents, had been bought by the Emmerson Foundation, the charitable organization started by Liz's grandparents. Rob Andrews had had the job less than a year when a routine audit showed there was money missing.

"I remember," I finally managed to say.

She looked past me, over my shoulder into the darkness, or maybe into the past. I wasn't sure. "I kept thinking I was going to wake up and it would just be a bad dream," she said, her gaze coming back to my face.

Michelle's dad had died in prison, less than three months after he'd been sentenced, from a fast-moving form of cancer that no one had known he had.

"Nobody seemed to understand how I felt." She stopped and swallowed. "Except you. And then I heard what you said about him to Nick."

And just like that I understood why Michelle had stopped talking to me. Just like that it suddenly all made sense. Why hadn't I figured it out before?

The night Maddie had given me my dad's guitar, and two months after Michelle's father had begun his four-year prison sentence for embezzling from the Sunshine Camp, Nick and I had sat on the rock wall at the back of my grandmother's yard and I'd told him that Michelle's father was a horrible person and that it wasn't fair that he was still here and my father was gone. And then I'd said, "I wish he was the one who was dead!" A couple of minutes later I'd taken it all back, but obviously Michelle hadn't stayed around long enough to hear that. And a couple of weeks later, her father was dead.

"I don't understand," I said rubbing the palm of my right hand with the thumb of my left. "You had chicken pox. You were in bed."

She ducked her head. "It was your birthday. I wanted to bring you your present. So I waited until everyone was asleep. Then I snuck out."

The next day Michelle had ended up in the hospital when she'd come down with some kind of secondary infection—probably from wandering around town late at night. I'd been baffled when she didn't want to see me and when she wouldn't even look at me during her father's funeral sixteen days later.

"I'm sorry," I said. "I was a thoughtless, self-absorbed teenager."

She gave me a small smile. "I think that's part of the job description. And you'd just gotten your father's guitar. You were missing him."

"You were my best friend," I said. "I was supposed to be on your side and I wasn't."

A strange look came over her face. "I think someone set him up," she said. She straightened up and brushed her hair back from her face. "I've been trying to figure out who it was."

"Have you found anything?"

"You're not going to tell me I'm tilting at windmills?" she asked, running a hand over the railing.

"I've been driving a group of senior citizens who think they're Charlie's Angels all over town. I'm the last person who's going to tell you that." I chose my next words with care. "And I'd like to be a better friend than that."

Michelle hesitated and then she leaned forward and hugged me. It was clumsy and awkward but it still felt pretty good.

"Could we have dinner some night and catch up?" I asked when she let me go. I was hesitant because it had been a lot of years since the two of us had been friends.

She nodded. "I'd like that." Her mouth moved as though she was testing out what she was going to say next.

I bent down to pick up Elvis to give her a minute.

"I'll do what I can to help Maddie," she said. "I'll look at every piece of evidence a second time. I give you my word."

I nodded. "I know that," I said.

She let out a breath as though a load had been lifted off her shoulders. "I have to get going." She leaned over and gave Elvis a scratch on the top of his head. He tipped his head to the right, looked up at her and murped. "Good night, Elvis," she said.

She smiled at me and there was nothing tentative about it this time.

I watched her walk back to her car, and as she drove away I raised a hand in good-bye and she did the same.

Chapter 25

Rose arrived about quarter to nine Monday morning, carrying her red-and-white tote bag, and looking like the cat that swallowed the canary.

"Did you get it?" I asked, even though I knew the answer.

She nodded and set the tote bag at her feet. She lifted out something swaddled in a towel and set it on the counter and began to unwrap it. Elvis, who had been sitting there, reached over with a paw and swatted down one edge of the towel.

"Thank you, Elvis," Rose said. Underneath two of her best peach-colored towels was a curved, squat gravy boat.

"I hope this is okay," she said.

"It's more than okay," I said. I threw my arms around her shoulders and hugged her. "Thank you."

"Go call Daisy," she said. "Let's see what we can find out."

I rewrapped the gravy boat and took it up to my office. Then I called Daisy Fenety, crossing my fingers that she'd be interested enough in the china gravy boat that she'd come to the shop.

"It's on consignment," I explained. "I can't promise the owner will take your offer or any offer, for that matter."

"I could stop by about four thirty this afternoon," she said. "Would that work for you?"

"It would," I said.

The day dragged.

About quarter after four I went downstairs. Charlotte had found new shades for the lamps I'd gotten from the motel and Avery had finished scrubbing the chairs. The lamps were on top of a squat wooden bookcase and the chairs were grouped in a semicircle, each with a bright pillow that Jess had made propped against its back.

Charlotte was just ringing up a customer. I waited until she was finished and then walked over to her. I set the china gravy boat on the counter by the cash register. She cleaned her hands with the bottle of sanitizer I kept by the cash register. "Avery and I are going to wait in the sunporch," she said. "I think Daisy might be more likely to talk to you if we're not all in the room. Mac will be around in case there are any customers." She laid a hand on my shoulder for a moment. "Just get her to talk to you if you can."

"I will," I said. I felt as though a dozen tap dancers were hoofing it up in my stomach.

Daisy Fenety walked through the door exactly at four thirty. Charlotte had made tea and I had the pot, covered in a quilted cozy on a tray, along with cups and cream and sugar, sitting on a small folding table beside the tub chair.

"Hello, Sarah," Daisy said. She was elegant, dressed in a caramel-colored sweater over a robin's-egg blue shirt and chocolate brown trousers.

"Hello," I said, walking across the floor to meet her. "That's the gravy boat." I pointed to the piece of china sitting next to the cash register. Her eyes lit up. We walked over to the counter.

"May I?" she asked.

I nodded. "Of course."

She picked up the gravy boat and turned it over in her hands, examining it from every angle.

"As you can see it's in excellent condition," I said.

"The daisy centers have faded somewhat," she pointed out.

"Which is typical for china of this vintage," I countered.

"You know something about this pattern," she said, her eyes meeting mine.

"I try to learn about the things I sell." I'd spent an hour online Sunday afternoon researching the china.

Daisy set the gravy boat down on the counter. "How much are you asking for it?" she said.

I gave her my best professional smile. "As I told you on the phone this is a consignment piece." I named a price that I knew from my research was about fifty percent more than the piece of china was worth.

"Is there any flexibility?" she asked.

I nodded. "I think a little. Would you like to make an offer?"

The price she named was a good twenty percent less than the average selling price of a piece of the vintage pattern.

"I think the owner is asking way too much," she said, reaching out to trace the curve of the gravy boat's handle with one finger. "People tend to put a dollar value on sentimentality."

"Yes, they do," I said. I pointed at the teapot. "I was going to have a cup of tea. Why don't you join me?"

"Thank you," she said.

I poured a cup for each of us. Daisy took the tub chair and I carried over one of the hotel chairs with its bright-banded cushion.

"How did you first get interested in the Daisy May china?" I asked.

"My mother had a tea set in that pattern," Daisy said. "She used to call it my china because of the daisies. She left it to me when she died. And I started collecting. Arthur used to tease me about it. I was a tomboy. The china was the only girly thing I was interested in. Never dolls or frilly dresses."

"You must miss him very much," I said. "I'm sorry."

"Thank you," she said. "I know that you want to believe Madeline's innocent."

"I do," I said. "It's hard to believe she'd hurt anyone."

Elvis wandered in from the storage room and came over to us. He sat down in front of Daisy and looked up at her.

"Oh, my goodness," she said. "You poor thing. What happened to you?"

Elvis hammed it up for all he was worth, dropping his head and giving her a sorrowful look.

"This is Elvis," I said. "I don't know how he got the scar. The vet thinks he was in a fight with a much bigger animal."

He jumped up beside Daisy on the tub chair.

"Get down," I said.

Daisy smiled. "It's all right. I don't mind." She reached over to pet his fur. I was wondering how I could get the conversation back to her brother when she looked at me and said, "It seems clear to me that Madeline must have had some kind of mental breakdown. I can't help feeling I should have been there. I could have done something."

"It's not your fault," I said, taking another sip of my tea.

She looked at me, still stroking Elvis's fur. "Are you familiar with the proverb 'For want of a nail the shoe was lost'?"

I nodded.

"If it weren't for my cracked tooth, Arthur would be alive."

Out of the corner of my eye I could see Elvis, sitting so well behaved next to Daisy on the tub chair, with that look on his face.

I could suddenly hear my heartbeat thudding in my ears, and at the same time tiny pieces began to fall into place. I took a sip of my tea, hoping nothing showed on my face. "I cracked a tooth once biting down on a pit in a date square," I said. "I remember it was really painful."

Daisy nodded and put a hand to her cheek. "So was mine. Arthur insisted I call the dentist and take the car."

The cat's expression hadn't changed. I needed to keep her talking. "How far away did you have to park?" I asked. "I had an appointment in the building the next day and I had to park on the street almost two blocks away because they were working on the parking lot." It was a lie, but at least I wasn't petting the cat, so hopefully Daisy couldn't tell.

"It certainly was poorly planned, wasn't it?' she said. "Doing that work on a Monday morning. I found a parking spot in the Legacy Place lot next door." A look flashed across her face like she'd just bitten into an apple and discovered half a worm.

"Did something happen to your car while it was parked there?" I asked.

She shook her head and stopped petting Elvis long enough to pick up her cup and drink a little of her tea. He gave her his most adorable gaze and she started stroking his fur again. "I had a bit of a distasteful experience but it's not important."

I shot a quick look at the cat. Nothing on his face suggested she was lying. I tried not to focus on the fact that I was relying on a cat to tell if Daisy Fenety was lying.

"I don't want to pry," I began a little hesitantly. "But my grandmother is thinking about taking an apartment in that building. If there's a problem"—I held up a hand—"I don't want her to live there."

Daisy's lips were pressed together in a thin, tight line. "I think you'd be wise to encourage your grandmother to look for somewhere else to live." She leaned toward me. "I saw a naked man walk by the windows."

I put a hand to my chest. "That's awful," I said. "Thank you for telling me. I don't want Gram to live in a place like that. Did you call the police?"

She gave me a cool, gracious smile and touched her free hand to the side of her head. "Some people when they get old go a little . . . funny. I didn't want to get anyone in trouble just because they're old."

"You're kinder than I am," I said, hoping my face looked appropriately judgmental.

Daisy looked at the delicate gold watch on her arm. "I have an appointment," she said. "I need to get going." She got to her feet and smiled at me. "Thank you for calling me about the gravy boat. And thank you for the tea."

My heart was pounding so loudly it seemed to me that she should have been able to hear it. "You're very welcome," I said. "I'll speak to the owner of the china tonight and give him your offer."

"I'll talk to you soon, then," she said.

I walked her to the door and stood there until I saw her car drive away. Elvis wandered over and rubbed against my leg. I bent down and picked him up. He looked at me with his wide green eyes and meowed once. "Good job," I said. "There'll be a little something extra in your bowl tonight."

That got me another, way more enthusiastic meow.

I turned around to see Avery peeking around the side of the storage room door. "Is she gone?" she hissed in a stage whisper.

I nodded and set Elvis down. "She's gone."

"The coast is clear," she called over her shoulder. She

bounded over to me, followed a lot more sedately by Charlotte and Mac.

"Did you find out anything that could help Maddie?" Charlotte asked.

"I did," I said. "I know who killed Arthur Fenety."

Three pair of eyes stared at me.

"Who?" Charlotte asked.

"Yeah, who?" Avery echoed.

Mac just looked at me, frowning slightly, and I could see him make the connection.

I let out a breath. "Daisy," I said.

Chapter 26

"No sh— No!" Avery said.

Charlotte stared at me, stunned. "Daisy?" she said.

Only Mac seemed to have all the pieces put together. "I heard most of your conversation," he said. "She saw Mr. P., didn't she?"

I nodded.

"But the timeline's wrong."

"It is," I said.

Charlotte looked confused. "I don't understand," she said.

"Daisy saw Mr. Peterson when he walked down the hall in his—"

"Naked glory," Avery finished. "I told you someone would see him." She had a very self-satisfied grin on her face.

Mac shot her a look and she wiped the smile off her face.

"If Daisy's appointment was when she said it was, she would have been finished and long gone when Alfred did his little walk of shame," I said.

"But I thought Alfred checked on that appointment time?" Charlotte said.

"He did," I said. And I was really hoping he'd done it more or less legally. "But he checked the computerized appointment schedule. It's possible there's a daily paper schedule that they use in the office and it has cancellations and any other changes."

"I'll call Rose," Charlotte said. "Maybe she and Alfred can find out."

"Good idea," I said.

Charlotte headed over to the counter.

"I'll close up," Mac said.

I nodded. "Thanks. There's something I need to do."

"What?" Avery asked.

"Let's just say Mr. P. isn't the only person who knows how to use Google," I said.

In the end it took a lot less time than I'd expected. When Mac tapped on my door I was leaning back in my chair, looking at the computer screen, with Elvis sitting on the desk, craning his neck sideways so he could see, too.

"Any luck?" Mac asked.

"Yes," I said.

"What did you find?"

"Arthur Fenety Senior—actually he was Edward Arthur Fenety—was a groundskeeper at a cemetery. He would have likely used pesticides. Years ago most people did. Daisy could have known about the napthathion. If Liz could find out that a lot of people still have it in their sheds and garages, so could Daisy."

"Are you going to call the police?" Mac asked.

"I don't really have a lot of proof," I said with a sigh. "Mr. P.'s backside isn't really evidence."

Mac smiled. "No, it isn't." He studied my face. "So, what are you going to do?"

"Gram says you catch more flies with honey than you do with brown sugar."

"You're going to sweeten the pot," he said with a smile.

I smiled back at him. "More like the gravy boat."

Daisy Fenety arrived at the shop at twenty minutes after eight. I should have worn a track in the floor, I'd walked back and forth so many times after I hung up the phone.

"I can't believe you got an answer so quickly," she said to me as I let her in.

"Well, between you and me, money is a little tight for my customer."

The china gravy boat was nestled in a box of paper shavings. Daisy smiled when she caught sight of it and walked over to the counter.

"I really do have to thank you, Sarah," she said as she picked up the box. "The gravy boat is a very difficult piece to find."

"You're very welcome," I said. I reached under the counter for the fake bill of sale I'd prepared.

"I'm actually a tiny bit sorry that I'm going to have to shoot you," she said.

I turned around to see a small silver gun pointed at my chest.

"Take it easy, Daisy. You've been under a lot of stress in the past week," I said, slowly taking a step backward.

"Put the gun down and we'll talk." It sounded lame even to my ears. Could I run to the storage room before she could shoot me? I got a crazy mental picture of myself bobbing and zigzagging my way to the double doors. Panic was making me stupid. I took a shaky deep breath and let it out.

She shook her head. "You're a tedious young woman," she said. "Although you are loyal, I'll give you that."

"Shooting me isn't going to fix anything," I said, putting my hands in my pockets so she couldn't see them shake. "How do you know I haven't already gone to the police?"

"And told them what? You think I killed my brother because I told you I saw a naked man when I went to the dentist?" She gave me a condescending smile. "Do you know what happened after I got home this afternoon?" she asked. "I had a call from the dentist's office. The receptionist had e-mailed a statement that showed exactly when my appointment had been and how long it had lasted, but she wondered if I wanted to stop by the office for a copy signed by the dentist himself." The smile reminded me of a crocodile. "Such a conscientious girl."

That had to have been Rose who had called for the statement. There was no point in bluffing anymore.

"Why did you kill your brother?" I asked. I glanced at the front door.

"You can try to run if you'd like," she said. "Daddy taught me how to shoot when I was a little girl. I won't miss."

I took a shaky, deep breath. "You didn't answer my question. Why did you kill Arthur?"

"You're right, I didn't answer you," she said. The hand holding the gun didn't waver and I knew she had every intention of shooting me. I, on the other hand, had every intention of getting out of this alive, and part of that meant keeping Daisy talking. "He'd gone soft. He'd fallen in love for real with that little Florence Nightingale and her organic garden." She rolled her eyes.

"For years I'd kept the money safe. I invested it. I turned it into more money than any of those vapid women he romanced would have." Her blue eyes flashed with anger. "He wanted to give it all back. With interest. I was his sister but his newfound conscience didn't have a problem leaving me with nothing."

"You set up Maddie."

She shrugged. "It seemed appropriate. The whole thing was her fault."

I tried to swallow down the lump in my throat. "Where did you get the bottle of pesticide?"

She gave me a smug smile. "The little stone church down the street from my house." She shook her head. "The things they have in the groundskeeper's shed. Heavens. Someone could take out this entire town."

"So, you followed Arthur to Maddie's?"

"Yes, I did," she said gesturing with the little gun. "And I did a much better job of it than that young man Arthur dumped into the bushes." She smiled. "I waited until Madeline went into the house, and then I went to speak to Arthur." The smile faded. "I was fair. I gave him a chance to change his mind. He wouldn't. So what else could I do?" She shook her head. "He was never very observant. He was so busy proclaiming his true love for her that he didn't see me slip a little something into his coffee. I just walked back through the park and went to the dentist." She gave me that confident smile again. "I told them I had car trouble. I was very upset. They were very accommodating." She studied my face for a moment. "Your grandmother isn't moving, is she?"

"No, she's not," I said.

She nodded. "I thought about that afterward. I'm slipping, almost getting taken down by that repugnant, naked little man and you."

"There's nothing repugnant about Mr. Peterson," I said. "But there's a lot repugnant about you."

"You're getting on my nerves, Sarah," Daisy said, frowning at me.

She was getting on my nerves, as well. My stomach had tied itself into a knot. I heard a sound behind me and Elvis came into the room. He had something large . . . and furry in his mouth. He headed right for Daisy and dropped the furry present on her foot.

She screamed. I dove for the cover of the counter. And Michelle and two other police officers came through the front door, guns drawn.

It was over.

I got up slowly. I'd banged both knees and scraped my hand. But there were no bullet holes in me. Or Elvis.

Nick hurried across the floor to me as I unbuttoned my sweater and pulled at the tape holding the microphone hidden just below my collarbone. "Are you all right?" he asked, putting a hand on my shoulder. He was present only as a civilian and I was surprised that Michelle had agreed to let him be involved at all.

I nodded. "I'm okay," I said. "Did the police get it all?"

He smiled. "Every incriminating word."

Michelle was reading Daisy her rights while Elvis watched, one black paw on what I could now see was a stuffed toy, not a real mouse.

The two other officers led Daisy out and Michelle came over to Nick and me, trailed by Elvis.

"You okay?" she asked.

"I'm fine," I said, buttoning up my sweater again. "Is Maddie in the clear?"

"Yes." She handed me the china gravy boat. I set it on the counter behind me and bent down to pick up Elvis.

"What did you do?" Michelle asked. "Why did Daisy scream? I thought we agreed no heroics."

"It wasn't me," I said. I gave Elvis a scratch under his chin and he sighed. "It was him." I pointed to the stuffed toy on the floor. "He came in with that in his mouth and dropped it on Daisy's foot."

Nick leaned sideways and squinted at the furry gray lump.

"It's just a toy," I said.

"No," Nick said slowly. "It has feet and they're moving."

I took a couple of steps backward. Elvis gave me a self-satisfied smile. It was the only way to describe it. Then he licked my chin and wriggled to get down. I put him on the floor and he walked over to whatever was lying there, picked it up and headed for the front door. No one stopped him.

"Smart cat," Michelle said to me.

"Don't tell me you think it brought that mouse in on

purpose to distract Daisy Fenety?" Nick said. "C'mon. It's a cat."

"I know," I said. If Elvis could tell when someone was lying—and I was convinced he could—then it wasn't that much of a stretch to believe his little stunt with the mouse was more than a coincidence.

Nick must have seen something on my face.

He shook his head. "Seriously, Sarah. You don't really think that cat knew you were in trouble, do you? What? You think Elvis is Lassie and you're Timmy stuck down a well?"

I frowned at him. "Of course not," I said. "Elvis is much smarter than Lassie."

Chapter 27

Sam had saved a big table for us at the back of the pub and we crowded around it to celebrate: Rose and Mr. P.; Liz and Avery, even though it was a school night; Charlotte; Maddie, of course; Mac; Jess, who had called Sam and organized the spontaneous celebration; Nick and even Elvis, riding in style in Rose's canvas tote bag. We'd invited Michelle but she had paperwork to do. "Thank you for believing me," I'd said to her as we stood in the shop parking lot.

"Thank you for trusting me," she'd replied.

Sam brought a bottle of sparkling cider to the table and handed it to Jess. "I don't think this bunch needs any alcohol," he said.

He laid a hand on my shoulder. "I'm glad you're safe," he said. "Don't ever do something this stupid again."

I rested my cheek against his hand for a moment. "Don't worry, Sam," I said. "My detective days are over."

"I can't believe Elvis came in and dropped a dead mouse on that woman's foot," Jess said as she poured the cider.

"Oh, I can," Rose said. "Elvis is a very intelligent cat. And technically it wasn't dead."

He poked his head out of the bag and looked at us all, clearly happy about the praise.

"I can't believe I let you talk me into bringing him," I said. "What if the health inspector finds out about this?"

"I don't see a cat," Liz said. "Does anyone else?"

"Not me," Avery said with a grin.

"All I see is family," Charlotte said.

I looked around the table. That was what I saw, too. Family. A bit of an odd one, but family nonetheless.

"Are you glad you came back?" Nick said quietly. He was sitting to my right.

I nodded. "Yes, I am. What about you?"

He looked at me and smiled. "Very glad," he said.

Jess stood up and raised her glass. "A toast, everyone," she said. "To Sarah and Elvis for catching Arthur Fenety's killer."

We clinked glasses and took a drink.

"So, are you going to make another career change and become a full-time investigator?" Nick teased, his brown eyes sparkling.

I shook my head. "No. This was my first and last time playing detective."

Rose came around the side of the table, bent down and put her arms around my neck. "I'm so glad you're all right, sweetie," she said. "We won't let this happen next time."

Nick looked at me. I looked at Rose. "Next time?" I said.

Rose nodded. "Don't worry." She reached into the

pocket of her sweater. "Our business cards came," she said. "With all the excitement I forgot to show them to you."

She handed me a cream-colored rectangle with black printing. It said CHARLOTTE'S ANGELS in cursive, with DISCREET INVESTIGATIONS underneath.

Rose beamed at me. "We've decided to open up a business. Isn't this going to be fun?"

ABOUT THE AUTHOR

Sofie Ryan is a writer and mixed-media artist who loves to repurpose things in her life and her art. She also writes the national bestselling Magical Cats mysteries under the name Sofie Kelly.

CONNECT ONLINE

www.sofieryan.com

COMING IN OCTOBER 2014 FROM
Sofie Kelly

A Midwinter's Tail
A Magical Cats Mystery

Winter in Mayville Heights is busy, and not just
because of the holidays. Kathleen has her hands full
organizing a benefit to raise money for the library....
and when a guest at the gala drops dead, her magical
cats, Owen and Hercules, are about to have their paws
full helping her solve a murder.

The victim is the ex of town rascal Burtis Chapman.
Everybody is denying knowledge of why she was back
in town, but as Kathleen and her detective boyfriend,
Marcus, begin nosing around, they discover more
people were connected to the deceased than they
claimed. Now Kathleen, Marcus, and her cats have to
unravel this midwinter tale before the case gets cold.

ALSO AVAILABLE IN THE SERIES
Curiosity Thrilled the Cat
Sleight of Paw
Copycat Killing
Cat Trick
Final Catcall

Available wherever books are sold or at
penguin.com

facebook.com/TheCrimeSceneBooks